The Fiddle

Natalie Cumming

D1331698

Michael Terence
Publishing

First published in paperback by
Michael Terence Publishing in 2018
www.mtp.agency

ISBN 9781912639083

DEDICATIONS

To Caroline Mylon...

Without your guidance, this book would not have been completed.

To my husband David, my sons Richard and James and my sister Debbie.

ACKNOWLEDGEMENTS

Ricochet for arranging the restoration of the violin by John Dilworth.

My grateful thanks to Carol Fugler for introducing me to Michael Terence Publishing (MTP).

All at MTP for believing this story should be told.

Cliff Anderson for his encouragement over the years in insisting I finish this book.

Fox Ensor for her continued support.

The Fiddle

Natalie Cumming

Tsar Nicholas II ruled from 1894 until his abduction on Thursday, March 15, 1917. The family were imprisoned in the Alexander Palace at Tsarskoye Selo, then in the Governor's Mansion in Tobolsk and finally at Yektarinburg in the Ipatiev House. The Tsar and his wife, son and four daughters, family doctor, the Tsar's valet and the Empress' lady-in-waiting and family cook were all killed in the same room on July 16/17, 1918.

PART ONE – ABRAHAM

Abraham David Levinsky took his role as violin teacher to Alexis, the son of Tsar Nicholas II very seriously, but, try as he might, he could not teach him to play as well as his own son, Israel, or his daughter Rosa. Both his children would pick up their violins and with a flick of the bow they could make it sound like a rare and beautiful thing. Rosa had the edge on her brother because she was the eldest and had been playing longer. Abraham taught all Tsar Nicholas's children music, which brought his family many comforts and privileges. They had a beautiful home in St. Petersburg and his wife Anna was a wonderful mother to their three children. She did not have the worries that so many of their Jewish relatives and friends had. They were not persecuted and hounded, but poor Nathan, Abraham's brother, and his wife Rula were very frightened by the current events. They had two children, Mala and Moshe, and they also lived in St. Petersburg.

"Come now, Alexis, you can do much better than that. That's right, tuck the fiddle under your chin more firmly, and hold the bow in a more slanting position. There, that's better. Now, begin again." Little Alexis could not hold his violin for very long as he tired so quickly. Abraham knew that all the child ever wanted to do was to rough and tumble with his sisters, particularly Anastasia, but his parents wouldn't let him. No, he had to sit around like a doll on a silk cushion in case he fell, in case he knocked himself, in case he should cut himself. Oh! what a panic if anything like that happened. What Alexis did not know was that he was a very sick boy, a haemophiliac, and if any of these things should happen to him he could bleed to death. Abraham had been hired by Tsar Nicholas II and the Tsarina to tutor their five children in music. They knew he had little ones of his own and would, therefore, be familiar with their tantrums and often boisterous manners, but their children were good at heart and respected him. They did their practice, somewhat sketchily at times, but Abraham was quite pleased with their progress, particularly Anastasia and Olga who had grasped music more easily than the others. Abraham's particular favourite was Anastasia, with her beautiful smile and lovely curls, and whenever she came for her lesson she greeted him with real enthusiasm. Knowing that Alexis was not very strong, and that great care had to be taken at all times to ensure he did not become injured, he still tried to treat him as naturally as Israel, his own son, who loved to bounce up and down on the couch, or run helter-skelter down the hall at home in a game of chase, and knew that this was what Alexis really yearned to do when he saw his sisters doing it. Abraham could not help but fear for the little boy's future, as new waves of terror ran through the city.

He heard the shouts and screams in the streets: the shooting and the sound of breaking glass; the Bolsheviks had arrived. It was the second week of March 1917. There was a dreadful shortage of food in Petrograd, and Abraham had heard that thugs had caused rioting and looting. His brother, Nathan, who was a tailor by trade, was finding it increasingly difficult to feed his wife and two children, but Anna was good to them, helping all she could. She must be careful, he thought. If anyone finds out they might tell the Master of the Tsar's household, who could think that he was stealing the food. Of course, that was not the case, for they were well provided for, but in these terrible times I must not take that chance, he said to himself.

After teaching the girls that afternoon he stepped out into the freezing air. It was Shabbas and getting late, so he decided to take a shortcut past St. Isaac's Cathedral, with its vast golden dome, to make his way home. They were all meeting at his house that night as usual; Nathan and Rula, with their little ones, and as he had long adopted the role as head of the family, he felt good at the prospect of a fine meal, the company of his brother, whom he loved dearly, and some music afterwards.

He heard shouting in the distance and wondered what had happened. He heard shooting. The noises increased and as he started to run he heard the pounding of horses' hoofs. "Oh! God," he said under his breath, as his pace quickened. "What is happening, what is happening?" As he rounded the Arch of the Permskaya Zastava the troops began to fire into the crowd massed ahead of them. He crouched behind a pillar for safety. Mounted horses had been grouped and were waiting in a solid line behind the foot soldiers. The animals impatiently pawed the ground, sensing their riders were sitting with swords drawn. "Charge!" went the loud cry, which was echoed by the riders, and with loud whoops and yells, they thundered down the long street, getting nearer and nearer by the second to the huge crowd of protestors in front of them. In those brief minutes before the charge, Abraham had realised that many of the people gathered there were Jews, for the marchers were now outside the Synagogue, where the service had just finished. Surely his people had more sense than to stand in groups like this. They knew there was a curfew and dangerous to be out once dusk fell, even for groups of two or three. As the horses drew nearer, the crowd tried to run, but there was nowhere to go. They had their backs to the square. There was no way out. The screams were sickening, and Abraham wanted to drag his eyes away from the sight, but he couldn't. "Oh! dear God, he thought, my people; my people." The troops were now also firing into the crowd and the Cavalry had reached their destination. Mingled with the cries and screams of men, women and children were the screams of horses which were being dragged down to the ground by those men brave enough to even try to defend themselves and their families. Abraham dropped his violin and clamped his hands over his ears, but nothing, nothing could reduce that sickening noise of people. People being massacred before him. People badly injured and dying. As the horses and riders completed their hacking of the people with their swords they turned and galloped away, the riders shouting with pleasure at their easy victory over so many. Abraham was shaking. Shaking as he had never done before. He looked at the sight before him; at the unspeakable horror of people lying on the ground. Countless bodies were strewn around the square; men, women and children; some trying to get up, some calling for help, but mostly just lying there, the dead and dying. The gutters were running with blood, and where the machine gunners had taken their toll there were bullet holes sprayed across the fronts of the surrounding buildings and the Synagogue. Apart from the moaning and wailing which was now pouring from those who had managed to escape and hide, all else was engulfed in a dreadful silence. Abraham felt the hairs on his neck stand up. Strange, he thought, how I can hear the silence even with the cries of our people.

He stood up, and with trembling hands picked up his violin, cradling it in his arms as if it was a precious child, perhaps in an uncanny way sensing that it might one day save his life. He half-ran, half-stumbled to where the Rabbi was lying on the ground and, kneeling beside him, he gently cradled his head in his lap. Someone was running, and suddenly there were the Guards again, but only soldiers this time. They shouted at Abraham and the other people tending the dead and wounded "Get out of here, go back to your homes, these people will be taken care of. Go back to your homes or you will be arrested." A cart came rumbling into the square, with two soldiers on board. They immediately jumped down, and with guns at the ready, pointed at all those who were trying to help. Abraham slowly rose to his feet, calling out to the crowd "Come, let us go. Our people can't be helped if we stay. Do as the officer says, go to your homes." His heart leapt with relief as he heard the Rabbi thank him - at least he was not dead. The people started to leave, the women crying and wailing for their loved ones, children calling for their mothers. The soldiers promptly started picking up the bodies, throwing them into the cart with no regard for either the living or the dead. Abraham knew he could do nothing without risking his own life, and what would then become of Anna and the children. No, he must not interfere, but he wished desperately there was something he could do. He quickly walked away, making for home, hoping against hope that Nathan and Rula had not been amongst those massacred after leaving the Synagogue. Oh! How he wished he had just had time to look, but he knew that within a very few minutes he would know, for they should have reached his home by now. As he opened the door his heart leapt with joy to hear the cries of children - not only his own

Israel, Rosa and Helena but Moshe and Mala, calling out "Uncle Abraham, Uncle Abraham. Papa," as they all crowded around him. This meant that, for the moment at least, his family was safe - but for how long, he thought. Determined not to let the women and children know of the terrible sights he had just witnessed he knelt down, carefully placing his violin on the table, and opened his arms to let the children run at him. "You are so late, Papa." "Where have you been, Papa." "Have you brought us any sweets, Uncle." As the children were enfolded in his arms he held them close, as if he knew there would not be many more occasions when he could do this. "You are hurting me, Papa." This from little Rosa. "Why are you crying, you always say it is not manly to cry and we should leave the tears for the girls," said Israel. Abraham stood up, pulling out his handkerchief. Anna, Nathan and Rula had all come into the hall and Anna immediately sensed that something was terribly wrong, for Abraham would not let his children see him upset without very good reason. "It's only that I am very pleased to see you all, and I had something in my eye." He wondered just how gullible they would all be, and hoped his white lie would pass undetected - if not by the adults. He looked up at the three of them, briefly frowned and shook his head, indicating that they should say nothing, praying they would follow his lead. He saw Nathan looking at him, and realised he had instantly sensed something was wrong. Although he was only a simple tailor, he was a very intelligent man, with piercing brown eyes, which saw through any situation – real or imagined. Abraham was taller than his brother, but he had the same black side curls and the Levinsky nose, which Rula always made fun of. "One day your nose will get in the way of the sewing machine when you bend down to thread the needle, and you will sew your hair to the cloth." He knew Nathan had loved her from the moment he had first met her as a young girl of 17, with her lovely petite figure and melting hazel eyes, her brown hair piled on the top of her head. Their daughter, Mala, took after her, but she would probably be taller when she grew up.

"Come, Dushka," said Anna. "You are very late and we should have started Shabbas supper a while ago. Quickly, have a wash and come to the table. Hurry children, all sit down and we will have our meal." It was wonderful to see his wife instantly take command of the situation, and so remove some of the burden from him. He glanced in the hall mirror – his ashen face peered back at him and it was obvious that he was extremely upset. He knew she would be wondering what had happened to affect him in such a way - for he was usually an unflappable man. However, he thought, I will tell them all later when the children are in bed. He went into the dining room, and quickly taking his place at the table they began their prayers for the Sabbath and ate their meal.

The women had put the children to bed, topping and tailing them in one big double bed as they did on Friday nights, for Nathan and Rula always stayed overnight so they could all go to the Synagogue together the following day. Whilst they had done this and cleared up the supper, Abraham had been so engrossed in conversation with Nathan, he realised they had not gone upstairs for their usual rough and tumble with the children before they climbed into bed. He could see that the two wives, whilst not mentioning it to each other, were both anxious to know what it was all about and so, wiping their hands on their aprons, they went into the living room, drawing up a chair either side of the men. Abraham had talked to his brother and they decided to be absolutely frank with their wives and so he proceeded to tell what he had seen in the square that evening. The women recoiled in horror when he told them of the protesting marchers, whose arrival in the square had caused the willful massacre of other innocent people, whose only crime was that they had been to the Synagogue or walking in the street. He told them how he had tried to help the Rabbi and others, but the soldiers had forced them all to leave. He watched in helpless silence as the women cried. Abraham then went on to tell them of the other worries he had concerning the very real threat of a Revolution, which was on everyone's lips. "As I am employed by the Tsar I will automatically be under suspicion, without taking into account the fact that I am Jewish. There is going to be real trouble. We know that Kerensky is becoming more and more powerful, and I am frightened - very frightened - of what will become of me, and more than that, of you, Anna, and the children." Anna continued to cry, and Rula comforted her. Nathan was sitting there dejectedly, wringing his hands in despair. "I don't know what we can do. Without the help and food you constantly give us we would have nothing. No-one has the money to come to me for new clothes now, and many would not run the risk anyway, in case it is thought that they are sympathisers with us or with the Bolsheviks. We have nothing - absolutely nothing. This is not life - it is the slow death of our people, incessantly hungry and persecuted." Abraham looked at him in astonishment. His brother, his mild, meek brother, talking like this. He was encouraged by this sudden spark of feeling, for

Nathan was usually quite content to let life go by and any problems go by with it. This gave Abraham the courage to speak his thoughts, and to recount the ideas which had been going through his mind for some weeks now, ever since he had witnessed the dreadful looting of the Jewish quarter when the soldiers were dragging bales of cloth, sacks of flour, books, jewellery, anything they could find of value, into the streets. They had been fired with lust and destruction, born of their fierce hatred of the Jews in St. Petersburg and of Bolshevik sympathisers, whom they thought were being harboured there.

"Anna, Nathan, Rula. I am going to make a suggestion. I want you to listen carefully, and not interrupt until I have finished. I stress it is only a suggestion - but one I think that, as head of this household, you ought to accept and agree to it." Abraham then proceeded to outline his plan. He suggested to them that they should immediately gather up their belongings, taking only what could be put into a suitcase each and a handcart between them, bringing all the rest of Nathan's possessions, which were not many, to their home to store. He pointed out that they would then retrieve them at a time when they could return to St. Petersburg, secretly knowing this would probably never be. He said the children should all wear the thickest clothing they had, and he would go out next morning and buy boots for everyone, no matter what the cost. He had some money put by, not much, but had some things he could sell which would be of no use to them at the present time. They could not take much food, of course, but any money left would have to be used to keep them over the coming weeks. His plan was to walk to Minsk, see whether they could peacefully stay there, and if not, move on to Lvov, where he was sure they would be able to settle down quietly until the troubles were over, and the talk of Revolution had died down. They would have to do whatever work they could, jokingly saying no-one would want a fiddle player and anything they earned they would pool to try and make some kind of life for the little ones. He thought they might be away for six months or so, and would then return to pick up their lives and carry on as before. He did not say that he knew that once he left his violin teaching at the Palace there would be no chance of going back - someone else would always be ready to jump into a position like that.

The talking was over. There was silence. The clock ticked, ticked, ticked. Funny, Abraham thought once again, how I always hear the silence even when there is a noise. Anna looked at Rula, who had picked up her husband's hand, which was nervously plucking at the arm of the chair. Rula looked at Abraham with that steady gaze of hers. "I am ready to do whatever you and Nathan think best. All I want is the safety of our children and ourselves, and I know you are a good and wise man, Abraham, and will only do what you really think is right. I am with you." Nathan smiled. "She is right. You are a good man and a good brother. We will do whatever you suggest. I have no money though, for you know how little I have earned recently, and all my savings have slowly been eaten up with food and fuel, so all I can offer you are a few small possessions which you can hopefully sell and raise some money on. Do you agree, Rula?" She smiled and nodded her agreement. Abraham turned to Anna. "You are not saying anything, Dushka. What do you think?"

Before she could answer there was a pounding on the door. Whoever it was urgently needed to be let in, for it was now past midnight and the curfew was on! Abraham rushed to the door, with the others following. Pulling it open he gasped in astonishment. Standing there on the step was Gospodin Polkovnik, an elderly Colonel from the Palace who knew and respected Abraham. He pushed past them and grabbed the door, slamming it shut. "Forgive me, I had to come. You are in grave danger and must leave. The Tsar and little Alexis were arrested yesterday on a train at Pskov, and the Tsarina and girls have been taken by the guards. I don't know where they are, but the crowds have been shouting for the Tsar's head all night and I am terrified that they will have harmed the children. I know Kerensky suspects me of being in league with the Tsar, which I am, and has said they will kill all those who are sympathisers. They have already killed the two tutors, and Professor Ovetchkin and Ivan the manservant are both dead. Abraham, it won't take them long to discover where you live and I am sure they will come for you. You must flee St. Petersburg immediately. Here, I have a little money, take it. You will need it." Abraham pushed Polkovnik's hand away, saying "I cannot accept your money. I will not be able to repay it, and if we leave the city God knows when we will be able to return." "No," said Polkovnik, "Don't be proud, take it, and consider it a loan. Of course you will be back and then you can repay me." He smiled ruefully at this. Abraham hushed the women, who had begun to ask questions in a rapid stream. "Quiet, quiet, let us get things straight. What are you saying about the Tsar?" The Colonel then again repeated that the Tsar had secretly boarded a train with Alexis, bound for Mogilev, with the hope of getting across the border and into exile. He instructed Colonel Babel, Igor and their Doctor to accompany the Tsarina and the girls to Zailet in the province of Viatka, where he thought they would be safe for the time being, and this would throw a smoke-screen on his own departure. What he had not realised was that he already had many enemies within his household - enemies who would stop at nothing to see him overthrown and Alexander Kerensky put in power. Consequently, the train had been stopped and boarded, the Tsar and Alexis arrested, and the army apparently had submitted promptly to the new authority.

Abraham quickly looked at the others. "Well, Anna, you were about to say what you thought - what do you think now?" Without a moment's hesitation, she said "You are right, we must go, and now; immediately! Thank you so much, Gospodin Polkovnik, you are indeed a true friend to come to us like this, putting yourself in danger. May God grant you safety. You must leave now, for if they do come and find you here they will surely kill you immediately. We will always remember what you have done for us." The old Colonel took her hand and smiled. "I am an old man with no wife; the Tsar and his family have been my family. If I live through these terrible times that would be God's will - if not, I will be in a better place. We might have different religions but I think we have one God." He grasped Abraham's hand tightly, pushing the money into it, released it, and disappeared into the night. As the door closed on their friend Abraham turned and faced them. "The decision no longer rests with any one of us - we must all see this as God's will. We must get ready to leave as soon as it is light, for we cannot chance going out whilst the curfew is on. Nathan, I want you to go to your home at dawn, get together all the things you need and anything of value which you think we can sell. I know where there is a small handcart you and I can easily manage to pull, which I have been keeping at the back of my mind for a few days. I will slip out in a few minutes, up the rear alley where no guards will be patrolling and bring it back." He knew very well what Anna's next warning would be, and to prevent any more fears than were absolutely necessary on her part, he quickly added "Don't worry, I will take some old sacking I have out the back and tie it around the wheels so the noise on the cobbles won't be heard." He must keep up this facade of bravado. He must not let the others see just how terrified he really was - much more for them, and the children, than for himself. Nathan would do anything he said but needed to be led. Perhaps they would stand a chance, however slim, of getting away, but go they must. They could not run the risk of staying for that would mean their inevitable slaughter, even for Nathan and Rula, along with the other members of the royal household. Very sensibly Nathan led his wife to the kitchen so that Anna and Abraham could have a few moments alone. They placed their arms around each other, looking lovingly into each other's eyes. "We have a chance, Dushka," he softly murmured. "God will help us through this and show us what we must do." She kissed him tenderly on his cheek, not saying a word, to show him that he had her love and that she would do whatever he said. In the kitchen, Abraham could see Nathan and Rula were doing the same thing!

"Come on now, we must get organised. There is much to do," said Abraham. With these words they all started to gather the basic kitchen utensils together; a saucepan, kettle, some plates. The samovar? No, he thought, shaking his head, what use will we have for that - it must stay. Next came the blankets and extra clothing for each of them. "It is a good thing Rula and I are almost the same size," said Anna ruefully, "we will have to share what I have." They got out the warmest of the children's clothing. They would dress them in two of everything and hope they would be able to get some boots or shoes as soon as they had left the city. Anna turned to Rula. "When Nathan goes to the house tell him to bring some more clothing for the children. We must try to keep them warm at all costs. And some blankets." The two women then went to the pantry. What a blessing it was Shabbas as Anna had done some baking for the next day. There was enough food for a few days if they were careful and, packing what she had into a large wicker basket, she took some jars of pickles and preserves. If nothing else it would help bread taste better! Little did they know that in the days and weeks to come they would be glad of even bread to eat and if they had known the journey which lay before them would probably have made the decision to stay in their home and risk whatever the consequences that came to them. At the sound of the rear door closing Anna jumped with fear, but to her relief it was Abraham. He was brushing snow from his coat and stamping his feet. "What a blow. Just as we thought the weather was improving it has begun to snow again. Anyway, I have the cart and several sacks. We can put the spare bedding in them and hang them underneath. That way perhaps we can put the children on top. Anna, have you anything ready to start packing away yet? You, Rula?" Both women nodded, and quietly, without fuss, started to bring bundles of clothing and blankets to the door. Abraham took charge. "We should put the spare things in the bottom and what we need all the time must go on top. We must take the Hanukka candle if nothing else. Take the brass candlesticks, they might be of value. Oh, and get my prayer shawl. I will wear it. Nathan, get some sleep if you can, for in a couple of hours it will be daybreak and I want you to get off home." At this, Nathan nodded and went upstairs. Even if he doesn't sleep, thought Abraham, he will get some rest, for he was beginning to look terrible as if the true impact of what they were about to do had just hit home. When they had loaded the things they wanted to take on the cart the three of them sat down and tried to get some sleep. After a few hours, they heard Nathan go down the stairs and quietly leave. "God keep him safe," thought Abraham. He loved his brother dearly and remembered his last words to his father before he died - he had promised he would always look after him.

A couple of hours later, just as daylight was really beginning, they heard a noise outside and, rushing to the door, were all immensely relieved when Nathan walked in, clutching two cases and with a large rucksack on his back. "I have brought what I could, but there is very little of value other than our candlesticks and a few pieces of jewellery." "Don't worry," said Abraham, "with the bits of silver we have, our jewellery, the money from Polkovnik and my own, and other odds and ends, we will have enough to last us until we can find work and a new place to live." A new place to live, a new place to live - these words were to keep him from giving up on many occasions in the months to come.

The children were dressed; complaining bitterly at having so many clothes on, but excited at the prospect of the "journey" they had been told about. All knew they must keep very quiet whilst leaving the city, but had been told that once they were in the country they could run in the snow if it was not too deep and make snowballs. The cart was loaded, and Abraham had very cleverly made up a harness of sorts from two long leather straps he had found where the cart had been kept. He proposed to put this around his shoulders so that it could be pulled from the front, whilst Nathan would push from the rear. They had hidden as much as they could down in the cellar, locked it and he had placed the key carefully in his pocket. "Please God, one day I will be back," he thought. Touching the Mezuzah on the door one last time, he turned his back on the house and they were off.

Abraham had chosen a route out of the city which he hoped would be the least patrolled, particularly at this early hour, and whilst the snow would hamper their progress if it got any worse, at least it muffled the sound of the wheels on the cobbles, for he could not leave the sacking round them now the cart was fully loaded. He was very pleased with it. What luck he had spotted it in the old stables. He went over in his mind the things they had brought with them: his fiddle, of course. The Hannukah candle. Anna's few pieces of silver - they would be useful. He felt sure they would end up selling them. The family Bible. And little Rosa had insisted on bringing her doll. They had left their beautiful china and other lovely pieces in the cellar, and he knew that Anna had been particularly upset leaving her precious Samovar - it had come from Nijni Novgorod when they had married.

He sighed; shook his head; he knew he must not dwell on these things, but get on with the business of living.

They were in luck. They were out of the city and had apparently gone undetected, for no one had challenged them - in fact, they had only seen a couple of people, obviously hurrying about their own business, only casting an inquisitive glance their way. "What a comical sight we must look," he thought, with their cart, five children, and all of them wearing so many clothes they appeared to be really overweight. He was getting very hot wearing two overcoats and pulling the cart, even though it was so cold, but he would not take one off yet in case they were stopped by the soldiers and the cart taken from them. This was a real fear to Abraham: one he had not mentioned to the others. Their sole possessions were on it - he must guard it with his life, if necessary. The children had been so good, leaving the city, and had played a game - who could be quietest for the longest. It never failed! Little Rosa was sitting there, on top of the cart, clutching her doll, with her mittened hand clamped across her mouth, giggling. She had won. Israel had spoken first!

A faint morning mist lay over the landscape as the clear, cold daylight came up, with a watery sun shining down. The snow had stopped and as the little party went down the road the forests stretched ahead of them. Abraham had set himself a target of twenty miles a day. He didn't know if they would keep that up - it would depend on the weather, but if they were to get away to the safety of the countryside they must put as many miles between them and St. Petersburg as possible. After a while, they were right in the forest. The trees were mainly pine, but Nathan pointed out a few birches. They had passed a team of labourers hacking away at the frozen ground, who had casually looked up at them, called out a greeting and continued with their digging.

So far, so good. No-one had stopped them. In the forest, the road was much easier to travel, for there was not so much snow here and by the middle of the first day he estimated that they had gone several miles. The children had been able to run ahead, skipping and jumping on the road, but had now begun to tire, and all pleaded to clamber up on board for a ride. Anna indicated to Abraham that they should stop and eat whilst they were in the shelter of the forest, and as soon as Nathan saw a track he pulled off the road on to it, slipping the harness off his shoulders with a grunt. He had been getting very tired, but would not say a word to Abraham who had pulled the cart for the first four or five hours. They lit a fire of dry kindling which they found in plenty at the base of the pine trees, and very soon all were eating hot soup and drinking tea. The children were given a Homentasha as a very special treat, but Anna pointed out that they would not be getting any more once this batch was gone. The adults had been content with a hunk of bread with their soup. The scent of the pine in the wood-smoke was sweet, and for the first time in many hours they began to relax. Whatever lay ahead was unknown but Abraham never wanted to re-live the terrors he had experienced in St. Petersburg over the last two days. He went over to the cart and carefully took his fiddle out of its case. Sitting down on a tree trunk he began to play, quietly and with sadness. The others looked at him and began to hum the tune, then Nathan was singing the words. Soon, the woods were ringing with the singing of those people - those four brave people who were ready to face the unknown rather than be slaughtered in their homes.

By nightfall, they had left the forests and passed through a few small, sleepy hamlets. No one had bothered them, and apart from buying some milk, they had kept going, fearful that if anyone got too inquisitive they might be reported to the authorities. The Bolsheviks were everywhere. The snow was falling again and a fierce wind had sprung up. They found some shelter in a small wood and built a large fire. The men collected as much bracken and wood as they could, encouraging the children to help them. Then using the cart as a windbreak, they ate a meal of hot soup, finishing the last of it, with some bread, tea and the last of the cakes. The wind's force increased but the fire was still burning brightly. The hardy grass in the wood, tall and broad, bent under the impact of the gale with a constant swishing noise. They huddled together and put the children between them to keep them warm. They slept, but the adults dozed fitfully, constantly woken by the crackle of the fire and the snap! of falling logs. A wolf howled in the darkness. Abraham shivered; as much with the cold as the fear which that noise evoked. What a terrible sound - what a lonely sound, he thought. The wind eventually lessened as day broke, and the children started to whimper as they woke, stretching their cramped limbs in an effort to get up. Helena was crying with the cold, but Abraham rubbed her hands gently, to and fro, and soon the warmth was back and she smiled up at him. "Papa, does this mean I don't have to wash?" she said. What a wondrous thing is a child's mind - it certainly gets its priorities right, he thought, with a smile. The women busied themselves, folding up blankets and piling their things back on the cart. Breakfast was very simple, but Rula made some porridge over the hot ashes of the fire for the children. The adults ate a chunk of black bread and sipped the hot, sweet tea. They were ready to start another day.

After they had been walking for a couple of hours they heard a noise. Abraham was scared - horses hoofs! He yelled to the children to come quickly, and they all huddled together at the side of the road, fearfully waiting to see the riders approaching. To their immense relief, the riders turned out to be reindeer. Reindeer! Dozens of them, all running across the field and making straight for them. They laughed at one another, and the children were jumping up and down. "Catch one, catch one, we can use it to draw the cart." Abraham laughed, shouting too, knowing he had no chance of catching one of the beautiful creatures. He had to make a pretence of trying, though, just to keep the children happy, so he and Nathan ran after the smallest ones, trying to jump on them and grabbing at their antlers. What a sight they were, laughing and shouting, being dragged along by the reindeer, who had no intention of letting themselves be caught. The whole escapade was the tonic they needed. The children were laughing; the women were laughing, and so were the men. But the reindeer had gone. They averaged about fifteen miles that second day, and Abraham knew they were doing well. He knew they would soon be approaching a town and if it was possible he was going to try and sell some of his and Nathan's valuables to buy some new boots for the little ones. They all had them, but these would soon be holed with all the walking. He worried about them all a great deal, although they were not complaining. They had taken turns on the cart, which to them was a great game, and had saved some wear on their boots. As they entered the town they began to get very worried. Would they find the Bolsheviks here? Would Jews be baited as they were at home? They had all agreed on a story - their home had been burnt by accident and they were making their way to Minsk where they had a brother. Abraham knew they were on the right road for that city, and hoped the story sounded plausible. Of course, it was obvious they were Jewish and he and his brother had even discussed whether to rid themselves of their beards and curls, but they were proud of their race and, for the moment, decided to retain their true identity. After all, there were many Jews in this part of Russia. Abraham and Nathan left the family with the cart and went into town alone, taking what they thought could be sold. Anna and Rula had given them a list of things it was essential they had, but had both begged for "a few sweets for the children." The men went into the store. It appeared to be the only one of its kind on the main street, and a genial-looking man came out from a back room. "Good day," he said, eyeing them both, not without friendliness. "Strangers in town, are you? Abraham told him their story which the shop-keeper, nodding with sympathy at their hardship, seemed to accept. He turned the candlesticks over and over in his hands. "They are nice, very nice. They would look good on the mantle in the sitting room. "What did you want for them?" he asked. Abraham looked at him. "We really do not want money, as there are many things which we need because we had to leave our home so quickly. The children need boots or shoes, then there is this list of food and some kerosene for our light. If you have any heavy canvas, and some light wood and nails, we can perhaps rig up a rough shelter at night or if we get caught in a sudden snowstorm." The man looked at the list and, smiling, he said "Done. Pick up what you need over there and I will get some canvas from the storeroom. My wife is the best one to help with the boots if you tell her the sizes you want." He disappeared into the back of the shop, where voices could be heard, and a plump little bustly lady came through, smiling. "I understand you want some boots or shoes," she said. Abraham nodded and told her the sizes they needed. She had some very stout boots for the boys and some good, heavy shoes for the girls. The man reappeared with a roll of heavy canvas and some thin planks of wood under his arm, placed them on the counter and said "I have a bit of oilskin here, if that will help." Nathan smiled and nodded at him. "You are very kind. We need everything we can get hold of to keep our wives and the five children dry. Thank goodness it is March and the better weather is ahead of us." The grocer placed all the other packages on the counter, not forgetting the sweets as Abraham had said, and wished them well. They turned to go, laden with their goods, and the grocer called out "Mind how you go, the Bolsheviks are roaming the woods and forests and I understand they are robbing any travellers they meet. Keep to the side roads if you can - you will be safer." They thanked him and went out, but as they were just about to step into the road the grocer's wife ran out, clutching a small package. "Here," she said. "Take this. I have just baked it and the children will need some hot food in them." The men were speechless. What kindness, what generosity. Nathan found his tongue first, and thanked her again and again. She kept telling him it was nothing, and then went inside.

Abraham knew the women would be anxiously waiting for them to return, worried that they might have met some trouble in the town. As they came down the road absolutely groaning under the weight of all the goods, the women ran towards them, smiling and laughing. "You got it all then?" asked Rula. "You must have got a good price for the candlesticks," said Anna. "Not only a good price, but some oilskin, wood, oil for the lamp, and look, a home-made pie for the children." They were all amazed at the generosity of these kind people, and although Anna and Rula wanted to stop on their way through to thank them personally, Abraham told them about the grocer's warning to keep to the side roads, and so they decided to skirt the town as they carried on.

It was nightfall. The day had been reasonably mild, but at sunset, the snow had begun to fall again, and the wind had sprung up. They had been walking all afternoon as the weather was good, but had anxiously looked for shelter for the night. Nathan had spotted an old barn in the distance and so they quickly made their way to it. They found it was mainly dry, except for one end where the roof was leaking, so they settled themselves in a corner, huddled together to keep warm. Abraham lit a small fire, but the smoke would not go upwards and out of the roof at first but insisted on staying inside the barn, choking them horribly. He thought to himself it was lucky he knew how to make a fire as Nathan had given it up after several attempts. As a boy their father had shown him how to light a fire, pulling the thick fungus called gubka off the trees in sheets, which they then boiled and dried to use as kindling. On their first day, he had sought the gubka out, and they now had a fairly plentiful stock. Not having anywhere to dry it now they were on the road he had put it between his two coats and it had dried successfully. He had placed a small pile of gubka on the ground, then rubbed two pieces of flint together until a spark caused the gubka to smoulder, gently blowing on it to get a flame going. He knew the only way to survive the nights in the sub-zero temperatures was to keep a good fire burning if they had no shelter, but as he lay there, listening to the breathing of the others who were all asleep out of sheer exhaustion he knew they had been lucky to find this place for the night. They would not find such a shelter very often, he thought ruefully. He could not sleep. He could hear the wind roaring outside, almost as if it wanted to blow the place down. He pulled his fiddle to him, opened the case, and lifted it out. "Whatever else I sell, I will not sell you, my beauty," he said under his breath. He ran his hand lovingly over the strings, gently plucking them, so as not to disturb the others. He would really have liked to play but knew he could not for fear of waking them.

The next morning big-flaked snow was falling heavily and it was very cold. After a discussion they decided to stay in the barn until mid-day at least, to see if the snow would stop. They all agreed that it was one thing to walk in the icy, sub-zero temperatures which would now obviously follow, but they could not subject the children to the wind-driven snow. Abraham went to the other end of the barn and lit another fire. This time the smoke did go upwards, even though a fair amount of snow was coming through the roof, but at least they could heat some water for tea and make porridge for the children, who were very unhappy and restless this morning. They were tired, and all of them were beginning to itch unmercifully inside their clothing. The two mothers had talked about this and decided that they would try to warm some clean underwear near the fire and very quickly strip each child and put clean clothes on them. This they did, and all went quite well until they came to little Rosa. She was shivering very badly and obviously running a temperature, for her eyes were over-bright, and her face flushed. She wriggled out of her Mother's grasp and ran to her father, begging him not to let them take off her clothes. He picked her up, cuddling her to him "Hush, little one. Your Mother knows best. You will feel so much better if you have some clean, fresh clothes on. You will be a new woman." She smiled up at him, with those big blue eyes, and trusted him. At this, Anna called her quietly to her, and she meekly allowed her clothes to be changed. There was no chance of washing the clothes they had taken off the five children, so they did the next best thing. They rubbed some clean snow all over them, which thawed in the heat from the fire, then rubbed them together in a scrubbing movement. After they had done this, the clothes were rung out and placed near the fire to dry. Abraham was very worried about keeping themselves clean, but at least he knew that in this terrible cold there would be very few germs lurking.

The snow had stopped, and a watery sun shone in the cold, grey sky. Several days had passed since they had sheltered in the barn and had decided to make a move, even if they only achieved a few miles each day, for the men were anxious to put as many miles as possible between themselves and St. Petersburg. They guessed they had come about one hundred miles so far, which was no real distance, and so on they went, with Nathan in the harness this time. Abraham had noticed that one of the straps was beginning to wear thin, and knew he must try and get a new one, or a strip of leather, when they reached the next town. The snow was piled up around the untrodden ground on either side of the icy road, making it very difficult to manoeuvre the cart, which was slipping and sliding behind Nathan. The women were trying to push, but every now and again they would lose their footing and fall in the snow. "They are marvellous," thought Abraham, hearing them laugh. "How brave they are being. We could not wish for better wives." The wind was very fierce, but at least it was blowing the new, soft snow off the road, leaving it clear. By nightfall they had made reasonable headway and saw a forest ahead, showing white-clad trees. They made for it, stumbling and falling in the soft snow as they left the roadside. They found themselves in a shallow depression amongst the trees, where they were quite widely spaced. The snow had started to fall again, but thinly this time, and the wind was just a gentle moan, shaking the branches of the trees so that the snow fell in soft sheets, like a waterfall. They found a very large tree with a huge base, and, clearing a space under it, gathered some of the dead bracken lying all around. Nathan placed the canvas over this to make a base and by now Abraham had plenty of practice in erecting his make-shift canvas tent, which he promptly began to do again, hammering and knocking the nails into the soft wood. He hoped and prayed that the wind would not spring up again, at least not here in the woods, for he knew the flimsy shelter could very easily be blown down. "There, it is finished," he thought, and with the help of Anna and Rula he placed it over the canvas base. How well it worked. They had a shelter, and it was very cosy. Nathan had been busy gathering wood for a fire, which they now proceeded to light with the gubka. Very soon they had a good blaze going, feeling the warmth from it creeping into their bones.

The next morning dawned bright and clear, although the sub-zero temperature was chilling them through now that the fire had died down. The children were warm enough, lying between their parents, but Abraham knew Anna was worried about little Rosa. She was obviously still running a temperature and had a very bad cough. During the night she had been fretful and slightly delirious and it was obvious she was sickening for something. He watched the branches of the trees swaying and, as a gust of wind sprang up, flurries of snow fell off them. He whispered to Nathan "How in God's name will we ever reach Minsk? It is miles away, and we have already been walking for days." With a sudden jolt he realised it was Friday and tonight would be Shabbas. They had actually been walking for two weeks. The cart has stood up very well, and Rula has been a tower of strength to himself and Anna, he thought. He loved his sister-in-law very much - he had never had a sister of his own, only a brother. It was good that there had always been a closeness between them from the moment they first met, and with the births of all the children, this had strengthened. They were one family. Anna stirred. Gently tugging at Abraham's sleeve she whispered "Dushka, the fire is almost out and we must get it going before we all freeze to death." He stretched his cramped body, yawned, and gently rolled away from the children, crouching in order to get out of the front of the rough shelter. "It works," he thought, "it really works." He knew, however, that it would never stand up in a fierce gale, but also knew that Spring was not that far away - perhaps only a matter of three or four weeks, and the worst of the weather was now behind them. Maybe if he and Nathan could find work in the first big village they came to they could afford to pay for lodgings for a few nights. He knew the women were very worried about the children, and the fact that they were not getting proper meals, or washing, for that matter. He smiled ruefully. "Strange how when we are at home the first thing they always try to get out of is washing," he thought. He stood up and then was joined by Nathan, who had woken early after a very fitful doze.

Rosa's coughing had kept Abraham and Anna awake much of the night and he was worried about it. He hoped she was not going to become ill, for that would really be a problem and one which he did not know how they would overcome. She was such a sweet child, and he was thankful that all of them had been so good, so far. The women had woken the children, and soon Anna had porridge and tea going on the now brightly blazing fire. Abraham and his brother made several treks into the forest and came back each time with armfuls of kindling and dry branches. Anna looked at them. "I think we all need a rest today. We have been walking for two weeks and it is Shabbas tonight. The wind is not too bad, and if we stay here Rula and I can make some food for our evening meal. There is still some meat left from the village the other day, and with the vegetables we have, I can make a good stew. We could all do with that, and I can make some scones on the fire. It will also give Rosa a chance to rest, for she is obviously not well." They all agreed, and once the other four children had eaten some food they all raced off into the woods, with a warning from their mothers not to go too far, shouting to each other "let's build a snowman; let's make a snow house." The adults smiled, pleased the children were obviously happy at this break from the walking. Abraham sat down in the tent. He knew that one of the wheels of the cart needed some attention, and as he sipped his tea and ate his bread he figured out how best he could put it right. He looked up at the top of the tent and worked out what extra wood was needed to make it stronger if they were forced to stay out in the open in a fierce wind. "Nathan, when you are ready we must look at the cart and then must find three branches which we can cut and smooth down to make this tent secure. If we can, we must buy some more rope at the next village, for the little we bought is not sufficient to tie it down in a gale." Nathan nodded. He never said much but thought a lot. "Abraham, I have been thinking. The weather has been reasonably good to us so far, but it could get worse suddenly, as we know. The next time it does and we are without shelter why don't we try to make an ice house like the peasants do for themselves and the goats. We have an axe and it shouldn't be too difficult." They all thought this was an excellent idea and Abraham suggested that, during the afternoon, they should experiment and see how they got on. That way, if they did need to build such a place, they would have learned the snags the hard way!

The women had melted some snow by the fire and were trying to wash some of the smaller pieces of underwear, but as soon as these were wet, even with the heat of the fire, they froze like boards. They found, though, that by rubbing them between their mittened hands near the heat of the fire they soon became pliable, and they then placed them under their coats to dry. How they would get them on the children was something neither of them mentioned - not in these temperatures - and outdoors. Maybe they would be lucky, though, and find a barn as they had at the start of last week. They busied themselves cooking and soon there was a wonderful smell coming from the pot over the fire - a good, hot stew and newly baked scones. "Get the children please, Nathan, and come and eat. It will get cold very quickly," said Rula. There were whoops and cries of delight as the children, running at the call from him, smelled the food. They needed no second invitation to sit down and were oblivious to Anna's apologies for how hard the scones were, or how tough the meat might be. To them all, it was the best meal they had eaten in ages and very soon not a plate was left with anything on it. Anna had saved a small portion of sweets for them, and she dished them out to the five, with a warning these were the last. Abraham could see she was upset that Rosa refused hers, but she had managed to eat a little, even if not the meat. A good rest was what she needed. That afternoon, whilst Rosa was sleeping and there were still a few hours of light left, they collected the other children together and proceeded to make a game of showing them how to stack the large chunks of frozen snow they had cut. Neither of the men had the slightest idea how to build a snow house, but knew what it should look like when it was finished, and so it became very much a game of trial and error. They laughed as, time and again, the structure collapsed, sometimes with a child or two still inside. However, after about four attempts to stack the blocks of snow they found that, by staggering them in rows, and trimming them round as they went, they stayed put. Rula had thought it should be square, until she asked with a chuckle "What about the roof, it will cave in." Her husband dived at her in fun, and they rolled over and over in the snow, laughing loudly. This gave the children an excuse to join in, and soon there were four children and four adults all roughing and tumbling on the ground. Abraham sat up, oohing and aahing. "I am too old for this, let me go. I give in. I give in." The children were determined that their game was not finished yet, though, and soon they were pelting the adults with snowballs who were running backwards and forwards amongst the trees, trying to get cover. "Truce, truce," cried Rula. "Let's finish the job. We have had a good game, children, but we must finish." Abraham smiled. She was such a sensible woman, and the little ones had needed that bit of fun. They started again, and soon, to their immense pleasure they had finished. It was a little lop-sided, and a bit small, but they could all squeeze through the opening to get inside. Anna stayed with Rosa, who had brightened up enough to peer inquisitively at the goings-on, and could hear the giggles coming from the house. "Oh, that's my foot." "Ouch, you dug me with your elbow," and various other exclamations. One by one they all emerged backwards from the house and, standing up, Abraham said "We've done it. Now if we have a problem we can build a shelter." "Papa, can we light a fire in it," asked Israel. At that, they all started to laugh again, and Abraham was happy to see Israel joining in, obviously realising what a silly thing he had said.

Night had fallen; the children were all asleep and had eaten their Shabbas supper. The wind had died right down, and although it was bitterly cold, they were all warm and cosy inside the ice house, where they had decided to spend the night. Abraham picked up his fiddle and tucked it under his chin. He drew the bow across the strings and began to play the 1st movement of the Brahms Violin Concerto. Nathan, Rula and Anna gazed at the man they all loved, as they sat listening to the music coming from the instrument, which sounded as it had never sounded before, giving them all a few small moments of joy. Anna and Rula had tears running down their faces, and Nathan quickly blew his nose. How they loved to hear Abraham play. He played for about an hour, his mittened fingers plucking at the strings and the bow sliding across them, and playing with such feeling and tenderness that the fiddle seemed almost alive. He played gay folk tunes, and they all joined in the singing. He played lullaby's, though the children were sleeping soundly after all the excitement of the day. He played boisterous Hebrew music, at which Abraham excelled, and at one point Nathan got up and, crouching, danced in the tiny area, with Anna and Rula both clapping time. Eventually, Abraham's fingers got too cold and he wiped his fiddle over with a cloth and gently slid it back into its case. He was anxious that it was played often, for that kept it at its peak, and was worried that Rosa and Israel, who played well for their ages, had not done any playing since they had left St. Petersburg, as their small violins had been left behind in the cellar. He knew, though, that he would quickly get them back into the routine of both practice and playing as soon as they reached their destination and he could get new violins for them. The fire outside the snow house was stacked with logs and all slept.

Little Rosa had definitely improved, for she coughed very little through the night, and her Mother knew that by morning she would be well on the mend. The next morning was fine and clear. Very, very cold but with that extraordinary clarity you sometimes get in winter - a day when the breath froze as you spoke, but the eye could see for miles and miles. They set off, Nathan in the harness and Abraham pushing, with three children on the cart and the two eldest walking with their mothers. The women hoped to pass through a village during the day, or certainly the next day, for they needed food, and hopefully some milk. They crunched along in the fresh snow, stamping out a trail as they walked. The snow had drifted high on either side of the roadway, and as far as the eye could see was snow, snow and more snow. Vast fields, which Abraham and Nathan reckoned would be potatoes, but no shelter or building of any kind in all directions could be seen. They searched the horizon for signs of woods or a forest, for Abraham was anxiously looking for cover by nightfall. The men reckoned that the snow lay at least two feet deep on the fields, and Moshe suggested that they could always build another snow house - theirs would never blow down! They all laughed and trudged on, their feet crunch, crunch, crunching as they went. After several hours Nathan shouted "Look, isn't that a spire or something ahead." They stopped, and peering into the watery sunlight Abraham could see something. The women were relieved, for they had begun to think they would not reach a village or town by nightfall. It cheered them up, and they all began to quicken their pace. As they got nearer and nearer they could see that it was quite a big town, but had no idea of the name of it. Neither Abraham or his brother had ever ventured far from St. Petersburg, only to go to Moscow when he had gone there with the Tsar's family. Rula took Nathan's hand, and together they started to push the cart to ease the load up front. Anna was carrying little Moshe, and Mala was holding on to her skirt. Like this they entered the town, Abraham knew they must present a sorry sight. He smiled through his snow-caked beard at his wife, and she brushed some of the snow off his eyebrows and hat with her free hand. They all straightened up their shoulders and walked ahead. It was obviously a very busy, bustling place, as there were many people about, even though it was nearly sunset. Goats and cows were standing in pens at the side of the road, under a rough shelter, and men were loudly bartering for them. There was much shouting and slapping of hands at the completion of a deal. As they advanced through the street people stopped and stared, aware of their coming by the clanking of the few pots and pans from under the cart. A butcher's shop displayed some cuts of meat in the window, and close by was another with vegetables laid out in profusion. The hardware shop had brooms, bowls, basins and a variety of goods hanging from the lean-to roof, and stacked up outside the windows on either side of the door. The main street had been cleared of snow, and chickens were running squawking to and fro, being chased by a cockerel. Abraham thought ruefully "He would make a nice Lokshen soup," but dismissed the thought, for there was no way they could afford to buy a chicken. They stopped outside the hardware shop and looked about them. Those people who had been staring looked away in embarrassment, not wanting to be thought nosey. "Who can these people be? Where have they come from? Do you think they have stolen those children?" Those were some of the words heard in the clear air, but Abraham took immediate charge of the situation and, putting all the children up on the cart with an order to stay put, he walked over to a group of men, suggesting to Anna and Rula that they purchase anything they urgently needed. "Good day," said Abraham. "My name is Abraham Levinsky, and this is my brother, Nathan. We are on our way to Minsk, where we have relatives. What is the name of this place?" Someone stepped forward. "Good day, comrade. This is the village of Bechonsky, but you are many miles from Minsk yet. How long have you been travelling, and when did your horse die." Abraham smiled. "We have no horse. We have pulled the cart between us. Our home caught fire and so we had to leave suddenly, with only the clothes we wear and the few possessions we could grab before the flames burnt everything down. We have been travelling for two weeks now, but are fine, and all we need is to replenish our stores. Of course, we have a long way to go yet, but with God's help we will soon reach our destination." "You all look as if you could do with a good wash," shouted someone, at which there was a loud roar of laughter from the other men standing there. "We don't want you bringing your lice into our town," shouted someone else. "Clear off, we don't want beggars in Bechonsky." The jeers and cries were loud, and the men hoped their wives could not hear. Suddenly an old man pushed through the crowd which had now gathered and, holding up his hands, he quietened the people. "My friends, my friends. What is the matter with you. The stranger has told us he had to flee because his home was burnt. Are we that uncharitable that we would force him to leave our town before he can buy some goods. If he has money, who are we to deny him the things he needs. Look at the children. See how young they are. From the way this man speaks he is no beggar, so come on, where is your sense? We ought to be offering our help in weather like this, for how many of us would have the courage to leave our homes if disaster struck and try to make our way to our families." He turned to Abraham "My friend, we cannot offer you the hospitality of our homes, for we are mostly poor farmers, but if we can help you, let us know." At these words all the villagers stopped their heckling and, looking very crestfallen, saw the sense in what the old man said, and murmured their assent to what he was saying. Abraham went up to him, grasped his hand, shaking it warmly. "Thank you, friend, for those words. We certainly are not beggars. In fact, my brother is a very fine tailor and I am a musician. We are no threat to you, and certainly have no lice or any disease. True we have not bathed or washed for a couple of weeks, other than with melted snow, but our wives have kept the children as clean as they could. Of course, none of us adults have been able to change our underwear because we have been in the open." A woman stepped forward. "You are Jewish, aren't you, friend." Abraham nodded. "Come. Come with me. Bring the little ones. The Rabbi lives down the street and he has a small community here. Between us I am sure we can provide you with a bath, so you can change your clothes. How are you managing for food?" She took Abraham's elbow and, still chattering on, asking a million questions, she propelled him towards the cart and to Rula and Anna who had completed their purchases. They watched in astonishment, not knowing what had been going on, as they saw their husbands and the woman, followed by others, coming towards them. Rula gasped, fearing trouble. "Rula, Anna, this kind woman is going to take us to the Rabbi. There is one here in town with some of our people. What a piece of luck." The men got the cart and, following the woman, walked after her down the street. They came to a few wooden houses, very shabby but clean, and the woman stopped at one and knocked on the door. The Rabbi came out and she quickly told him what she knew. They all stood, with the children, and waited to hear what he would say. At the noise, others had come out of their houses. The woman called everyone to them, and apparently enjoying bringing some news to their quiet lives, she again told what she knew, embroidering it with her own little titbits. Anna, Rosa and Helena went to one house, Rula and Mala to another, whilst Abraham, Nathan and the boys went into the Rabbi's house. They were all able to wash, change their clothes, and sit down on soft, oh! so soft chairs. Was it really such a short time since they had known such comfort? Anna and Rula had quickly realised that none of these people had much money, and so had brought what little food they had into the homes, sharing it with them, supplementing what was available, and in this way they did not feel that they were begging. Just to sit at a table and talk was a relief. Abraham had warned all of them, especially the children, not to tell why they had really run away in case any of the villagers were Bolshevik sympathisers who might turn them over to the authorities. The story of their flight was believed and they were shown a great deal of kindness.

After they had eaten they all congregated in the Rabbi's house and his wife, whose name was Esther, said "Did you say you were a musician." Abraham nodded, and someone asked what instrument he played. "The violin,"he said. "Play for us, please." "Oh, yes, play for us,"said a couple of the other villagers. Nathan smiled and, getting up, went over and picked up the fiddle case from the pile of possessions they had felt they could not leave on the cart. "Here, brother, play for these people. Give us a tune." Abraham took out his instrument, wiped it over with a cloth and tucked it under his chin. He played. The crowd grew silent. They thought they would hear an amateur fiddler but soon realised that they had a true master in their midst. They listened, enraptured, as the music rang forth. As he finished his first piece, the Vivaldi Concerto in C, il Piacere, and put the fiddle down, you could hear a pin drop, and then suddenly the clapping started. "Wonderful. Wonderful," came the cries. "Play some more, please, you must play some more." The applause went on and on until Abraham, with some embarrassment, picked it up again and played. He played Hebrew music; he played Tschaikovsky; he played Mazurka's; he played non-stop well into the night. Each time he finished the people begged for more. In the end he was too tired to go on and the Rabbi, sensing this, held up his hands and said "Good people, you have been generous to these travellers today, but you have been more than repaid with the wonderful music you have heard. You indeed have a rare and wonderful talent, Abraham Levinsky. You should put it to good use." Abraham smiled, but he was not a vain man and would not dream of boasting of his past life. He put his violin away, after wiping it and putting it in its case. Saying goodnight, everyone went to their homes with Rula, Anna and the children. Abraham and Nathan laid down on the floor of the Rabbi's home and for a little while they talked about the day's events, until drowsiness overcame them and they fell asleep. The next day they left Bechonsky at noon, waving goodbye and calling out their thanks. The women had promised to write when they reached Minsk to let them know they were safe, for they had quickly struck up friendships with the kind people who had taken them in for the night. Feeling clean and fresh and, with renewed vigour, they left the town to set out once again for their destination.

The next few days passed uneventfully, with very little snow and only a light wind. Each night they erected the tent in the shelter of trees or a small wood, but now they were running out of food again and had not seen any sign of life, nor the prospect of a village. Nathan's feet were now covered in blisters where his boots had rubbed and he was finding it increasingly difficult to keep up the pace. Rula had bound them up and put oil on but the pain was excruciating. "If only they could stop for a day or so and he could rest," she said. "Once the blisters heal I will be alright," said Nathan, when Anna had looked at his feet in horror. Abraham was very worried, but didn't say anything. He knew they must keep going at all costs, for the sky was much heavier today, with low, leaden clouds, and he knew this meant a blizzard was coming. The temperature had dropped considerably and the children, all sitting on the cart, were crying how cold they were. Anna got them all down and started to run on the crisp, hard snow. "Come on, all of you, let's play tag. That way we will get warm and have a game at the same time." Rula joined in and soon they were all puffing and panting, falling and sliding in the snow, their breath freezing as they shouted out to each other. Abraham was glad, because he was now looking for somewhere to stop. He said to Nathan "I think we are in for a blizzard and, by the feel of the air, it has got much colder. If one comes we could be in it for a couple of days. We should try and make a snow house, don't you think." He knew Nathan would be relieved and guessed he had wanted to stop, but had not dared to suggest it. He quickly agreed with his brother and, seeing some large snowdrifts to their left, he said "Abraham, let's go over into that field where there are a few trees, and if we are going to build a snow house there is all the frozen stuff we want, and a high hedge. We can easily do it there." At this, they proceeded to drag the cart to the drifts and, placing it a few feet away, started to cut the blocks of snow they needed. The women, seeing what was happening, encouraged the children towards their fathers and, carrying Moshe, they clambered through the thick snow and started to help. The exertion helped keep them warm, but Abraham kept casting anxious glances at the sky which was getting heavier and greyer by the minute. Calling Anna to him he said, quietly, "Make a fire and use the flour you have left to bake scones, and anything else you can cook. We might be in for some bad weather and not be able to have a fire for a day or so." He knew Anna had sensed the panic in his voice, which he had tried to hide from her. She called Rula and together they started to light a fire with the gubka and some dry kindling they had now always got with them on the cart. They sent the two eldest children to the other side of the snow drift, where the bushes were, to see what wood there was, for the little they had would be gone before they could finish baking. The children found a little, and Rula joined them to speed up the collection. She called to Nathan to chop down a couple of small spruce trees from the hedge with his axe, but when she saw the difficulty he had walking towards her she quickly sprang forward and took the axe from him and cut them down herself. He gave her a bleak, watery smile and she smiled back at him to let him know she understood. Once they had collected enough kindling and wood they baked a small batch of scones and some flat cakes, using the last of the flour, and at the insistence of Abraham and Nathan, quickly unloaded the cart and took their few possessions into the small finished shelter. The two men then upended the cart and packed snow either side of it to keep it upright to make a form of windbreak in case the blizzard should come from the other direction. Finally they were finished; their progress hampered by Nathan stumbling on his blistered feet and the wind which was getting stronger and stronger by the minute. The children were already inside, and the two women had taken the last of the things in through the opening. Then suddenly, with a deafening shriek, the gale met the two men head on.

They were blinded, and could not open their eyes in its force. The impact was so great that they could not believe they, or the shelter, were still standing. Within minutes snow covered them, freezing on beards and eyebrows. It was a searing blizzard, hitting them with its fury and hurling the full weight of the snow at all in its path. They stumbled, fell, got up and stumbled again towards the snow house. It briefly went through Abraham's mind that if it was still standing in the path of this gale, it would probably keep standing. It was indeed a miracle. They scrambled in through the small opening, packing the entrance with the bundles they had ready. Abraham looked around them and, in the light of the lamp lit by Rula, he saw the terrified, whimpering children huddled around their mothers, who in turn were looking wide-eyed at Nathan and himself. "Don't be frightened, children, we are safe in here. The storm will soon pass. Come, Nathan, let us look at your feet whilst we have the chance. At least you won't get frostbite in here, we are so closely packed in that we will all be as warm as toast before long." He knew that no-one really believed him but he had to keep their spirits up. When he saw his brother's feet he shuddered inwardly for they were in a terrible mess; bleeding and red-raw. Some of the places had become infected and were swollen and inflamed, but there was nothing they could do, for they had no ointment to put on them. Rula had some oil and rubbed this on them. "Keep your feet loosely covered and in a little while they will get better," said Anna.

Their snow house worked. It really worked! The full fury of the blizzard was hitting them time and time again, but they were still safe. "Oh God, please keep us safe in here," prayed Abraham, and he knew this was in the minds of all of them. They stayed there for what

Abraham guessed to be a couple of days, eating, sleeping, dozing and coping with the call of nature as best they could. The women found this acutely embarrassing, but the men tried to make light of it, turning their backs whenever it was necessary. Moshe and Israel did as their fathers' did, but the girls were much more uncomfortable at relieving themselves in front of their fathers. Still, there was no alternative and, sensing this, they scooped away the snow from under them and then pushed it back again when they had finished. The blizzard was still raging, but Abraham felt he must get out and see if there was any lessening in its force. He stumbled out and was hit by the screaming, lashing wind and the sub-zero temperature. It took his breath away, and he gasped, clinging on to the snow house. "Thank God, that huge mound of snow against the hedge is still there," he thought, "it's taking the main force of the gale from us, and the other heap must be the cart, covered up by another large drift." His ears, although covered by his scarf, were soon frozen, his nose icy and red, and his eyes flooding with unwanted tears. He shook uncontrollably with the intense cold and quickly scrambled back inside. "It's terrible out there, it is the worst weather I have seen for years," he said. The storm lasted for days and they had no food of any sort left, and as they had no means of heating water they could not make tea to warm them. The children were fractious, hating being cooped up in such a small space, which by now stank unmercifully from excreta and vomit, for Helena and Moshe had both been sick several times that day. Abraham knew this was because their stomachs were empty but was powerless to do anything. They could not get out until the storm died down. He was glad Nathan's feet had begun to heal as Rula had constantly tended them, knowing that when they got out of this place he would need to be fit and well for the rest of the journey. They all agreed that they would never want to experience such cruel and bleak weather ever again. Abraham said "Quiet. Ssh. Listen." They all sat very still. "What are we listening for?" said Nathan. "What have you heard?" Then they appeared to realise at the same time that the wind had died down and what they could hear was the silence. They all started to leave the shelter, Abraham and Nathan pushing and shoving their way through the snowed-up entrance, the women carrying the two sick children and, although there was still a keen wind, it was nothing in comparison to the hammering of the blizzard which they had experienced for the past few days. They had no way of knowing how long they had been inside, but Abraham knew none of them ever wanted to go back in there again.

They were all stiff and cramped, but how relieved they were to be out in the fresh air. It was very cold, but the sky was clear and the sun bright. Abraham reckoned it was about mid-day, which meant they had some hours of daylight ahead of them to get on the move. The two sick children were a worry, but he knew that if he could light a fire so that Anna or Rula could make some porridge and tea for them they would probably begin to feel much better. He got out the last of his gubka and, together with Nathan, they kindled some of the dried moss and eventually had a small, meagre fire going. "What could they use," he thought. They had nothing which would burn. Then Rula had an idea. She quickly went back into that hell hole and retrieved the oily rags which she had used to bind Nathan's feet with knowing the oil would ignite, and the cloth would burn. It worked - they had a good blaze going and soon the porridge and tea was ready. Oh! how welcome the hot food was, and Anna chided them to eat it as slowly as they could, so as not to make themselves sick again. The adults were all as hungry as the children, but there was nothing left for them, and so they made the best of the tea, thankful for its warmth and feeling it reviving them as it went down. They dismantled the snow house to get their belongings, rather than face going back into the stench, and Rula called Moshe and Israel to help her scoop the snow away from the cart, thankful for its protection during the storm. All the bundles and packages were retrieved and they started to load the cart, anxious to be on their way in order to obtain food before nightfall. Abraham knew they could not be too far from a village, for it had been some time since they had left the last one. Suddenly they heard a noise - sounds of voices yelling and shouting in the distance. They all turned in the direction of the sound, fearful of what they would see. "Bolsheviks!" thought Abraham. "Soldiers!" Said Nathan. As the riders got nearer they all shouted out their surprise and the children started to jump up and down in excitement. It was reindeers again. Dozens and dozens of reindeers, but this time with sledges and men. What were they doing here? Where had they come from? As they came nearer and nearer they could see that the sledges were being pulled by two or three reindeers apiece and when they had almost reached them, with loud shouts to the animals to stop, many little brown men with grinning faces jumped down. They were the primitive herdsmen from the area Abraham knew he had read about. He remembered they were called Ostyaks. He called out a greeting, wondering if they would understand, but they did and soon about twenty or so of the little men were all crowding around the family. There were apparently no women with them, but they had obviously been on a hunting trip for they had several dead rabbits, two deer, and large birds strapped to the sledges. Abraham told the leader of their plight and the little man, who was only about five feet tall, told him that the storm had raged for four days, and that was how long they must have been in the shelter. The Ostyaks were busying themselves releasing the reindeer from their shafts, which amused the children, who begged to be able to stroke the beautiful animals. First, they took away the neck collar, then the two long shafts which went down to the ground to form the runners of the simple sledges. All the children pleaded to have a ride on the reindeer, but the leader told Abraham that no-one could ride on their backs as this was their weak area, but that their necks and shoulder blades were strong. Israel, Rosa and Mala pleaded with them. "Please let us have a ride, we will be very careful and do not weigh much." Then Moshe and Helena joined in, quickly forgetting their recent bouts of sickness, so the men lifted them all up, chiding them to remember to sit well up on the neck of the animal. An Ostyak each led a reindeer with a child on its back at a run on the hard, crisp snow, and the children thought it was wonderful. "Can't we have one to pull our cart, Papa," called out Israel. "We would look after it," said Mala. The brothers smiled and said "We'll see, we'll see," knowing full well that there was no possibility of using one of these lovely creatures to pull their cart. The little men had plenty of food with them, and when they heard how the two families were without any they promptly gave them bread and presents of meat from their hunting. Anna and Rula were overjoyed and thanked the

Ostyaks over and over again. Now that there was no immediate reason to be off in search of food they stoked up the fire with some wood and kindling which the Ostyaks had with them, and sat around, sharing the tea which was all the family had to offer in return for the generous gifts of meat and bread. Two hours later, having said goodbye to their new-found friends, and with some fur skins to make gloves for the five children, they were on their way again. Nathan's feet had completely healed, but this time he wrapped his feet in some soft linen from Rula's petticoat so that he would not get blisters again. Abraham had done the same, for he had noticed that his feet were getting very sore, and he encouraged them all to copy him. "Fine thing, my best petticoat being used to wrap around your feet," said Anna in fun. "I will buy you a dozen new petticoats when we reach Minsk and settle down," said Abraham. She smiled at him lovingly. The Ostyaks had told them that Minsk was still many miles away and, as they started off on their journey again, they all wondered how long it would take to get there.

Everywhere was bright and shining as the sun shone down on the newly fallen snow, and the wind had now stopped. The silence was all around as they made their way through the forest, relieved that they would have shelter and a warm fire that night. They had been walking for several days since their meeting with the Ostyaks and had eaten the last of the meat given to them the day before. In a small village they had passed through they had replenished their supply of flour and oil and had used the last of the money to buy some ointment in case they developed any more foot problems. Abraham was keeping the Hannukah candle for when they reached Minsk and knew that Nathan had the same idea with his few meagre possessions. "So far, so good," he thought. "We have been lucky. We can do without meat for a few more days and will be in Minsk soon." They pulled off the road, making for a clearing in the trees. The children, now used to the nightly routine, ran about gathering small branches and kindling from under the trees, whilst Anna and Rula started to prepare food. Abraham and Nathan rigged up their tent with amazing ease and very soon they were all sitting around a huge fire, eating and talking, but eager to reach their destination. They woke early the next morning, and after a hurried breakfast in the bright, early spring sunshine, they were all aware that they should soon reach Minsk. They were now all very dirty and their clothes needed changing. Abraham wondered if they smelled, but it was impossible to tell if it was themselves, or the clothes they wore. He knew there was nothing they could do, though, and he shrugged the thought off. As they approached the town they could see smoke, and as the wind blew it towards them they could smell the burning, searing smell of death. They stopped, and the hairs stood up on the back of Abraham's neck. "God in Heaven, what is ahead of us?" he said. They walked on and saw, coming towards them, a line of people. As they grew closer to each other they saw that it was women and children, with no men to be seen amongst them. They all carried bundles and some had small cases. They had fled from something or someone, "But what? Whom?" thought Abraham. Stopping as the first woman reached them he gently said to her "What is wrong? Where are you going?" The woman looked up at him with tears in her eyes and told him what had happened. Their town had been suspected of harbouring some royalist supporters and there had even been a rumour that Grand Duke

Michael had been hiding there. Kerensky's troops had come and taken all the men and shot them in groups, in this way hoping that someone would say where the traitors were hiding. There were no traitors in the town, no royalist sympathisers, and no Jews, who the troops were also seeking. In their fury at coming on a wild goose chase, once they had killed all the men they had raped the young girls and a few of the women, and actually ridden off with some of them. The women had been powerless to do anything and had stood by watching both the slaughter of their husbands and sons, and the rape of their daughters and sisters. Many of the soldiers had looted and stolen vodka, then drunk themselves into a state of wild hysteria, culminating in the burning of all the houses and had stood, laughing, whilst their colleagues had thrown the dead men into the flames. Abraham turned to his brother and said "These women and children in the road are in the same plight as we are but they have no men to help them." Nathan turned to the leader "What can we do to help you?" but she ignored his question and, seeing their wives and children, and realising they were Jewish, said "You must not go into the town. It is very dangerous, the troops are everywhere and they are looking for Jews and royalists. You will be murdered as soon as you are seen." Abraham and Nathan looked at one another. "We were heading for Minsk and this town is on our route. We only have another twenty or thirty miles to go and we will be there," he said. "You must turn round. You must not go on if you value your lives. We are going to head for Lvov on the Polish borders, and then we will get across into Poland, where we will be safe," said one of the women. "Abraham, we cannot go all that way. It is miles and we have been going for so long already," Anna was pleading with him. He turned to face her. "Dushka, these people would not be fleeing if there was no danger. We have to do the same, and change our course. We must also make for Lvov and see how we get on there, but we cannot risk our lives and that of the children's, after having come through so much already." She and Rula nodded miserably, knowing that they had no alternative but to change their route and make for Lvov.

They walked for several days, the two brothers trying to be of what little help they could to the forty or fifty women and children that had joined them. The days dragged on in the same never-ending pattern, with each night stopping, lighting fires and eating what little food they had. Fortunately, the women from the town had managed to bring some with them and had survived so far, but Abraham knew it would soon all be gone. Four of the women and children had already died and Abraham and Nathan had tried to bury them, without success, because of the frozen ground. All that could be done was to heap snow over them and hope that, by the time Spring came, the wolves would have disposed of the bodies. Abraham knew that they must separate from this body of people, for they were in grave danger whilst they stayed with them - not for being Jews, but of starving! The women refugees were sitting dejectedly in the shelter of the woods so he went up to their leader, a woman called Ushakova, and said "I am sorry, but I think my family must go on alone as we have run out of food now and can move quicker with our cart to reach a town. As there are so many of you I think it would be better if you split up into groups of ten or so, for no village or town will be prepared to help fifty or more refugees, but would perhaps be more kindly disposed to helping a few women and children." Ushakova saw the sense in this, knowing that they had very little chance of surviving if they continued as they were. She said to Abraham "You go on, and we will all rest here today. From tomorrow we will leave in groups as you suggest and make our way to the border. You are right, Abraham. We all wish you Godspeed and thank you for what you have done for us." The other women all murmured their thanks and, with cries of "Good luck and God go with you" and the children waving to each other, they set off.

That afternoon Abraham and his family reached a farm, so he went to the farmer to see if there were any jobs they could do in exchange for some food and shelter. He and his wife were very kind and when they heard their story, and that of the savage massacre of the men whose wives and children had been forced to flee their homes, the wife cried and said that they could take shelter in their barn for the night. The farmer, whose name was Oskar, put down some fresh, clean straw for them to sleep on and they were given a wonderful meal by his wife of hot beef stew, black bread, sweet cake and tea. They hadn't had tea for some time. What a treat! After a while, Oskar came to see if they were alright and had everything they needed. He told them that it was not often he had the chance for a conversation with outsiders in this remote area so he wanted to be friendly, particularly as he realised that both the men were not labourers, but cultured and well-bred, so he turned to them and said "What work did you do before your house was burnt down and you had to leave the city?" Abraham replied and said "Nathan was a tailor before we left St. Petersburg and I was a musician." Oskar was very surprised, and grasped Abraham by the hand "Come into the house, I have something to show you." He led them into his home, which was a wooden building, entered from a central porch, heaped up high with cords of wood ready for burning. There were mats scattered on the polished floor, and a large fireplace giving off a warm heat, with two old armchairs either side. This was obviously the kitchen, with a soot-blackened pot hanging over the fire and a large family table and benches in the centre of the room. Everywhere was bright and very clean. Oskar led them into another room, which was obviously only used on special occasions and proudly pointed to their prized possession - an old upright piano! Abraham immediately went over to it, lifted the lid and ran his fingers over the yellowed ivory keys. It was sadly in need of tuning, but it played. Oskar explained that his eldest daughter was the musician in their family and she would be very pleased to meet someone who had the same love. His wife quickly ran out and called her. "Lara, Lara, come. Someone is here who you will want to meet." There was a light tripping on the stairs and a beautiful young girl entered. She was about eighteen years of age, with her blonde hair plaited around her head in peasant style. She had a fresh, pink complexion and her figure was just bursting into maturity. "Come child," said her father, "play for the gentleman. He is a musician from St. Petersburg." She sat down at the piano and, without music, began to play some Chopin. She played exquisitely and Abraham gasped with delight as the music filled the room. Nathan and the rest of the family had all come in, and they sat down, awed by the sounds coming from the piano. Her mother proudly smiled at Anna and Rula, as only a mother could. Lara stopped playing and placed her hands in her lap.

Turning to Abraham she said "Do I play well enough to be a musician in the city, sir." He stood up and, going over to her, he put his hand on her head. "You play beautifully. Chopin himself would be proud to hear his works played so well. Let me see if I can tune the piano for you a little." He tinkered with it for almost an hour and, when satisfied that it was the best he could do with the old faithful, he called Lara in and asked her to play again. She sat down and played a Polonaise and as she heard the chords emitting from the keyboard she sighed with pleasure. "Oh, it is a thousand times better. Thank you so much." She turned to him. "What instrument do you play?" He told her it was a violin and she begged him to play for her, and her parents urged him to do so as well. Abraham looked at Anna, who had come back into the farmhouse after putting the children to bed, and she nodded to him. "I will go and get the fiddle, Dushka," she said, and quickly went out. When she returned she told him "Rula and Nathan are with the children. They are alright." She handed the fiddle to Abraham and he took it out of its case, wiping it, as he always did, with the cloth which covered it. He played some of his most favourite pieces for them and the girl gasped in delight at his playing, as he had done when he heard her, and soon the two of them were playing duet after duet, Oskar and Maria clapping after every piece. She had a perfect ear and could play almost anything from memory. If she was not familiar with a piece he would play the melody through for her once or twice and she could then play it. "What a gift she has," he thought, "what a gift." When they had played for a couple of hours Abraham and Anna said goodnight to the three of them and, before making their way to the barn he turned to Oskar and said "With such talent you should do everything you can to encourage Lara to become a pianist. I am sure she could get a scholarship to study at the Conservatoire in Moscow. Once all the troubles are over promise me you will do all you can to help her." Abraham could see the pride in the man's face, that a musician such as him thought his daughter was so talented. He nodded and promised that he would try to arrange something very soon. He had known his daughter could play but until tonight he had never realised just how well.

They left the next day, feeling they had made yet more friends and were laden with food, flour, oil and some clean strips of linen. The farmer would take no money, and when Anna and Rula tried to give his wife a small gift of jewellery she would not hear of it, telling them both they would need whatever possessions they had when they finally reached their destination. She had hastily added the clean linen when they had told her of the trouble with Nathan's feet, but saying all the while "I hope you won't need it." Abraham turned from the harness position of the cart and waved, thinking to himself that there were still some good people left in this world after all. They headed in the direction that Oskar had indicated, which he said would lead to Lvov and the Polish border. He had known nothing of the Bolsheviks or Kerensky's troops and only hoped that there were none in Lvov. Whilst saying their farewells he had again promised to send Lara to study music, which pleased Abraham a great deal.

For several days they continued, with the weather being reasonably kind to them, but Abraham knew that it could not last. Sometimes March was a notoriously bad month and early April, with the sudden gales, not much better. They had now used up nearly all their food except for some tea, and he knew they would soon have to acquire flour, milk and maybe some vegetables. There was nothing of value left, except his precious fiddle, and nothing on this earth would make him part with it. He had told Anna to ration out the food and it had lasted until now, with the children having more than the adults but he knew it was vital they all be kept well-fed in these still cold conditions. The brighter days which they had been having had caused them some extra problems - that of the sun's glare off the white snow. He was becoming increasingly worried about Rula, as he was certain that she was suffering from snow-blindness, and had suggested she tie a thin scarf about her eyes, holding on to the cart for guidance. Wherever possible he had led them through shade, but more often than not their road led them through wide, open plains. The children had also been complaining of the brightness and were all suffering from headaches, but he was not sure if this was, in fact, from the sun or the icy cold hitting them on their foreheads, which were exposed under their hoods.

Abraham saw a wide river ahead, and they quickened their pace in order to be over it before nightfall. As they approached he saw that it was completely iced over and, to his horror, the once-flimsy bridge had been almost entirely swept away. He turned to the others. They, too, had seen the bridge and knew that they must cross this river to get on to the road for Lvov. They had no idea what sort of diversion they would have to otherwise make, for they were following the directions given to them by the farmer and a few people they had met on their travels. Anna, overcome with fatigue and weak from lack of food, started to cry, and Rula was soon doing the same. The men stood abjectly by, unable to comfort them, wishing they could cry too. The children, not knowing why their Mothers were so upset, were tugging at their skirts "Mama, Mama, don't cry. What's wrong. Tell us, please." Eventually, first Rula, then Anna, pulled themselves together and knelt down and drew the little ones to them and soon they were two little groups, tightly enclosed in the circle of arms. Abraham turned to Nathan. "We should try to cross the ice. It must be pretty thick and unless it is a fast flowing river it should take our weight." Nathan looked across to the other bank. "It is not too far and I think you might be right, but I don't think the cart will make it. I should hate to lose our things, so it might be wise if we unload it first and carry what we can across, giving each child a bundle too and then, if we are lucky, we can come back for it and take it across empty." Abraham saw the sense in this, so they all unloaded the cart. Nathan crossed first, very warily, putting his feet carefully one in front of the other. He knew that the danger would be in the middle if the ice was going to crack at all, where it would be at its thinnest, but soon he was across at the bottom of the bank and called out to send the children over one by one. They all started to cross, each clutching a bundle, but then the difficulty arose. The bank was steep and covered in ice and snow, with no bushes or tree stumps to hold on to. Nathan called across to the others to send the axe over with the next child and when he had it he hacked chunks out of the bank for footholds. It was still very slippery, but he managed to crawl and slide his way up, huffing and puffing with the exertion, sitting down with a thump on reaching the top. He had tied some rope around Moshe, who had come across first, and promptly started to haul him up. By the time he was safely on the top of the bank, Anna and Rula had joined the rest of the children and they proceeded to bring each one up in the same way. Their bundles were tossed up, but Anna gently handed the violin up to Nathan, and soon all of them, except Abraham, was safely up on the bank. They all watched anxiously as he started to make his way across, dragging the empty cart behind him. He was in the centre. He was testing his way carefully. He heard a crack like gunfire and looked in horror at the water which had begun to swirl around his feet. He heard the women screaming, and the shouts of Nathan. "I have to get across, I have to," he thought. He started to try to run, but the water was making the ice more and more slippery. The cart was going under. It was pulling him with it. He could not hold it. "Oh! God, help me," he shouted. "I can't lose the cart." The ice was creaking and banging all around him now and he knew that to plunge under it would be certain death. He heard Nathan shouting to him. "Leave the cart. Drop it in the water. Run, Abraham, run. Come on, you will drown. Come on." He was vaguely conscious of the shouts and screams. His one thought was to save the cart. He kept trying to go ahead, but to no avail. He had to pull himself free of the harness and he watched in sickening fury as the cart began to sink and, in the very strong current running under the ice, he saw it being dragged along, breaking the ice in its path. He reached the bank safely, but his feet were frozen to his boots, and he could hardly walk. "Thank God you are safe, Dushka. Come on, brother, tie the rope around you and come up." Words of encouragement from his beloved family, when he had failed them and let their precious cart sink. He sat down on the bank and then it was his turn to weep!

Nathan built a huge fire on the bank from the wood remaining from the wreck of the bridge and Anna had taken Abraham's boots off. The linen had frozen to his skin and she looked in horror at the red, raw feet. How could he walk like that? His boots would be really stiff when they dried in the heat of the fire and he would be crippled by them. She then remembered the small bundles of raw wool which one of the many kindly villagers they had met had given them to help insulate their feet against the cold. She rubbed some oil into the raw skin and placed the last of their clean linen strips on his feet, wrapping them loosely around with a blanket until his boots had dried. Meanwhile, Rula started to prepare the last of the food. Abraham had been anxiously watching the weather, noticing that the sky was becoming very grey and overcast, which to his now seasoned senses indicated to him that there was some more bad weather on the way. He looked around the landscape and spotted some large rocks some distance away. "They would make a good shelter," he thought, and as soon as they had eaten and he could instil some enthusiasm into them, they started to pack up their belongings ready to make their way over to them. Abraham put handfuls of the soft wool into his now dry boots and, pushing his feet into them, found that it did indeed help. However, he did not say to any of them how painful his feet really were and he wondered to himself how on earth they would be able to move on the next day with him in this condition and no cart to carry their belongings. The wind suddenly sprang up, leaving them gasping for breath, and between them they half-dragged, half-carried the children and their bundles. Nathan and Rula said they would go back for the remaining few things, but Abraham knew that it would not be very long before these would be totally covered over by the snow which was now falling in large fluffy lumps - just like the wool in my boots, he thought ironically. "Leave them. We know where they are. We will get them back when the storm has passed," he said. The snow was blotting out the landscape and the wind was hampering progress but luck was on their side, as the rocks which they had seen turned out to be three in a group, with a cave-like formation and an overhang forming part of a roof. The wind was too strong to allow them to erect the tent, and they had lost the stout staves with the cart. With the greatest difficulty they managed to light a new fire with the last of the gubka, but there was plenty of dry wood in the hollow of the rocks and so all through that raging night they kept the fire going, each adult cuddling a small child to them in order to keep them warm. They knew the fire must be kept going, whatever else, but the storm was increasing by the minute and soon the wind was even penetrating their shelter, freezing their backs, whilst they were warming their fronts from the heat of the fire. Not one of the four adults slept; as soon as they began to doze they would be gently roused, for they all knew that to fall asleep would be instant death. As they held out their numb hands and feet to the flames they pulled them back quickly with the agony of their blood flowing again. The pain of the cold was as severe as the pain of the heat. At last it was morning and, with the dawn, the wind had died down and the snow stopped. The sun began to rise and they all knew that they had survived another night.

The day was fine and bright, and although they had no food the women made hot tea which they all sipped gratefully. Abraham's feet were very sore but not as bad as he had feared. After a short discussion they all decided that, after the fright they had experienced on the icy river and the rigours of the night, they would stay and rest in the rocks for the day. This would enable them to retrieve the bundles by the river, and sort out their few possessions into packages which they could all carry. What they could not take they would have to leave behind. Abraham could also rest his feet and Rula was already rubbing the last of the oil into his boots in an effort to soften them. As the sun rose higher in the sky it grew warmer and warmer. "Spring won't be long, thank God," thought Abraham and, as if she had read his thoughts, Anna said the same. All the children were running about amongst the rocks, playing hide and seek and it was good to hear their squeals and cries as they dashed hither and thither. Suddenly Israel called out "Papa, Papa, come quickly, there is a man coming." They all jumped up, at the same time hearing a dog barking. Nathan climbed up on to the top of the rocks and, shielding his eyes in the glare of the sun on the snow, he peered in the direction Israel was pointing. Then he saw him. He crouched down and shouted to the children "Go back to the others and keep very quiet." He watched as the man and dog came nearer until, getting their scent, the dog ran straight towards them, barking and yapping loudly. The man was also running, wondering what had caused his dog to get so excited. As he got nearer to them Nathan saw that he was quite old, with a white beard and a wrinkled brown face; wrinkled, no doubt, because of the constant peering into the sun and snow. He was well wrapped up against the weather and obviously fit and well-fed. When he saw Nathan he stopped, holding up his arm in a welcoming gesture. "Who are you? Where have you come from?" he called out. Nathan, sliding back down the rock, called out to the others "It is an old man; he is alone; I am sure there is nothing to be scared of." The dog had stopped its noise and was standing beside the man, snarling at them as they approached, with its hackles standing up along its back. The little man had a long white beard and wore a coat and trousers of sheepskin as protection against the cold. On his head, he wore a fleecy cap but his hands were bare, red and gnarled, showing that he had always worked hard for a living. He was obviously very pleased to see them all and started talking very quickly, asking where they had come from, where were they going, what were they doing here? Abraham introduced themselves and briefly told him their story, and when he reached the point where they had lost their cart in the river the old man was very sympathetic and said how sorry he was. Being proud by nature they did not say all their food was gone but the old man, as if guessing their real plight, said "Follow me and I will take you to my home, where you can rest and have a meal with me before going on to Lvov. My name is Mischa, and my dog just answers to Hey." Gathering up their bundles, helped by the old man, they made their way across the flat snow-covered land. Ahead they could only see hills and rocks and, search as they might, they could not see any sign of a house. "How far has he come? He is so old he must live fairly near," whispered Abraham to his brother. They were making for some rocks ahead and Mischa told them to start climbing up the narrow footpath. They asked him where his house was and he started to laugh. "I don't live in a house. I am a shepherd, and I live with my friends in a cave." Rula and Anna looked at one another in fright. "Could this man possibly be a bandit? He talks of "friends" - were they thieves and robbers hiding in the hills for the winter? He is pretty old to be a bandit but he might have to cook for the others - he had mentioned his friends," thought Abraham. With all these thoughts going through their minds they proceeded to climb up the narrow path, helping the children over the difficult parts and leaving Abraham to manage as best he could with the large staff he had cut himself from a dead tree. His feet were worse than he had thought and he stumbled several times, falling over and cutting his knees on the rocks. He didn't cry out, for he knew Anna was worried enough about his condition. "Thank goodness she is at the head of the line with the youngest children and has not seen how many times I have fallen," he thought. The old man stopped and, pointing at a huge rock to his left, they saw it was a large cave, partly hidden by several bushes which hung across the front. The dog was running, yapping happily, towards the entrance and he was following, beckoning them to hurry and join him. It was with trepidation they all did so, the children clinging on to their parents, but soon realised they had no reason whatever for fear - his friends were sheep! Dozens and dozens of them, all penned into the rear of the huge cave, bleating and baaing their welcome, their little rudder-like tails moving quickly back and forth. The smell was really overpowering and the children were very quick to point this out in no uncertain terms! Anna and Rula quickly shushed them, telling them not to be so rude, but Mischa just chuckled and said "Little ones only tell the truth. I am sure it smells in here, after all we have been penned up together for some months." The two women tried to pretend it was fine, much to their husbands' amusement, all the while keeping their scarves across their mouths. The old man stirred up the fire, so that it was soon blazing merrily in the middle of the huge cavern and, in the light of the torches which he lit around the area, they could see bundles of hay stacked up against the walls. This was obviously food for the sheep, carefully stored by the old man for the winter. There were some large cooking pots, too, and when he knew they had not been able to wash or change their clothes for some time he asked Nathan to help him and they proceeded to fill up one of the pots with snow, packing it in tightly, then placed it over the fire to thaw and heat. The water was soon boiling so their mothers stripped the children of their dirty clothes, proclaiming at the state of them. Their hair was dirty and the way they had been scratching lately, Anna had told Abraham she thought they may have lice. He tried to console her by questioning where on earth would they have picked them up from? They had not been with anyone. "Maybe when they had their hair washed it would feel better," she agreed. It was so warm in the cavern, Abraham knew they would come to no harm whilst undressed, even though the temperature outside was still low. Anna and Rula had smiled at each other when the old shepherd had gone outside when they started to undress the children. One by one each child had an all-over wash and then, using the same water, so did the men. Another pot was heating and when this was ready they turned their backs whilst Anna and Rula washed themselves and put on clean underwear. Abraham suggested they should bundle the dirty clothes together and then, if the opportunity arose to wash them before leaving this shelter, they would. If not they would do so at the first opportunity they got. He felt they had imposed on the generosity of Mischa enough and, if they were to mention that they had washing to do, knew he would be out there very quickly shovelling more snow into a pot. As soon as they had finished their washing and cleaning, as if by instinct, the old man re-appeared, clutching a large flat-bladed knife in his hand. Abraham stood up, pulling Anna behind him, and saw Nathan do the same with

Rula, with the children huddling in a frightened group when they realised their parents were afraid. Mischa stopped and looked at them, realising they were all very scared. "Don't worry, I have just been sharpening my knife. I have work to do." With that he walked through to the first pen of sheep and, with much bleating and baaing, he grabbed a small one and brought it through the cavern. All the children watched this procedure in horror - fully aware of what he was now about to do. Moshe and Mala began to cry, and Israel ran after the man, crying out "Don't hurt him, he is only little." His father called him back and, gently pulling the children on to their laps, the two men explained that if you needed to eat then you had to kill an animal and, unfortunately, the only ones they had were the sheep. Israel cried "I won't eat it, I am not hungry," and his two sisters soon took up the cry. Their fathers' smiled and kept quiet, knowing that once the children smelled food cooking their stomachs would soon take over and they would forget their refusal to eat. The shepherd came back with a skinned carcass, which in no way resembled the sheep. It looked more like a big rabbit. "See, little ones, I lost the sheep. He skipped down the path, but I found this hare lying injured in a trap so I had to put him out of his misery, didn't I, and thought he would make a very good supper for us." The children actually believed him! Abraham was astounded, but they did. The sheep had been cooked on a spit over the fire and they had all eaten their fill, licking their fingers, the juices running down their chins. Nothing had ever tasted quite so good! The smell from the sheep pen was over-powering but the warmth which they created was worth it, for they were all so cosy and warm that soon Abraham and Nathan were dozing in the firelight. Anna tucked the children up, all fast asleep and well-fed, and she and Rula chatted to the old man, who told them how he lived here every winter, tending his sheep, and in the summer moved down to the plains to graze them. His worst enemies were the wolves, but his dog, Hey, was very good at scaring them off. He pulled out a long thin pipe and started to play a slow little melody. Abraham woke and, recognising the music, picked his fiddle up and softly started to join in the music. Mischa was astonished and smiled his toothless smile, signalling to him to continue. They played together for a while, by which time Nathan had also woken, and then Abraham played some music on his own. The old man was nodding and beating time to the melody, obviously enthralled by the music and glad to be in the company of humans and not sheep for a change.

They stayed there for three days, resting and talking, and the old man made them wash and dry their clothes but, most important of all, it gave Abraham time for his feet to heal with the ointment which Mischa gave him, and for Rula's eyes to improve. Now the time had come for them to be on their way, however, as the weather appeared to be settled, so they thanked Mischa over and over again for his hospitality and for the gifts of food and meat he had given them. He pointed out the route they should take to Lvov and told them they should reach their destination in about three days and that the rest of the journey would be easy. He proved to be correct, for on the third morning, after a fairly early start, they could see the city ahead of them, about five miles in the distance. The weather was good, with no wind and a bright sky, and they walked quickly, eager to reach their destination at last. They could see the sunlight flashing on the roofs and spires of the city as they marched briskly towards them. About a mile on they came across a few small wooden houses, obviously lived in by peasants or farmers. As they approached, three small children ran out into their path and looked at them curiously, not saying a word. Some men and women came out, obviously inquisitive to see what their dogs were barking at, and Abraham introduced them all, saying they had come to Lvov from St. Petersburg, adding the now familiar story. One of the men, a tall well-built man, wearing the traditional Russian winter clothing, was obviously their leader and asked if they were Jewish, to which Nathan nodded. Abraham shot him a warning glance, although he thought it was fairly obvious who they were with their long black curls and beards. Abraham then said "Our names are Abraham and Nathan Levinsky, we are brothers, and these are our wives, Anna and Rula." The man gripped Abraham's hand and said "My name is Peter, we are pleased to meet you. It is not often we get visitors from so far away," then beckoned them inside his house, suggesting that the children stay outside and play with their own little ones. They followed him inside and a plump, middle-aged woman came towards them, her hair parted in the centre with the traditional plaits piled on top of her head, rosy cheeks, a twinkle in her eye and a beaming smile. Peter introduced them and said "This is my wife, Valentina." She was wearing a thick shawl over her shoulders, and her long skirt brushed the floor. It was obvious to Rula that her clothes were home-made, comparing them straight away with the type of skirt or top which Nathan made for her. She greeted them in a friendly way "You are welcome in our house, make yourselves comfortable." There were some low bench seats around the wall and the four sat down, glad to be able to rest at last, and

Valentina offered them tea, which they gratefully accepted. By now several other villagers had come in to meet them, so there were greetings and handshakes all around. Some bread and little cakes were then brought out by an old woman, bent double with the years, who smiled a toothless grin at them and bade them "good day" before she returned to the back of the house. Valentina told Anna that she was her Mother, and was 70 years of age. The room was very comfortable, with gaily coloured hand-made rugs on the walls and floor, and the shawls which the women were wearing were also brightly coloured. The people were all obviously quite poor, but the house was spotless and their appearances very clean. Once again Abraham recognised the smell of sheep and it turned out later that these were in a room attached to the back of the house, bedded down for the winter. Once they had eaten and drunk the tea Peter turned to Abraham and began to tell him why they must not go on into Lvov as it was extremely dangerous. It seemed that there had been many Jewish families in the next small village who, learning of the Bolshevik revolution and Kerensky's rise to power, had decided to get across the border and escape to Poland. They had entered Lvov and immediately been captured and imprisoned by the troops. As soon as word had spread that Tsar Nicholas and his son, and the Tsarina and the girls had all been taken prisoner and were feared dead, panic had overtaken the city and, as far as he knew, all the Jews, both those from the next village plus those already living in Lvov, along with all the known loyal royalists, had been taken out and shot by a firing squad, by order of Kerensky. He knew that the story was true for some relatives of his neighbour had arrived only two days ago from Lvov, anxious to be away from the city centre whilst it was under martial law. Abraham and his brother looked at each other and then at their wives. "What do we do now? Where can we go? We have no money, no food and hardly any possessions left." Abraham was talking to them all, and Peter listened, rubbing his chin thoughtfully. "Look," he said, "we have an old cart out the back which we are not using. You can use that and if you have walked this far already then I suggest you make your way to Odessa where I know you will be able to get a boat, then make your way to safety. From what I have heard from my neighbour's relatives there has been a mass exodus from the city already, and they are all making for that port. Why don't you do that? You have the better weather coming now and it should only take a matter of weeks." Abraham saw Anna, Nathan and Rula look at one another, and then at him, their own leader. He must make the decision. He had led them this far, he could surely lead them a bit further. They talked for some time to Peter and a few of the other men, quite forgetting that they should be planning their night halt, until Nathan, looking out of the window, saw that little Rosa was sitting on the ground, crying. He quietly got up and went outside. "Those other children are horrid. They said I am a dirty Jew. I'm not dirty, am I, Uncle Nathan? I have clean clothes on," she said. She was so young that, to her little mind it was more important not to be dirty than to be proud of being Jewish. She was to remember those words for many years to come. Her uncle picked her up, wiped her tears, and took her indoors. Her hands were freezing so he made a game of tucking them under his armpits in an effort to warm them. When he entered the room with Rosa in his arms Anna stood up to take her from him and this brought the conversation to a close.

It was done. They had made their plans. They would move on once again, and make for Odessa. Peter took both Nathan and Abraham outside, round to the back of the house and there, in all its glory, was a cart. Not as big or as good as the one they had lost in the river, but a cart! They whooped with glee and, pumping the man's hand up and down, they thanked him profusely. Both their wives, hearing the shouts, had also come round and they, too, were delighted at the gift and kissed the man on both cheeks. They spent a warm night sleeping on the floor of the house and the next morning they quickly loaded their bundles on to the new cart, accepting with many words of thanks the little flour and oil they were given, and newly baked bread, even though the villagers were so poor. They were ready to leave. Peter and a couple of other villagers escorted them about a mile through a small wood, in the opposite direction from which they had previously come. He said they must travel due south now and follow the sun at all times to keep to the right route. Once they were through the trees and out into the fields again he pointed to a small road, heading straight towards two hills, and said they must make for them, when they would be on the main road for Odessa. By going on this route he felt sure they would not encounter any troops. Abraham had long thought that they had been very lucky in missing all signs of trouble, even when they were as close as they had been to it at Minsk. He would never forget the sight of those poor women and children straggling along the road, following them day after day. He had felt guilty at leaving them, but knew that he had to do it, or else they would have all died. They said their farewells to the men, thanking them for all the help they had been given, Anna and Rula kissing them on both cheeks. Abraham was in the harness position, with Nathan pushing and the three smallest children on board, happy to be riding again. They set off down the road, turning after a few yards as the man called out "God go with you," to call the same words to him. Nathan was very quiet – Abraham could see that his brother had never realised until they had started out on this venture that people with so little could give so much, and he knew that he would never forget the kindness they had been shown by so many on their long and arduous journey.

Spring was here - really and truly here. The snow drifts were still high along the roadside, but where it had lain flat across the fields it was disappearing and the trees had little green flags sprouting from the branches. It was still very cold at night, but the days were lovely and, with the aid of the cart to take their load, they did not mind the walking. The children rode and ran, taking it in turns to ride on their large horse, as they called it, and the exercise was not doing them any harm - in fact, they seemed to be quite fit and well, thought Abraham. They had stopped for a few days and laboured for a farmer, helping him with the lambing, for which they were allowed to stay in his barn, given food and, wonder of wonders, fresh milk and a few roubles when they left. At first, they had been hesitant about trying to get work, in case anyone should report them to the authorities, but they knew that they were a long way from any major city, where the troops or Bolsheviks might be, and so they had taken a chance. Nathan had even been able to help the farmer's wife alter some clothing, and she had given him a little of the cloth left over from an overcoat, from which he made Israel a new pair of trousers - he had literally outgrown his own and had sprouted several inches during the last few months. Each day the weather improved and every night they noticed that it was less and less cold. The women left off their scarves, their hair blowing in the fresh breeze, gently whipping it around their faces. They removed some of the children's heavy outer clothing, so that they could move with more freedom and, now that the snow had gone from the roads, they took off their shoes and boots in order to run barefoot in the fresh spring grass. All around them the trees were bursting into leaf; birds were singing and over on the side of a nearby hill a mass of yellow indicated that there was a field of daffodils. The children wanted to run to them and pick some, but Rula said "We do not have a pot to put them in and they will soon die. Leave them for others to see, Mala, they are so pretty." Ahead of them they could see distant hills and hoped that the road would go through them rather than over the top. They had no way of knowing, and as it was still early in the day decided to keep going before looking for somewhere to stay for the night. As they got nearer to the hills the road started to rise up, and they soon realised it would indeed be a long climb. Abraham and Nathan changed positions on the cart and decided that soon they would choose their night stop. "There will probably be some caves in the hills," said Abraham. "Yes, but it might be dangerous, for there may be some wolves around and we don't have a dog to chase them off this time," said Nathan.

They saw a ridge up above them and Abraham pointed out an opening. "That looks like a cave," said Anna. "We'll go and see," said Rula. "You men stay here." "Be careful, Dushka, there might be wolves up there," said Nathan. "I'm not afraid of a little wolf," said Rula, trying not to show her husband that she was a little apprehensive. The two women picked up their skirts and climbed up the ridge. When they reached the top they slowly walked up to the front of the cave and peered in. They loudly called out, "Hi. Hi," knowing that there would be a reaction from within if there was a wolf inside, and to their relief, there was not a sound. They called out "It's safe, there is nothing here, and no animals we can see." Abraham then told the children to run up and join their mothers. They half dragged, half pulled the cart up and, panting, reached the cave. Inside they found a huge pile of dry kindling and wood, a sure sign that someone had made use of it at some time. Nathan lit a fire whilst Abraham and the children unpacked what they needed from the cart and when this was done he made some make-shift torches. They each took one and walked to the rear of the cave to see just how far back it actually went. The cavern was huge - not as big as the one where the shepherd had lived, but to their immense delight, running into the ground at the back of the rocks was a trickle of fresh water. It tasted so sweet when they tried it they knew it was pure, so ran to get some pots which they placed under its steady stream in order to get as much as they could. "We will make a good hot stew tonight and use up the last of the lovely vegetables we got at the farm," said Anna. "I wish we had some meat, Mama," said Israel. "Hush, you can only have what we have, my son," she said "and be thankful that we are still alive and well, and enjoying the beautiful weather after the terrible cold and snow we have been through." Nathan had disappeared out of the cave. He was gone for a long time and after about an hour they were all getting worried as it was nearly dark. Where could he be? It was not like him to wander off without a word. Just as Abraham had decided he would have to go out and see if he could find him they heard a scrambling noise outside and he appeared, grinning, at the mouth of the cave, clutching a large dead bird in his hand. "Oh, how did you manage to catch it?" they cried, the children jumping up and down with glee. "With difficulty," said Nathan, "but I got it, and now, my darling sister-in-law, if you would like to pluck it and add it to your pot we can have a real feast tonight. Do you realise it is Shabbas?" They were like children with the bird, all trying to pull the feathers off as quickly as possible in order that they could start cooking it. Rula was already making some flat cakes on one of the hot stones by the fire and, later on, when the wonderful smell started to rise from the pot and the food was dished up they all agreed it was a meal fit for a king.

In the morning, when they were all outside attending to their various needs Nathan suddenly called out to them to come and see something. He put his finger to his lips and said "Be very quiet and do not make a noise. Look what I can see. Make the children stay behind at the mouth of the cave for the moment." Anna and Rula crept to where he was crouched down in the bushes, with Abraham closely behind, and followed the direction of his pointed finger. "Look, what do you think they are?" he said. There, on the grassy slope, were two large brown objects, moving slowly across the hill. As they got nearer it was soon obvious to them all that they were bears, the first they had seen. Abraham said "I think this is a good sign we must be getting nearer to our destination, as I do not think brown bears live up in the far North as it would be too cold for them up there." The bears lumbered around, back and forth, seeking food and then, to their absolute delight, one of them stood up on its hind legs and started to scratch its back on a young tree, almost bending it double with his huge weight. Anna had gone back for the children, telling them to be very quiet, so they could watch too. They could not see the bears' face of course, but it was easy to imagine his look of sheer delight with the ecstasy of this back-scratching exercise! Abraham could see Rosa wanted to laugh out loud at its antics but held her two hands across her mouth to keep the giggles from coming out. Israel whispered to his father "Can they see us? Will they come and carry one of us off, as neither you nor Uncle Nathan have a gun to shoot it." Abraham turned to him and said "We are quite safe. They could possibly come after us if they knew we were here, but the wind is obviously blowing towards us so they cannot smell us. We are safe as long as we keep quiet." It was some time before the bears lumbered away out of sight and, although they had enjoyed watching them, particularly the back scratching exercise, all were glad that they were ambling off in the opposite direction and had not got their scent, and headed towards them the whole time they had been watching. They stayed in the cave that day, resting, talking and trying to assess just how much further they had to go. During the afternoon Abraham got his violin out and called Rosa and Israel over to him. "Come on, you two, it is many weeks since you last played and you have not done any practice. Let's hear what you can do on my big fiddle." First Israel picked it up and, with difficulty, placed it under his little chin. It was a bit large for him, and heavier than he was used to, as he and Rosa had played on their own half-sized violins in St. Petersburg, but he took up the bow and started to play. He was very good for his age, but then he had been taught by a wonderful teacher – his father! He played the scales, at his father's insistence, with the cry of "Do I have to?" and then, after a while, his father let him play one of the pieces which he knew so well. The bow was also heavy for him and he soon tired, and gave the instrument back to Abraham. It was then Rosa's turn. She played beautifully and her father was secretly pleased with her progress. He had such high hopes for her when they lived in St. Petersburg, but all that was now gone. She took the violin from her father and, with no word of encouragement needed, her little fingers flew up and down the strings, not finding the fiddle or bow too heavy, plucking and pulling the melody from it, making even the simplest scales sound wonderful. Her mother came in from outside to listen, obviously thinking Abraham was the one playing, and stood there, smiling at her little daughter. She might not have played for a while but had not lost her touch – he could see that in Anna's eyes she could play almost as well as her father!

Slowly the spring turned to summer and all the time they kept on walking. The children were always hungry with the exercise and fresh air, so it became imperative for Abraham and his brother to spend a few days doing any odd jobs they could find in the villages they came to, in order to earn money to buy food, or be provided with food and shelter. Some of the people in those villages they passed through shunned them, for by now their clothes were very shabby and their shoes had completely worn out, so all were bare-footed. They had really begun to look a very penniless band of people. They had been able to discard their heavy winter top-clothes as the weather was so much warmer, and traded in their good clothes, which had been in bundles for so long, at the last village they had reached in order to buy liniment for both Rosa and Moshe, who had very severe coughs. Anna told Abraham she was worried about Rosa, who would probably always have a weak chest. Moshe, however, was a tough little fellow and they all knew that once he received a few doses of medicine he would be fine again. Abraham never ceased to wonder at how fit they all really were apart from the coughs. He guessed it was because they had never actually starved and been able to obtain food most of the time. He shuddered involuntarily when he thought of those terrible four days locked up in the snow house during the blizzard, and of the band of homeless women and children. "How many had survived?" he asked himself, trying to shrug off the guilt which he always felt at having left them. By his reckoning they were now about half-way between Lvov and Odessa and the days were warm, with gentle breezes sighing through the great conifers and birch trees which abounded throughout the countryside. It had not rained for several days but he knew there was some on the way, for over on the horizon the clouds were massing and the sky was not the same brilliant opalescent blue it had been. He hoped it would not be a storm, just perhaps rain, for they could nearly always find some cover in amongst the small woods if they had time or, if not, they could erect their shelter. Goodness, how well that had done and what stories it could tell of the places it had been, he thought to himself. He turned from the harness at the front of the cart to smile at Anna, who was walking with Mala, Rosa and Helena. She smiled back, her blue eyes twinkling. Israel and Moshe, who were now really firm friends, were playing boyish games in and out of the hedgerows and Abraham smiled at the sounds of their laughter, and their chattering. All this exercise was helping them grow and, by now, both boys had totally outgrown their pants and, to their great disgust, Nathan had made them into short ones so that the legs were not half-way around their calves. It was hot, however, and so the air on their legs would do them no harm at all. The two women wore their last remaining dresses, which had been washed so many times, and pounded on the stones by the sides of running streams, that the colours had almost completely disappeared, leaving only a faded impression of blues, greens and red. They were clean, however, even though some people had thought they were not. Abraham had one very constant dread - that of lice, but he was perfectly sure that none of them had any. By now, both he and his brother had become accomplished fishermen, for whenever they came to a lake or small river they would cut some forked sticks and catch fish. Nathan had tried it first; cutting a branch with a 'Y' at the top, and lying down on the edge of the water, had lain in wait for a fish. As soon as he saw one, he would quickly push the branch downwards and, whilst at first he missed the majority of them, he now caught most of them. Anna or Rula would then grill them over the fire, and all agreed they tasted better this way than cooked in a pan. Rula had sighed on the last occasion they had been eating such a meal. "Wouldn't you like to be in your own kitchen, Anna, and making gefilte fish. Do you think we will ever stop our wanderings?" She had been hushed by Nathan, who said "Don't let the children hear your worries, for they are in such good spirits at the moment that I do not want anything to mar this." Abraham nodded his agreement. Since the weather had improved, and they had been settling down before dark each day, he had taken on the task of teaching the children to read and write. Israel and Rosa had learned back home in St. Petersburg, but the other three had not, and whilst they had very little to write on, he had saved a few scraps of paper, and they had their Bible to read. Their progress was slow, but it occupied their minds, and he hoped that when they reached their final destination Helena, and Nathan's children, could at least write their names and read simple words.

They had reached a large lake and by now the clouds had started to mass and Abraham was sure he heard the distant rumbling of thunder. No one else mentioned it, however, and so he kept quiet - the two women did not like storms! The water was shimmering in the sunlight, and the ripples were barely visible, it was so calm. No one needed a word of encouragement to run to the edge, and the next moment they were all running and splashing in the cool water, Anna and Rula holding their skirts up around their knees, the children laughing and giggling, running in and out of the ripples. "Oh, it feels so good, Abraham, it is so warm," said Anna. "I would love to lie down in it and feel clean all over again," said Rula. "Well, there is nothing to stop you," said Nathan, with a twinkle in his eye. "Don't be foolish, Dushka," she said, with a mischievous toss of her head. "Now everyone," said Abraham, "I think we do all need to get clean, and what better chance than now. I have been watching the countryside over the last few days, and it seems to me that it is getting dryer and dryer and we have not even come to a stream. This might be our last chance to be near a lot of water for some time. I think that you, Anna and Rula, ought to take the girls, whilst Nathan and I will take the boys, and we will go to separate ends of the lake. We can then strip off all our dirty clothes, wash them, and the heat of the sun will soon dry them. I am sure we can find a few odd garments left on the cart to put on in the meantime for decency, once we have had a good swim and splashed around in the water." The children were jumping for joy, of course. "Oh yes, please. Please, Uncle Abraham. Please, Papa," came their cries. Anna and Rula looked at one another. They were not too sure about the idea but Anna, seeing the sense in this, turned to Rula and said "Well, we will certainly feel much better after a proper wash, and you did just say you would like to lie down in it." They all laughed, and getting their few remaining clean clothes from the cart, set off in two different directions, laughing and shouting to each other. "Oh my, how good it feels. I never thought I would welcome a wash so much. It is so warm in the water you would think it was heated." Rula lay in the shallows, splashing the girls playfully, whilst Anna was more adventurous and had gone out from the bank into the deeper, colder water. It was sheer bliss and they stayed in much longer than they should have done. Suddenly, a large "plop" sounded on the water beside Anna and, thinking it was a fish biting, she turned in the direction of the sound. Then there was another, and another. Suddenly there were hundreds - it was rain! Huge blobs of it falling from the sky which had suddenly become grey and overcast, and massed with large black clouds. Thunder was rumbling all around them, and it was clear they were in for a storm. "We haven't even started to dry the clothes yet," called Rula. "Never mind, we shall just have to wait until it is over. It won't be much - just a summer storm, and once it has passed we can light a fire and get the things dried." The men and boys were running along the edge of the lake now, coming towards them, and both women grabbed what clean clothes they had and put them on quickly, helping the girls to do the same. In minutes, however, they were all as wet with their clothes on as they had been in the water! They were soaked through. The children thought this a huge joke and ran about holding up their little arms and faces, as if they were drinking the falling rain. They had no shelter, nor were there any trees they could get under, so they started to rig their tent in order that they could at least have it up for the night when the rain had stopped, and could then concentrate on getting the clothes dry. By this time the thunder was right overhead and the lightning was zig-zagging across the lake, seemingly right over them. It lit up the now almost dark day with bright blue and green flashes, beautiful in their intensity, but terrifying in noise. The children quickly forgot their running about and scurried under the canvas, huddling up to their parents in fear, forgetting how wet and cold they already were. The wind had increased with the first enormous crash and was now blowing violently, so that they had to hold on to the uprights of their crude shelter with all their might to stop it from being torn from their clutches. The storm raged for nearly an hour, but gradually the wind and rain lessened, the thunder rolled away, and the sky grew lighter and lighter. Soon the sun was peeping through the few remaining clouds, giving out a little warmth, and the birds had started to sing.

The storm had completely died away and the sun was shining brightly again. Anna and Rula laid out the wet clothes to dry, whilst the men and children searched for kindling to light a fire. Everything was sodden, so try as they might they could not get a fire started, which was very worrying as Abraham always ensured they lit a fire once it was dark, particularly now they were in such open countryside. There was always the constant threat that wolves, or maybe even a bear, would attack them, drawn by their scent and hungry for food. There was nothing they could do this time, and so they could only eat the last of the flatbread which had been baked a couple of days before. "Thank goodness it had been under the canvas," thought Abraham. He knew that, as long as it was hot and sunny the next day, the kindling would soon dry out and, who knows, they might reach some forest land and find what they needed under the trees. However, the landscape was growing increasingly barren, with very few trees in sight, and the earth had a dry, parched look as if to discourage anything from growing on it. He knew from the little he had read that Odessa lay in a very dry, arid area of Russia, but he was surprised at how desert-like it actually appeared - probably because it is summer, he thought to himself. The next day they decided to move on very early and put plenty of miles between the lake and their final destination. It was hot and sunny and the air was clear and fresh after the storm. Not a cloud could be seen in the sky and so they all wore as little as possible, putting the newly washed clothes into the cart. These were all they had, and none of them knew where the next lot would come from. Abraham and Nathan often talked well into the night about what they thought they would do when they did reach Odessa, but both were certain of one thing - to flee from Russia and the persecution of the Jews, which they now knew to be as important an aim of the Bolsheviks as the arrest and rumoured murder of the Tsar and his family had been. Where they would go they could not decide, for they had no money to pay for the journey and would either have to hope to work their way for a free passage on a boat, or get employment for a few weeks in a town en route, or in Odessa, in order to earn enough money to pay their way. Both agreed if it was just the two of them, or even Rula and Anna as well, they could probably get work, but with five children this made the situation very different. Nathan was a fine tailor, and was proposing to get work in that line; there were always people needing alterations, or new clothes if they had the money, but Abraham was now secretly worried - who would have the money to pay a fiddler to play when there would doubtless be hundreds of their people in the same plight when they reached the city? Now their chief aim was to settle in a new land, where they would be free to follow their own religion and beliefs, and where their children could grow up and someday raise their own families without fear of being hounded from their homes.

They had been walking for several days. It was midday and the sun was now at its highest point in the sky. They had not found any shelter; no trees or bushes, only a dry parched land, with nothing apparently growing or living on it. Rula had begun to hobble and was lagging behind. Nathan stopped the cart when she called out "Please help me," and Abraham ran back just in time to catch her as she swayed, her knees giving way as she fell to the ground. They gently laid her up against the cart, getting what little shade from it they could, and placed a bundle behind her head. She lay with her eyes closed, her mouth open with short, rasping breaths coming from it. When they looked at her bare feet they were horrified to see that her ankles were swollen and discoloured and, lifting her skirt, the swelling reached the knees on both legs. She was clearly in great pain and they realised just how ill she was. "Poor Rula, not a word has she said, not a complaint of any kind," said Abraham. When Anna tried to rub her ankles she moaned and they were appalled to see the deep impressions left in the skin. "She needs salt," said Anna. "It must be lack of salt that is doing this. We have a little, let us give her a drink and put some in." Nathan sat wiping his wife's brow, saying nothing, but obviously very disturbed at the condition of her feet and legs. "Is there any way we could put her on the cart. She is such a little thing, surely we can manage to push and pull it between us." "Of course," said Abraham "we must try, anyway. But I think we will put up the shelter now and at least take cover from the midday heat which will give us all a chance to rest. I will go with the children to see if we can find any kindling for a small fire. We won't need much, just enough for Anna to make some tea. Once we have heated the water it can go out." Rula lay there for nearly an hour before she started to revive and tried to sit up. She was full of apologies for causing them to be so worried. "It's just the heat, it is nothing, nothing. I feel fine now. Please, let me get up and we can start off again." "Hush, Dushka," said Nathan. "We have rigged up the shelter and are resting here for a while. You can lie in there, which will keep the sun off you. I am sure you have a touch of sunstroke, that is all, but drink this. It is some salty water, as your ankles and legs are swollen, which Anna thinks means you need more salt. There is a fire, and we are also making some tea." She drank the liquid down, grimacing as she did, for it was very unpleasant. Abraham was secretly very worried about her. He could tell she felt terrible and guessed her feet and ankles throbbed incessantly, and that walking had become a very real problem, but she could not bring herself to mention any of this to them. They had enough problems without her being ill, and so she smiled, drank all the vile tasting liquid and patted her husband's cheek in an effort to dismiss the doubts he had for her health. As the heat of the mid-day sun started to lessen they took down their tent and, taking some of the bundles off the cart and giving one to each of the children to carry, they tried to persuade Rula to get on to it. She was adamant that she was alright and would not hear of it. "I am fine now we have rested. Please, don't make the little ones carry the bundles in this heat. They cannot manage them and we mustn't let them get like me. I am truly alright so you must let me walk." Try as they might to persuade her, she was adamant, and so they all set off once again; the children clutching their mothers' skirts and Israel helping his father to push the cart. By evening they had walked a few more miles. Rula said nothing but Abraham could tell she was obviously in agony, putting each foot to the ground causing her intense pain in her legs. He wondered if she had any feeling in her feet or ankles. They found a large clump of scrubby bushes by the side of the road and decided to make camp for the night. They were now desperately short of water and the men said they would go off in opposite directions to see if they could see any signs of a stream or small lake. They both returned an hour or so later - no water to be found! The children were settled for the night, but in the still, warm air they were very restless and fretful. They were sleeping on top of the cart, which had been emptied, in order that they could feel the slight night breeze, but the four adults erected their tent and sat outside it talking well into the night, with Rula pretending she felt better. Not finding any water would cause them a serious problem, as they had now almost run out, with no way of knowing how many more miles it would be before they reached a village or town, or even Odessa itself. It had been several days since they had left the last village so they hoped and prayed they did not have many more to go before reaching another.

The next day was just as hot, with no breeze and no clouds in the sky to hide the sun for even a few minutes. They set off in the early morning in order to cover as many miles as they could before mid-day, when they would have to rest. Rula walked without any comment, occasionally holding on to the side of the cart, but Abraham watched her carefully for he felt sure that she was very ill indeed. She stumbled, but quickly righted herself, and continued. It was reasonably cool in the early morning and walking was as pleasant as it could be, but soon the sun was blazing down on them and the children started to cry, asking to stop or be carried. Suddenly Rula fell, face down on the ground. She was shivering but totally unconscious. Her cut and swollen feet joined her ankles in one elephantine lump and her legs were almost the same size, a dark reddish-blue in colour. Nathan was cradling her in his arms, whilst their two little children were crying out "Mama, mama, don't die. Please wake up." Anna pulled them to her and took all the children round to the other side of the cart. "Your Mama is not well. You must be quiet and brave and not let her see you are upset, for that won't help her get better. We will put her up on the cart and I want all of you, even you, little Helena, to carry a bundle each. I know it is very hot and we will stop as soon as Papa says, but we must get your Aunt to a village or somewhere where we can get help for her." The children all nodded as if they understood, but clearly little Moshe and his sister did not know why their Mama should be lying on the ground asleep as they had not known her do this before. Anna could not tell them just how ill she really was. Rula opened her eyes after a while and looked up into their anxious faces. "I am sorry. I really am being a nuisance. Really, I will be alright. It is just my legs, they won't take my weight any more." They half-lifted her up and sat her against the cart, giving her little sips of the last of the precious water. "Do you think you can drink any more of the salt water, Dushka?" said Nathan. "No, save the water for the children. I know we have very little," said Rula. Her legs were now swollen to the tops of her thighs and when she lifted her skirt and saw them for herself her already pale face became ashen and beads of perspiration sprang on to her forehead. "I don't think I can walk any more," she whispered, and started to cry. With that, Abraham picked her up in his arms as if she was a toy doll and very gently laid her on top of the cart, quietly telling her to lie still and do as she was told for a change. She smiled up at this big, gentle man, whom she loved like a brother, and said "For once I won't argue, Abraham. I am very tired, but very ashamed to be such a nuisance." They all hushed her, stressing she was not a problem, and joking that soon she could take a turn at pushing the cart whilst one of them rode. They set off once again. Abraham knew they all had one secret fear now – what would happen if they could not find water? Try as he might he could not help thinking of flowing water and trickling streams, which made him feel even more thirsty and he knew the others felt the same way, although not one of them echoed these thoughts. The children now started to complain that they were thirsty and wanted to stop. Moshe said "I want Mama to walk beside me and hold my hand," and Mala repeated it, with tears flowing down her face. Anna knelt down and told them as gently as possible that Rula was just having a rest and that they must keep moving if they were to help their mother. Abraham knew in his own heart that if they did not get help soon the dreadful swelling would spread through Rula's body and she would surely die. They could not let this happen now, not when they had come so far, through so many of the dangers they had faced, and were now nearly at their destination.

They were passing through a rocky valley, strewn with boulders that had fallen away from the sides over the years. No bushes or trees could be seen and no rocks were big enough to give them any shelter - it was just a barren desert-like terrain. Abraham's heart sank. He had hoped that when they rounded the hill before entering the valley they would see some signs of life - but nothing. He was in the harness, with Nathan pushing, and although Rula weighed very little it was desperately hard work pulling the little cart over the rough ground. Nathan called out. "I must stop and just go up into the rocks for a minute." As he went, so did the two boys, anxious to copy their fathers' at all times, whilst the girls went behind a nearby rock with Anna. Rula stayed on the cart. Her eyes were closed and her breath was coming in short, sharp bursts from her lips. She looked terrible and they all knew she would not survive much longer without help of some kind. "What I would give for a drink of cold, fresh water," she murmured to Abraham, who had stayed by the cart. Suddenly there was a loud shout from above. He turned to look up and there was Nathan, with both boys, jumping up and down, shouting and yelling, with their arms outstretched. "Water. It's water. Look, come and see. I nearly missed it." Abraham, Anna and the three girls all started to climb up the slope and, sure enough, there it was. A tiny trickle from a small crack in the rocks. The water was crystal clear and very cold and, as it bubbled up out of the crack it started to course its way over the hot stones, disappearing into the dry sand and earth before it could form into a pool. The children ran back to the cart and collected some small cups and pots, racing back to the water with them. Holding a small, flat pan under the trickle Anna was able to collect a cupful at a time and they were all touched when Israel, being handed the first cup, said "No, I will take it to Aunt Rula," He carefully carried the cup, brimming to the top with sparkling water, and handed it to Rula who, hearing the commotion, had raised herself on one elbow and was as excited as everyone else with their find. She lifted the cup to her lips, and let the cold, clear liquid cool her mouth before drinking it slowly down. Abraham knew her prayer had been answered! Anna gave water to the children first, telling them to drink it slowly, then she and the men had theirs, drinking several cups between them, until Abraham warned them not to drink too much as they might be sick. They all agreed that this was the most wonderful drink they had ever tasted! Nathan and Anna painstakingly collected the tiny trickle of water into two dishes to use straight away and now they had found the spring they decided to stop and rest there for a while, although no shade was to be seen. They erected their tent and, under Israel's direction, the children made a game of collecting the water in their containers which would last them for a few days, whilst Anna sponged Rula's legs and face, to help her feel a little better. There was some flour left and, now they had water to spare, Anna, with Rosa's help, made flat cakes of bread over the small fire and they brewed some tea which she hoped would refresh them all. By mid-afternoon they had collected as much water as they could carry and so they set off again having all washed their blistered, hot, cracked feet in the spring. They passed through the valley after a couple of hours and the landscape looked identical to that of the previous day. In fact, Abraham wondered if there was a chance they had been going round in circles. He quietly voiced his thoughts to Nathan, when they stopped to rest and change positions on the cart, so Rula and Anna would not hear, but Nathan laughed and said "We have only been through this valley once. If we were going round in circles we would be going through it again. Come on, brother, stop doubting yourself. It is easy to be fooled by the landscape, but we know we are following the sun and must be on course. Remember what the man in the last village said. "Follow the sun, always head south and that is just what we are doing." Abraham felt re-assured and, shrugging himself into the harness, turned to ensure Nathan was ready to start pushing.

They were on their way again. Suddenly there was a great rushing noise and, looking upwards, they saw two huge birds flapping their enormous black wings several feet above them. They soared and skimmed over the little group, wondering whether they were food or not, and were magnificent in their size, their giant beaks outstretched on long, thin necks. The children were very excited and were running around and around craning their little heads upwards. "Catch one, Papa, oh! please catch one," cried Moshe. Nathan laughed. "How do you suppose I can catch one of those, my son. I don't have wings to fly up there and grab it." The birds wheeled and dived, skimming over them, then made off into the distance just as suddenly as they had appeared. "What do you think they were, Abraham," asked Anna. "Oh, eagles, I think, Dushka, obviously looking for food. There cannot be much out here, only a sand snake or lizard, but they decided that we were not fit to eat. We probably look too skinny." They all laughed but were secretly pleased that the birds had gone. "If there are birds overhead, doesn't that mean we must be near a village or town?" Nathan waited for Abraham to reply. "Well, I was just thinking the same, but did not want to mention it in case I raised your hopes, but as you have spoken up, I think you might be right." At these words, they began to grow optimistic and hoped that before long they might see some signs of life. The men were scouring the horizon with their eyes, shielding them with their hands against the brilliant sun which reflected off the dry earth. Far in the distance, there was something out there. Wasn't that a plume of smoke rising straight up into the clear blue sky? Yes, it was a cluster of houses and that was smoke. Abraham laughed out loud and, turning to Nathan, he called out "Come on, little brother, push. We must make that village by evening and I think it is a few miles further yet." Anna and the children quickened their pace too, keeping up with the cart, everyone anxious to get out of this awful dry, hot land, but in all their minds was the urgent problem of Rula. "Oh please, let there be some help for her there," whispered Anna in a silent prayer which Abraham overheard. They grew nearer and nearer, and eventually could see that it was a small hamlet, made up of about eight or nine wooden houses. Smoke was coming from most of the chimneys, indicating that the women were busily preparing the evening meals for their families. The juices started to run in Abraham's dry mouth as he thought of chicken broth, or stew, or some hommentash - his favourite. They had no money with which to buy food and no possessions worth selling, but he and his brother were still capable of chopping wood and tilling the ground, and even the children could do little tasks to earn their keep. Most important of all, of course, was to get help for Rula and this would probably cost money.

As they neared the first of the houses they saw a boy milking a cow with some goats nearby. As if ejected from a gun a sudden rush of small children came out of some of the other houses and ran towards them - stopping suddenly in their curiosity to stand and stare. It was obvious they rarely saw strangers and Abraham's group really did look a sorry sight. Women and men had come out of their houses now, standing silently to watch them coming towards their homes. "What must they think of us. They could not possibly think we are a threat, could they?" thought Abraham. The village children soon decided that the children, at least, were friends as they were now walking along beside them, asking quick, innocent questions of the five with the cart. "What are your names," said one. "Where have you come from," said another. "Have you lost your horse," a small girl asked. A middle-aged man had come off the wooden porch of one of the houses and was standing in their path, his arms folded, his legs astride, as if to bar them from going any further. He said "Where have you come from?" his eyes darting from the children to Anna, and Rula lying on the cart, back to Abraham and Nathan. The two brothers went forward, extending their hands in greeting, but the man stood his ground, his arms still firmly folded, a stern expression on his face. Abraham briefly told him where they had come from, and Nathan, pointing back to the cart, told him how ill Rula was, and how they needed help and medicine for her. Abraham said "I am afraid we have no money. We have sold everything of value on our journey so far in order to buy food, particularly to feed the children, and have been very lucky in some of the villages we have passed through as they let us work for a day or two for food and shelter. We do not expect charity and would be prepared to work for anything that you and your village can spare." He was frank with him, not keeping anything back so that their position would be clear from the beginning. The man relaxed and beamed at them, stretching out his hand in greeting and, looking at the women, said "My name is Kolemenos and I am the head man of this village. I hope you understand why I was not very friendly towards you at first, but we see very few strangers here, and you do look a bedraggled group and I needed to be sure you would not attack and rob us. Now I know who you are, and realise that you need help, you are welcome to stay. We are a poor village but what we have we will gladly share with you. Bring in the woman on the cart. My wife will show you where to put her and will do what we can to help her. In this place we have learned to live without medicines, using the little knowledge we have, and trusting in God's will." He stood aside, ushering them all into his home. It appeared to be one large room, a curtain hanging at the rear which presumably separated the kitchen from the living area, and a narrow flight of rickety-looking stairs leading upwards, presumably to the sleeping quarters. A small, thin, middle-aged woman, who Kolemenos introduced as his wife, Olga, had followed Nathan into the house, who was carrying Rula in his arms. She promptly picked up her skirts and climbed the stairs, telling Nathan and Abraham to follow. They did so, and on reaching the top saw two small, low beds on one side of the room, and another larger one on the other. Bright red and yellow hand-made covers were carefully covering them all, and everything was clean and bright. Nathan gently laid Rula down on one of the beds and Olga hastily shoo-ed him down the stairs. "Don't worry, leave your wife to me. I will take care of her and see what I can do." Abraham said "Nathan, you go down to be with Anna and the children and I will stay up here and help. Olga lifted Rula's skirts, gasping at the dreadful sight of her feet, ankles and legs. "Oh, you poor child. You must be in agony. They are so swollen. Come, let me help you. My name is Olga and I have two daughters about your age, so do not be embarrassed." Rula was crying, more out of relief that they were somewhere safe at last, than at her own troubles, but the woman was being so kind and motherly that she allowed her and Abraham to take off her dress and tuck her under the covers. The room was cool and dark, only getting its light from a small window at the far end. She laid her head on the pillow and Abraham turned away whilst Olga removed the rest of her clothes and sponged her down with cool water. He knew she would now feel so much better. When he turned back he realised she was falling into a deep sleep, and at last giving in to her exhaustion. Suddenly he was afraid. This was not sleep, she was becoming unconscious, or worse, going into a coma. Before he could do or say anything she was quickly snapped out of this by Olga who gave her two sharp slaps; first to the right cheek and then to the left. "Come, little one, you must not fall asleep. Wake up, wake up. Come now, drink this, it will help you," she said, holding a cup of some hot liquid up to Rula's lips. "Try and drink this, it will help the swelling go down. Come child, drink, and then you can sleep." It smelt vile and Abraham could just make out something floating on the surface. He asked what it was, and Olga told him it was special herbs which they used for heat stroke and similar conditions. It would ease the swelling, but she needed much rest, and they must let her sleep. "There is no fear of unconsciousness now, for she has nearly drunk it all. Let her rest. She can stay here for the time being." Rula looked up at Olga through hazy eyes, knowing Abraham was standing at the foot of the bed. "I heard his voice, as well as yours, telling me to drink. I must do as he says. He is such a wise man," she said. She shook her head, as if to clear it, and let herself be helped into a sitting position by them both. After a time she had drunk all the hot, not unpleasant liquid. She turned to Abraham and said "I could feel myself falling. Falling deep into a dark well. I couldn't stop myself, nor keep my eyes open. I just wanted to give in to the wonderful glorious sensation of sinking and sliding into soft, deep mud. Then I was being slapped. No one has even slapped me before!" Abraham was very relieved that Rula was being cared for so well and could not offer enough thanks to the woman and started to try, but she quickly stopped him, stressing that it was nothing and she would help anyone in the same way. He knew, though, that the terrible sight of Rula's feet and legs had upset her very much, which was why she was now being so kind. Downstairs, Nathan, Anna and the children had settled themselves on the wooden seats built around the walls of the room which Kolemenos had offered them. Hanging from the shelves were bunches of herbs and dried meat of some kind or another - he suspected goat – and an Icon of a Russian Saint was hanging on a wall. Anna whispered to Nathan "Do you think they know we are Jewish?" He nodded and whispered back "I am sure they do, but it does not seem to have made any difference." A pair of lamps stood on the table under the Icon, and there was a profusion of coloured rugs, mats and wall coverings everywhere, all in brilliant colours and obviously hand-made. The five children were sitting quietly, as if afraid to speak, in case they were sent on their way again, Helena cuddled up beside Rosa, and Anna was embarrassed to be there. As soon as she saw Olga and Abraham come down the stairs she stood up and said "We do not want to beg, for we realise that you have little enough as it is, living here in this barren place, but we are all prepared to work in return for a little food and if there is any milk for the children, we would be very grateful indeed. You have already been so kind to our sister, that we do not like to ask for more, but the children are very hungry and have not had a good meal for several days. If you can at least spare something for them that would be sufficient." Olga and Kolemenos looked at her and he said "We are indeed poor people, but are amazed at the story of your long walk over the past months and your bravery and courage. We have flour and corn, and a little meat, and what we have you are welcome to share with us." He would not let them thank him, holding up his hand to quieten Abraham and her in a manner which made them realise that he was used to being obeyed as the head man of the village.

Over the next few weeks the children played and ran with the others, becoming firm friends, whilst Abraham and Nathan helped with a variety of jobs. Cutting wood, milking the goats and cows, getting the animals in at night in case a wolf or bear came along, and generally helping wherever possible to pay in some small way for all the hospitality they were being shown. Abraham had continued to teach their five children to read and write and was pleased that four others from the village had joined them for lessons. Nathan had told them he was a tailor and was literally besieged by the women of the village, begging him to cut down this pair of trousers, that coat, this jacket, in order to make something from the least worn parts of the material. Anna, too, had been busy; she had told Olga she admired the wonderful rugs and wall coverings in her house and some of the other's homes, exclaiming at the bright colourings and patterns so the women of the village, in their pride, showed her their crude loom. She was soon addicted to this and worked constantly at it, producing a myriad of designs and colours in rugs and covers. They all said she had a natural flair and tried to insist that she keep what she had made, but Anna, anxious to repay these kind people for their generosity, would not take them and said that if they were not needed they should sell them when they went to town and earn some money. Rula was still in bed, recovering slowly but surely. By now, her legs and feet were almost back to normal, although still very red in colour, but she felt fit and rested and each day asked to be allowed to get up and help with the chores. Olga would not hear of it, however, and kept saying "Tomorrow, tomorrow." The herb drink had no doubt been the reason for her cure, and she said she would make sure they took some with them when they left, although hoping they would not need it. Then came the final evening. Rula had been up for a few days so they all agreed that now she was better they would make their way in the morning. The weather was still fine, but winter was nearly here, with a slight breeze blowing inland from the sea, cooling the air at the peak of the day, and leaving a sharp frost in the early morning. The whole village had prepared a farewell party for them, killing a goat, some chickens and a sheep. These were all being roasted on spits over the fires, and benches had been dragged outdoors, together with tables, to form a huge ring around them. Word had spread that Abraham played the violin and, once they had eaten the wonderful food and drunk some home-made wine, which had miraculously appeared from nowhere, he was urged to get up and play for them. Secretly, he needed no second bidding, for it was some weeks since he had really played, and so without another word, he went to the cart and got the fiddle out of its case. He played mazurkas; he played lullabies; he played gypsy music. The villagers kept yelling for more and he played and played, watching them whirling and twisting to the music, hands clasped around each others' waists, laughing and tossing their heads, throwing their arms up to the night sky. It was a wonderful sight - these poor people, who could be so rich on so little.

The next morning they set off very early, their cart loaded with their few belongings, and two rugs which Olga had insisted Anna should keep. The whole village turned out to wave them goodbye, the children running and laughing alongside them for a while. They knew that Odessa, their final destination, was only about forty or fifty miles to the south and had been given enough provisions to last them for about three days, knowing they would soon be reaching the outskirts of the city after that. They all turned and waved at their new-found friends, so grateful they had saved Rula's life and given them all the opportunity to rest and relax after those terrible heat-ridden days. Cries of "Good luck. Farewell. God bless you," rang in their ears and they all had tears in their eyes as they waved for the last time. Rula was still sitting on the cart, much to her annoyance, for they all agreed that although her legs were better, she was still not strong and they did not want a recurrence before they reached Odessa in case the authorities would see this as a reason for not allowing them to leave Russia and board a ship for an unknown destination. Rula saw the sense in this but knew that her weight put an extra burden on the men. The land was changing. The sandy, dry soil was becoming more earthen in appearance and here and there were bushes and stunted trees. Birds flew overhead in various patterns, swooping and diving in the currents of air, which had now lost its hot, acrid dryness and was becoming more moist with the gentle cold breezes which seemed to blow all the time. They all knew that, as the miles passed by, they were moving out of the dry, arid land and approaching the coast, with the sea and, hopefully, safety. The clumps of rough, spiky grass gradually turned into the soft green of new grass and, with it, trees - wonderful shimmering trees, turning golden in the winter air. Larch, birch, conifer. Oh! how glad they were to see the wonderful vegetation again. They were now passing fields of corn and wheat, and other plants which they could not name, but took delight in standing just to watch the heads of the wheat blowing back and forth, to and fro in the wind, ready for harvesting, the red poppies showing their brilliant red hue through the stems. The grass was everywhere and for the first time in weeks, they spent the night in a small copse of trees, lighting a fire with brushwood and using as much kindling as they liked. Abraham and Nathan knew they must be very near their destination by now - possibly only another day's walk, and so they were eager to be off as soon as daylight came. This was no problem, for the children were just as anxious to end this "adventure" and, sensing the excitement of their parents, they were full of questions about what they were going to do, and where they were going. "Will we reach the sea soon, Papa." "Will we go on a boat, Uncle?" Israel, ever the practical one, said "How will we pay the fare if we do not have any money. Do we have to work in another village again, Papa." The men smiled and Nathan said "We should soon arrive in Odessa, which is on the sea, and hopefully we will find a boat to take us to another country. You are right, Israel, we do not have any money, but hopefully your Papa and I can work on board to pay for our passage." This seemed to satisfy him for the moment.

The trees and countryside were tinted with the gold and reds proclaiming the coming winter. Rivers and streams in abundance were plummeting and rushing headlong towards the sea, with wide valleys on either side of them. The countryside was a little more hilly now and they had climbed steadily for most of the morning. As they came over the top of the last rise they stood and looked down with amazement at the sight below. Wonder of wonders, the sea! Lying across the horizon, shimmering and twinkling in the sunlight, the deep green-blue sea. They all hugged each other, the women crying, and laughing, and crying again. The children cried "Hooray, hooray." They had never seen the sea before, but knew it meant freedom. The city, sprawling in front of the vast expanse of water, was shrouded in a hazy mist, causing it to look as if it was moving in the sunlight. They knew that it was a trick of the light, however, and continued to stand and look for what seemed an interminable age. Abraham could see domes and spires of churches, the sun glinting off the roofs, and smoke spiralling upwards from chimneys. To the right were the docks, with a profusion of ships lying at anchor, and others out at sea, either waiting to enter port, or just leaving. The whole sight took his breath away and they all stood - rooted to the spot. Finally, they started down the hillside and, once down in the valley, they stopped to prepare some food, but mainly to dress the children in their few remaining good clothes. The four adults had nothing more to wear, and looked a poor, sorry group, but hoped that when the authorities heard their story they would not think them paupers or beggars. After a very quick meal, anxious to reach the city by evening, they set off. All had a jaunty air and even Rula, who now insisted on walking the last part, was laughing and shouting to the children, she was so happy they had got this far alive. As they passed through the outskirts of the city they knew that all eyes were turned on them in curiosity and were secretly worried in case the Bolsheviks should also be here. Their kind friends in the last village had reassured them there were no troops in Odessa, and that the Jewish community was living side by side with the Russian Orthodox people with no problems. They stopped a couple of times to ask their way to the docks, proceeding through the suburbs until they came to them. On reaching the wire fencing surrounding the whole area they saw dozens and dozens of men, women and children, sitting and lying around the whole area, clutching small bundles and packages to them. It became obvious to them that they were not alone in their flight from terror! Abraham spoke to an official at the gates. The others could not hear what was said, but within minutes he was signalling for them to come and join him. The three adults left the cart with the children, telling them not to move away from it, and Abraham said "We are to report to people in those large sheds over there, where we have to give our names and where we are from. There are many people here, all waiting for boats, and we will have to wait with them. The cart cannot go in, so unload it and we must take whatever we can carry, leaving anything we do not need." Abraham called the children over, and the official smiled at them, not unkindly, and after asking the occupations of the men, he patted Rosa on her head. "Hello, little one. Have you come a long way?" She looked up at him with those big blue eyes "From St. Petersburg, sir." He looked up at the others in amazement. "From St. Petersburg? Surely not, it is hundreds of miles away." Abraham told him it was true but, anxious to get into the docks, he made light of it and they hurried inside, making their way over to the huge sheds to register.

That night they were given a hot meal of stew and bread which was prepared in one of the huge sheds, and an apple for each of the children. Steaming mugs of tea and coffee were handed out, made with tinned milk, giving it a sickly, cloying flavour, but they were all thankful for the food and grateful for the kindness they were being shown. They talked to those around them, hearing the plight of others but not mentioning how far they had come themselves, in case it created too much interest, for they were anxious to remain incognito and just board a boat as soon as possible. The next day several officials walked through the huge crowd of men, women and children, allocating lines they were to wait in according to the letter of their surname, and whether they had money to pay for their passage. Their queue was alongside the sheds which meant that they had some protection from the wind for much of the day, although the sea breeze blew constantly and, although mixed with the smell of oil and fuel from the boats, it gave them encouragement and hope that they would soon be on one, bound for who knew where. Many of the refugees who had been waiting several days gave them a variety of stories as to where they would end up. One said France, another Germany, another said "America - hooray," and some said England. They did not really mind, as long as they were together - and safe. Towards noon one of the officials came over to Abraham. "You are Jews, aren't you?" he said. "Yes," said Abraham. "You play the violin, is that right?" he asked. Again Abraham said yes. "Well, friend, you are in luck. The captain of that small ship over there is leaving tonight for England and has some friends making the journey with him. The hold is fairly large, but they are only carrying little cargo on the outward journey, so he has offered to take all of you in return for some music each evening when he entertains his friends. What do you think about that? Is England where you would like to head for? The Captain is a Jew himself and has learned of the plight of so many of his people that he wants to help. Are you interested or do you think the space will be too small for you and the children?" Abraham and Nathan looked at each other. They grabbed both hands of the official, pumping them up and down in their excitement. "Oh, thank you, thank you. We are so grateful to you. How did you know I played the violin?" Someone must have told him, thought Abraham. "You are too kind, so very kind." The official, quite overcome with this sudden display of emotion, smiled, pushing his cap firmly back on his head. His kindly blue eyes were twinkling at the pleasure of this little group as he bent down and, lifting up little Rosa, said "Look, would you like to go on that little ship over there?" She said nothing, but throwing her arms around his neck, she nodded and planted a huge kiss on his whiskery cheek. He clutched her to him and his eyes filled with tears.

"Friend," he whispered to Abraham "You must take this opportunity to get away. There is news from Kiev that the Bolsheviks have slaughtered hundreds of people there in the last few days, including many Jews, and the Tsar and Tsarina, together with their five children were reported to have been murdered at Yektarinburg in July, together with their doctor and some of the staff. Before we know where we are this place will be teeming with more refugees. Thank goodness you have got here ahead of them and will at least have a chance to escape, for there will be no stopping them from slaughtering even those who manage to reach Odessa if they decide to come this far south." Abraham turned and looked at Anna. His eyes were full of tears and he could hardly speak he was so distressed at the news. He said "They have murdered the Tsar and Tsarina and all the family. My dear little Anastasia and Alexei. They were children! What had they done to deserve such an end to their lives." Anna and Rula stood up, and both clutched his hands, seeing how distressed he was. Rula, ever the wise one, said "Abraham, you must just take comfort that they are at peace, and with God. Who knows what would have become of them in these terrible times if the family had been allowed to live – maybe prison in Siberia, a far worse fate." Nathan turned to the Harbour Master and said "We cannot thank you enough. You have saved our lives, and we will never forget your help." The four adults gathered up their bundles, calling the children to keep close to them. They carefully picked their way through the crowds sitting on the quay and made their way up the gangplank and on to the deck of the ship which was to be their home for some time.

The name was painted on the bow in bold, red letters. The word was "SHALOM."

Rosa Anna Levinsky

KRISTALLNACHT. GERMANY.
WEDNESDAY NOVEMBER 9, 1938

A date which will be remembered by the Jewish Nation for all eternity. The night when terror reigned throughout the land and the real persecution of the Jewish people began in earnest. When families were forced from their homes, separated, slaughtered or forced to work in concentration camps. A time when they never gave up their struggle to overcome the persecution which they had endured for centuries, and still continue to endure.

PART TWO - ROSA'S STORY

The concert which had been held in the Berlin Philharmonic Hall came to a close, the deafening roar of applause ringing in the musicians' ears. The Conductor bowed to the audience, whilst the violinists' tapped their bows against their instruments to acknowledge him. He turned to the orchestra and signalled them to stand, and again the audience applauded, over and over again until they finally stopped. The Conductor walked from the stage, the rest of the musicians following. The audience began to leave the Auditorium, and the lights went up.

As they finally left the stage Rosa's two friends from the second row of fiddles, Marian and Kitty, whispered to her "Don't forget our date later. It's about time we treated ourselves to a good meal, we have been going without for too long. Come to the flat as soon as you can." She smiled, nodding her agreement as she made her way to the dressing room to change and get her coat. As second violinist she was privileged so did not have to share with other girls in the orchestra and, although small, the room was comfortable, allowing her to relax after rehearsals and before the evening concerts. As she changed she glimpsed herself in the mirror. She pulled a comb through her long hair, renewed her lipstick before putting on her coat, and felt pleased with her appearance. Now aged twenty-eight, she was a very beautiful, tall girl, with a lovely figure, and her blue eyes and blonde hair made her a firm favourite with the men in the orchestra.

She picked up her bag and violin, left her dressing room and went out by the stage door, saying "good night" to the doorman. Once in the street she could hear a band playing nearby, so walked around the corner towards the noise, and was amazed at the scene before her. There were soldiers marching by, with the drum major leading, waving his baton. The song they were singing, "Denn wir fahren, denn wir fahren uber England," filled the air. As they passed her, seeing the armband with the Star of David attached to her sleeve, several men left the line, came towards her, pushing her into the gutter. They pounded and pummelled her about the head and body, savagely beating her in their pent-up fury on seeing the hated Star which she so proudly displayed, tipping the contents of her bag onto the street, kicking and stamping on the contents. Jeering and shouting abuse, they rejoined the line of men and marched on. Some people helped Rosa stand, supporting her on either side, asking if she was alright, but her immediate panic was to find her violin. "Oh, where is it, where is my fiddle?" she cried. With no thought for the blood running down from the cut on her forehead and the severe pain in her back, she frantically looked for it. To her immense relief, she saw the case lying intact on the pavement and she grabbed it up, leaving her bag and its contents strewn on the ground and started to make her way slowly out of the crowd towards her apartment. In the distance, she could hear shouting, yelling, sounds of glass breaking. She felt dizzy from the blow to her head, and both her knees were grazed but knew she would feel better once she reached home. What a shock when she arrived there! The Gestapo were out in force, already removing all the Jewish occupants from her block of flats. Too late – she had been spotted and, anyway, could not have run, for apart from the injuries she had just received she was rooted to the spot in terror. An officer approached. "Are you Rosa Levinsky, from the Berlin Philharmonic?" She nodded dumbly. "You are under arrest. Get over to that truck and get inside." She pulled herself together and cried out "You cannot arrest me, I am British. I am doing a concert tour here with the orchestra. You cannot take me, I have done nothing. Please don't take me. I know there is a curfew in a few minutes, but I have just come from the concert where I have been playing. Look, I have my fiddle with me." The SS officer gave her a cold, sneering look, and called over one of his men. "Take this Jewess. Make sure she is on the train out of the city by morning with all her friends." The maniacal laugh he uttered made Rosa go cold and the hairs on the back of her neck stood up. The guard grabbed her arm, dragging her to the waiting truck. Rosa was sobbing and becoming hysterical, pleading with him to let her go, and for some inexplicable reason, she hung on to her violin with grim determination as if it was her most precious possession – little did she know that it would eventually help to save her life.

The truck moved off slowly and in the darkness, Rosa saw there were several women and children huddled in the rear. Most of them were sitting there in abject terror, completely mute; much more frightening than if they had been screaming or crying. The bewildered children clung to their mothers and they too, taking the cue, remained totally silent. She felt ashamed that she was crying and by sheer will-power stopped the hysteria rising in her throat, which was threatening to emit in a long drawn-out scream. Instead, she started to gabble at them "Why are we here? What have we done? Are you all Jewish?" No one answered; they were too terrified to reply. There was utter chaos on the streets they went through. Panic, and screams from those who were being pushed into the roadway. She heard the lash of a whip and cries as it hit home on some poor person. The truck kept stopping, and the SS would shove more men, women and children in. As it moved through the streets huge bonfires could be seen everywhere, the soldiers laughing and shouting, throwing books, clothes and pieces of furniture to fuel the flames. There was the constant sound of breaking glass, and a Synagogue they passed was burning furiously. Suddenly a small bundle came flying through the open back. Everyone ducked, thinking it was someone's belongings, but when it landed with a sickening thud and started to cry they realised it was a baby. Someone called out "Is this your baby?" but as there was no reply from anyone they all knew the mother was certainly not in the truck with them. A woman close to Rosa, who said her name was Esther, picked up the child and started to rock it in her arms, crooning to it as if it was her own. Slowly the baby stopped crying and eventually was lying there quietly. She said "It's a little girl, a pretty little thing. I think she must be about eighteen months old. She seems to be alright, and not really hurt, so was just scared when she landed in here." How wonderful the baby had no idea what was going on all around her. As the truck started up after about its fourth stop, Rosa had been pushed to the rear and there were now about forty men, women and children on board, lying huddled together in the lorry. She could see that there were several other trucks behind theirs and someone said "We are leaving the city centre. Where can we be going?" Another whispered the dreaded word "marschbefehl" which meant transportation to an unknown destination. Panic spread amongst all the people in the truck, including Rosa, for they had all heard the stories being told about the vast numbers of Jews being sent to work camps, but no-one knew how true they were. Those who had been totally mute until now started to cry and wail, calling out to God to help them, and this was a signal to the children to start crying too. They sensed their mothers' were terrified - fear has its own smell, and this smell they were to live with for a very long time to come - those of them who had the courage and will to survive.

As the truck drove through the city they all realised with a horrifying feeling of dread that they were headed for the railway. They passed several patrols of German soldiers marching in the opposite direction, lorrys loaded with troops, machine guns and other weapons. Suddenly they came to a halt. There was a rush of booted feet running towards the trucks and the back of theirs was flung down. "Schnell, schnell. Raus. Raus." These two words, which Rosa and the others were to hear over and over again, were shouted at all of them, and they could hear it echoing through the line of trucks which had all come to a standstill. "Raus, raus," shouted the guards again. They thought the people inside the lorries were moving too slowly and began to pull the women and children from the backs of the trucks. There were screams as they fell onto the hard cobbles and the sickening thud as rifle butts hit the heads of those on the ground - mercilessly being clubbed to death. On seeing this, it made the rest of the people rush and they started to claw their way frantically past each other in an effort to be out of the trucks before they felt the lash of a whip or the butt of a rifle across their backs. Rosa jumped down, clutching her violin, and stopped dead in her tracks. There was Esther, lying dead on the ground, with her face battered in. The baby she had taken so lovingly as her own lay screaming once again, but she was still clutching it tightly to her. Rosa knelt down and although she felt the stinging, searing pain of a whip cutting through her clothes, prised Esther's hands apart and took the child from her. She got up quickly, just as a guard was about to club her to death too, and stood in front of him. She said "Have you never known love for another human being?" Her look seemed to unnerve him, for he lowered his rifle and pushed her, not too roughly, towards the group of women already standing in line - the baby in one arm and clutching her violin with the other. Rosa felt very faint now, and the pain across her shoulders was increasing with the cold. A woman standing beside her saw her sway and quickly took hold of her arm. "Let me help you; give me the fiddle." She said "No, no. I can manage, I am alright." The child was quiet in her arms and not too heavy and so they marched off. Suddenly floodlights were switched on and the whole station was illuminated. There were hundreds of men, women and children huddled together in the cold winter night. The men were being segregated and went to the left of the yard as they approached. The white armbands with the Star of David could be seen everywhere, and Rosa then realised that this was a round-up of the Jews of Berlin. There were machine guns placed at strategic intervals around the huge compound and she wondered why they were there. She did not have to wonder for very long, as suddenly a burst of gunfire rang out, amidst much screaming and shouting, and when what seemed like an eternity the firing ended, they could see that the dead bodies huddled on the ground were obviously the Rabbis and Elders from the Synagogues. Everyone started to wail in anguish and Rosa could hear prayers being said and calls to God, asking for help. The noise was deafening, but still above it could be heard "Schnell, schnell. Raus. Raus," and the barking of the Alsatian dogs, snapping and snarling, and straining on their leashes to try and attack someone.

Eventually, it was the turn of their group to board a train. They were pushed and shoved towards all the trucks hitched to the engine and the baby, sensing that Rosa was walking again, started to whimper – Rosa did not know if it was with fright or cold. She clung to her and felt very protective as she clambered on board the cattle truck, clutching the baby and her violin. Whilst Rosa could still see from the floodlights she realised there must have been at least fifty people in there and, quickly looking around, saw that there was some dirty looking straw on the floor of the truck. There was a roof, but no windows, and it went through her mind very briefly how would they all breathe in there once they shut the doors? An SS officer appeared and shouted to them to be quiet. "You will all be transported to an internment camp for resettlement. The men will be sent to labour camps. Do not worry, you will all meet again very soon." His smarmy tone lulled some of them into a feeling of false security, so one woman bravely called out "We will all suffocate and die in these cattle wagons. You can't do this to us. At least let the children go." He merely smiled and gave a final fling of his arm in the now-familiar salute, shouting out "Heil Hitler" and with a tremendous heave, slammed the door shut. Immediately, there was a horrifying sense of panic amongst all of them, with the fear of suffocation uppermost in all their minds. Chinks of light could be seen through the slats of the cattle truck from the floodlights outside and everyone tried to get near to them, knowing that they would at least bring the blessed relief of air. Suddenly, a strong voice called out "Please, for the sake of the children, let us be strong. We are obviously going to be in here for some time, so must make the most of it. Has anyone got any blankets or shawls with them?" "I have." "I have," said three or four voices. "Right," said the voice. "I spotted several hooks in the roof before the doors were closed. If we can sling the blankets from the hooks we can put the smallest children in them and they, at least, will not get trampled on and will make a little more room for the rest of us." With a tremendous sense of relief, the women realised they had a leader. She could not be seen in the dark, but they felt her strength coming through, which gave them all the spark of courage needed. As their eyes became accustomed to the darkness a small boy was held up to hoist the blankets from the hooks. They found eight in the roof, and with the shawl from the baby and three other blankets which were strung up, to their amazement they managed to get eleven small children, including the baby, into the new cots. Although all of the adults were terrified at the unknown prospect before them they took great delight in the chuckles from the children suspended above their heads, who were all enjoying this new game.

As the train moved off they began to speculate where they were going. Some thought the south, some north, but none voiced the thought that they were headed for that most dreaded of places - the name that had been whispered many times during the past few months as the new labour and "re-settlement" camp. Dachau! As the train lumbered slowly into a fast motion and the wheels made more noise it started to pick up speed. Rosa was rammed up against the wall of the truck and all through that first night, they hurtled along in the blackness. At least she could feel the cold air rushing through the slit beside her face - that oh! so pure, fresh air. Some of them were able to sleep standing up, but after several hours they devised a scheme which was to last the duration of the journey, where they squeezed up tightly against each other and allowed the rest to sit on the floor for a while, then changed over. As dawn broke and daylight started to filter through the sides of the truck they began to feel renewed hope that perhaps soon the train would come to a halt, but as the hours passed by, and it did not alter its hurtling speed along the tracks, they all realised they were trapped - totally. There were occasional stops when they guessed the train was being refuelled, or taking on water, but everyone remained locked in the trucks. The first part of the journey was a nightmare. They remained imprisoned in the truck for a night and a day and had to relieve themselves where they stood. There was no food, no clean nappies for the baby and tiny children, who had cried incessantly for several hours in their discomfort. The smell was foul and the air very foetid. When the train did stop everyone shouted through the walls of the truck "Water, food. Water, food. Help us, please help us," but to no avail. It moved off again and still kept up its hell-bent pace, causing those women standing to be rocked to and fro against each other, clutching at an arm or a sleeve to keep upright. Somehow Rosa managed to keep her balance and a firm hold on her violin, as she had her back pressed against the side of the truck. Three women had fallen down during that first day and everyone knew they were dead but there was nothing they could do except try and pull them to one side, which was an almost impossible task. Suddenly, the train began to slow down and they knew it was stopping. It finally drew to a halt and the hammering on the doors of all the trucks began again, growing louder and louder, with frantic cries from those locked inside. The guards were running along the train, pounding on the sides of all the trucks and shouting to everyone to be quiet. They had been imprisoned for over thirty-six hours when suddenly their truck door was slid noisily open, with the command to get out.

It was nearly dark, and all they could see was snow, snow and more snow. It gave them no clue as to where they were and no-one was prepared for the bitter weather. Rosa and the other mothers took the children down from their hammocks and clambered out, carrying them in their arms, whilst others who could get down more easily from the truck did so, helping the older ones and those too stiff from standing to move. After the stinking warmth of the truck the searing wind hit them with a blinding force. They all hobbled stiffly to the verge and started to rub their aching limbs to restore the circulation. The blow across Rosa's back was throbbing and she felt sick and ill, but clutched the baby and tried to keep her warm, whilst her other hand kept a firm grip on her violin. She was wearing a thin silk black dress, covered with a short coat, but neither was designed to protect her from the freezing conditions they were now experiencing. She knew the baby would feel cold as well, as her shawl was still hanging from the roof of the truck, so she pulled her coat around it to try and give her some more warmth. Someone pointed inside their truck, telling the guard there were some dead women inside and, at this he jabbed four women forward with his rifle butt, telling them to remove the bodies. They somehow managed to drag and pull them from the floor of the truck, covered in wet, filthy straw, and several of the women then laid them out as best they could in the freezing snow. There was no chance to bury them, even if they had been given spades, for the ground was frozen hard. The soldiers were laughing and jeering and called out "Take the clothes off them, you verfluchte Schwinebande, they don't need them now but you will." None of the women would do as they suggested, and all received more blows and cuts from their rifle butts. They were not allowed to move a small distance away to relieve themselves, which was very humiliating as the soldiers laughed at them trying to be as discreet as possible in the circumstances. None were yet at the point where they had lost their sense of decency - that would come later. The soldiers were jeering "Filthy Judenbande, you are animals," but suddenly there was a command from an officer standing a short distance away and they were all pushed, shoved and jostled back into the trucks. Rosa called out "Please can we have some food and water, at least for the children. We have been travelling all last night and today with nothing. They must have something, even if we don't." The guard looked at her but did not say a word. There was to be no food or water for them that night! As the doors were slammed shut once again the smell of putrid, filthy wet straw hit them and they knew it would be many hours again before they could breathe fresh air. Soon the train started to pull away, gradually picking up speed as it raced across the countryside.

They travelled for many hours again, through the darkness and into the dawn, during which time the train made an occasional stop. No-one came when people called out for food or water, only the guards who pummelled on the sides of the trucks with their rifle butts, shouting to them to keep quiet. Some had tried singing to keep their spirits up, but their mouths were so dry and parched that, before long, they gradually stopped. No one knew where they were going, but the whisper "Dachau" got louder and louder. Rosa did not dare to think they were really going to that terrible place she had heard rumours about. An icy shiver ran down her back - she was alive, but would she be able to survive in such a place, if that was where they were going. Towards the middle of the second day, they again came to a halt, but the doors of the truck remained closed. After what seemed an interminable time she could hear the shouts and yells from other parts of the train getting louder and louder, and so the people in her truck started to beat on the sides and doors, screaming to be let out, until in the end, after about two hours, they all seemed to realise this was useless and they were to remain prisoners. Gradually they became quiet, and the noise lessened, until all that could be heard was the whimpering and crying of children and the odd shout of "Quiet in there" from a soldier. They remained locked up until it was dark. The foul stench was indescribable and the cold crept into all their bones. Huddled together as they were did help, but their feet and hands were numb as they did not have room to stamp or swing their arms in order to get warm. The baby lay silently in her makeshift hammock and Rosa wondered why she had become so quiet and still, for she had been screaming for food incessantly until a short while ago. She could not nurse her, as mothers' of other babies could, and she had no food to give her. She reached her hand up above her head to touch the baby and felt the soaking wet hammock in the darkness. She whispered to a woman standing close by "She is quiet and very wet. Do you think she is alright?" "Don't worry, she has probably cried herself to sleep with exhaustion," she said. Suddenly, there could hear shouts outside, obviously of command, and the running of many feet. Rosa guessed it was the soldiers when she heard the truck doors being hauled open all along the train - it was their turn! It crashed back on its runners. "Austeigen, alles austeigen, schneller, los," cried the soldiers, as everyone started to pour out of the trucks into the blackness of the night. Rosa grabbed the baby down and, clutching the violin in her other hand, managed to pass her out to the crowd. Suddenly, the floodlights were all around them and Rosa saw there were hundreds of people swarming around the railway track. The soldiers were ordering them into batches of about fifty people and all around was the swishing of whips and the barking of dogs. Dogs such as they had never seen before - yellow fangs, great burning eyes and snarling snouts. They were straining and rearing on their leashes and the guards were doing nothing to pull them back. Rosa looked down at the baby as she was handed back to her "She is dead, you know, my dear," said a woman gently, thinking she was Rosa's. "She is quite blue with cold and there is no heartbeat. Leave her here in the truck with the others who are dead. It is useless to take her with you; you cannot help her now." Rosa hated herself for having to put the little thing back amongst all that filth, even though she was dead, and wished she could have arranged for her to be decently buried. The guards ordered them to march forward, and although there was a lot of snow on the ground, her feet stuck in the mud where it had been trampled on by hundreds of feet and had not had time to freeze over. They passed a floodlit fence, with lookout posts every few yards, occupied by sentries with guns which pointed directly at the crowds. It crossed Rosa's mind that they had no need to threaten them – they could not possibly fight back - they were all unarmed!

In front of them stood large iron gates, and the soldiers poked and prodded the women and children through, constantly yelling "Schnell. Schnell. Raus, raus." A female guard came marching towards them, swishing her cane against her hips, shouting at them to march inside, whilst other guards grabbed at the children who were with them. The mothers were yelling and shouting. "Don't take my child. Please don't hurt her." "He is only seven, please don't take him." All the mothers were distraught and calling out. The children were screaming and crying, sensing their mothers were desperately trying to keep hold of them. The guards were yelling. "You will see your children later. They will be safe with us," and led the children away. The women tried to run after them, slipping and sliding in the snow, some falling to the ground and being beaten senseless by the guards until there was no life left in them. Once inside a large yard, they were all herded together and more women guards surrounded them, brandishing their canes, shouting "All of you, strip, take off your clothes ready for disinfection. You will be issued with other clothes once you are clean." Rosa put her violin against the wall, where she hoped it would be safe. She had never undressed in front of anyone before and noticed that several of the women also seemed reluctant to strip, so stood there, trying to brave it out. "Do we really have to," she murmured to someone beside her. Before she could answer a whip lash caught her on the arm. Rosa screamed out, not so much in pain, but in fright. "You will undress. Now. That is an order, and if you disobey me I will shoot you," said one of the guards. This caused the others to quickly undress, and Rosa followed suit. It was very cold out in the open, despite the press of bodies all around her, so they huddled together – not just for warmth but also for support. Rosa was shivering as they were marched over to the other side of the yard, all naked, trying to cover their breasts and lower regions with their hands as best they could, but this did not stop the many male guards ogling them and calling out obscene names. They were formed into a long line and then came the final humiliation – the guards began spraying them from the front and back with a stinking white powder. They had no warning to cover their faces and so it clogged their mouths and noses, and they were almost unable to breathe. Their hair was covered in it. Their eyes were stinging, the tears running down their cheeks mingling with the thick white powder – and the smell. What was it? Then Rosa realised it must be some form of disinfectant. The guard had said earlier they would be disinfected – but this degradation was nothing compared with what would happen to them all in the future.

Rosa managed to grab her violin as they were marched into a large hall. Several female guards then entered, carrying huge bundles of clothing. Dropping them onto the floor one of them shouted out "Here are clothes for you to wear. Yours will be burned, as you Jews carry so much vermin we would all quickly be contaminated. Get dressed so we can get rid of your stinking bodies out of here. There are no shoes yet. We may bring some tomorrow." Rosa and the others ran over to the bundles to find out what there was. Skirts, woollen shirts, some bits of underwear, a few dresses, and some blouses. Nothing looked clean and was obviously well worn. The scrabbling then began as all the women suddenly realised if they did not move quickly they would have nothing to wear. Rosa grabbed a skirt, a top of some sort, a petticoat, then spotted a thin jacket underneath the pile she was sorting through. The woman beside her tried to snatch this, but Rosa clung on, frightened that between them the jacket would get ripped. Then it would be no use to anyone. "Let me have it," said the woman. "You have got enough already. I could only find a dress, and, look, it has short sleeves. I need something else to try to keep me warm." Rosa's conscience pricked her. They were all in the same boat. She let go and said "You are right. Take it. I will find something else." There was not much left in the piles, but Rosa spied another thicker looking top. She picked it up and held it tightly, not letting go this time. "Thank you. Thank you," said the woman. "What is your name? I am Elsa." Rosa smiled and said "Rosa." Elsa looked at her and said "You are so beautiful, even with all this filthy white powder covering your face. I noticed you before. I don't think you are German – you sound foreign to me." Rosa said "You are right. I am British. I shouldn't be here. I am a musician, playing with the Berlin Philharmonic orchestra. I have been here in Germany for three years and was hoping to get back to England very soon as I knew the situation was getting worse and we Jews were being hounded more and more, but I never expected this. Now, I don't think I will see my family for a long time, if at all." She stood up and started putting on the clothes. Nothing fitted, but at least she had a skirt, a petticoat and the two tops she had on would give a bit of warmth. Then the tears welled up out of her eyes. Not from the stinging as before, but this time with the sheer desperation of the plight she now knew she was in. Elsa put her arms around her to comfort her, but then felt the lash of a whip for trying to be kind. This type of treatment would soon stop any of them having feelings for their other captives. The crowd of women were a sorry looking sight in the assortment of clothing which had been doled out. Virtually nothing fitted, buttons were missing, some of the skirts and tops were torn – perhaps in the rush to be snatched up.

"Line up over here," called out one of the guards. "When you have given your name and where you are from to the guards sitting over at the tables move to the other side of the hall. Then take a bowl. Take care of it, you won't get another. You Juden can use it for everything." He laughed, turned and walked away from the long trestle tables. The women moved forward and after stating their name and where they were from each took a small metal bowl. The guards were then pushing the women back in line, shouting at them to move, and stood briskly to attention, saluting as a tall German officer entered the room. He stood, tapping his cane gently against his leg, looking at the women. "All of you. Listen, and listen well. My name is Franz Ziereis. I am the Commandant here in Mauthausen - Gusen Camp. You will be taken to your barracks which is where you will then spend the rest of your time here. You will be given some food, but from tomorrow you will work for it. No work, no food. Those of you who do not work will be put to death. Heil Hitler." With those words, he turned and left. The women guards then forced them out into the bitterly cold snow and marched them to several wooden huts. The snow was frozen on the hard ground and Elsa cried out in pain as she tried to walk without shoes. Their guard said "Stand in line there. The first fifty of you will go into Hut 1." She counted them out, roughly pushing them forward, until fifty had gone inside. Rosa and Elsa stood waiting, then it was their turn, and they went into Hut 2. Inside was dark and unlit, the only light filtering in through two grimy windows on either side. In the centre was a huge iron stove, with a row of two-tier bunks either side of the hut. As Rosa passed the stove she instinctively knew it was not alight. "Why is the stove not lit in this freezing cold weather," she thought. She turned to Elsa "Do you want top or bottom of the bunk?" Elsa said "I will go on the bottom. You are a lot younger than me and I might have trouble climbing up there." There was a slight covering of straw on the base, but nothing else. No pillows or covering of any sort. Rosa put her violin under the base, up against the wall, hoping it would be safe just as three female guards entered; two carrying a large bucket between them, the other holding a basket. "Here is your food. Share it between you. There will be nothing more until tomorrow night – if you have worked." The bucket and basket were put on the floor and the three left. The women surged forward – all had been without food for several days and were rushing to get their share. Rosa grabbed a piece of grey looking bread, and managed to dip her bowl into the greasy looking liquid in the bucket then moved out of the way of the others and perched on Elsa's bunk. The soup was revolting. Tepid, with bits of potato peel floating in it. She heaved as she swallowed the disgusting liquid but instinctively knew that eat she must. Eat or die. Elsa joined her but had only managed to get some bread. All the soup had gone. Rosa said loudly to no-one in particular "If this is all we are going to get to eat we will have to arrange rationing of some sort so that we all get a share." "Yes, we must. I only got bread," said one voice. "I got nothing, it was all gone," said another. "You arrange it. You be in charge," said another. Rosa looked at Elsa, who nodded. "Alright. My name is Rosa, and tomorrow when the food comes Elsa and I will give each of you a bowlful and a piece of bread. If there isn't enough to go round we will have to cut the portions down and halve the bread. Let's see." There was a loud murmur of consent. All the women could see the sense of this plan. They started to talk to each other; exchanging names, where they were from, how old they were, those with children crying - wondering where their little ones were; were they safe, when would they see them? They were locked in the hut, with no means of getting to the latrines. Several buckets stood by the doors, offering no privacy for the women, but this was what they had to use during the night, and all realised they must overcome their feelings, just as they had done in the carriages on their journey to this terrible place. All were still covered with the white powder, despite trying to rub it off their faces, but with no water to wash with they had not been very successful.

It was dark inside the hut and most of the women had grown quiet, each with their own private thoughts. Rosa reached under Elsa's bunk and grabbed her violin. She climbed up on to her bunk, opened the case and started to pluck at the strings to ensure none had been broken. She felt for her bow in the darkness, then softly drew it across the strings. All was well, so she began to play some Chopin. More to console herself than anything else. When she paused there were cries of "Please play some more." "That was beautiful." "How wonderfully you play," from all around the hut. Elsa called up to her "Not only are you beautiful, but your music is beautiful too." She played for a while, gradually realising she had lulled most of them to sleep, climbed down and put her violin away, then went up and laid down on her bunk.

Dawn. There was a loud banging on the doors as they were opened by the guards. "Schnell. Raus. Get up. Get to the latrines, and empty your buckets. Then line up ready for work." Rosa and the women stumbled, still half asleep, out into the icy grey morning. One guard shouted "Pick up the buckets. Take them with you." Rosa and a few others each grabbed a stinking bucket, covering their mouths and noses with their hands at the stench. Walking without shoes was very difficult in the thick snow which had fallen during the night and very soon Rosa could not feel her feet at all. "Surely they must give us shoes. Why couldn't we keep our own," she thought. The buckets were emptied. There were two cold taps in the yard and, despite the freezing cold, they formed a queue waiting to try and wash some of the disinfectant off their faces to feel a bit cleaner. Rosa's turn came and she gasped as she sluiced her face and neck with the icy water, quickly rubbing herself dry on the sleeve of her jacket. The guards approached, shouting their normal "Schnell. Raus. Schnell, schnell." "Line up, follow me. Quickly, we are in a hurry." One swished her cane, giving this as a signal to the other guards to do the same, and the women rushed into a line as quickly as they could on the slippery ground. They were marched back to the building where they had been the day before and urged inside by the guards, beating them around the head and back with their canes if they did not keep up. On several trestle tables stood piles and piles of boots and shoes. Rosa's first thought was where did they all come from? "Get moving. Find a pair of shoes or boots to fit you. There are enough for all of you, but make sure you wear them all the time so they are not stolen. There will not be any more," called out a Guard. They moved forward, all trying to find two shoes or boots which matched. Rosa grabbed two boots which looked alike, and some shoes, hoping they would fit. She sat on the floor with the others, all trying on what they had picked out. The boots fitted her, and so did one of the shoes. But where was the other one? Rosa kept the boots on, looking quickly among the rest of the pile on the trestle for the other shoe. Then she spotted it, and it fitted. "Which shall I keep," she wondered, then decided the boots would be better as they came up around her ankles and would give a bit more protection on the snowy ground. "Hurry up, get your shoes and get back outside. We have work for you to do," shouted the guard. Some of the mothers were crying, asking when they would see their children. "Your children are all together. They are being well looked after and you will be reunited when you have proved you can work hard. That will be your reward." "When will that be," cried out one woman. "When you have shown us you are prepared to work," was the reply. "Now, get outside and form a line."

They began to walk. In the freezing temperatures, they tried to hurry in order to keep warm, but some of the older women had trouble keeping up. As they fell back they were beaten and forced to run forward to join the line. They marched for nearly an hour and came to a group of men who were building what looked like a roadway up from the huge quarry they could see ahead of them. The line was halted. The main guard stood up on some raised ground and said "Here is where you will work. Your job is to carry the stones you see on that pile over there and take them to the men who are building a staircase to the top of the quarry. Each day the stairs must get longer. If it does not you will all be punished, not just those who drop the stones or fall, but all of you." And so the work started, and every day the same routine. Up at dawn, no food, working for more than twelve hours each day until it was so dark they could not see the stones, or where the stairs finished. The march back to the camp, so tired and exhausted that many fell by the wayside and, despite being beaten, did not get up and died there. The same meagre rations when they returned to their hut, but no thought of playing the violin. Not only was Rosa too tired and worn out; her hands and nails were so torn and bleeding she could not hold her bow, or pluck the strings. Nor did the other women want to be lulled to sleep – there was no need. They fell asleep as soon as they laid on their bunks. Those who were too ill or sick to work were removed to the Krakenlager, which was supposedly a hospital, staffed by a few prisoners with medical knowledge, but as there were no medical supplies only basic treatment was offered. If the prisoner did not improve they were either starved to death in a bunker or shot. Then they heard the new rumour – but was it true? Could it be true? There were now so many sick and dying that an improvised "death lorry" had been brought in. These patients were loaded inside the van, which was then sealed, with the exhaust tube connected to the inside. The engine was started up, when screams and shouts could be heard coming from the inside for some time, until eventually, all was quiet, and everyone was dead. No one who was sick ever came back to their hut, so all secretly thought it must be true. The mothers constantly asked when they would see their children, crying and pleading with the guards, begging to just let them see them until, finally, the Kapos told them that all the children had been put to death. The wailing and keening went on for hours. Nothing Rosa, Elsa and those without little ones could do or say could help them. One mother rushed at a guard, pummelling him on the chest, yelling and shouting at him, so that he aimed his pistol at her head and killed her. A nun from their hut called out "What has happened is terrible and not something any of us thought could happen. Of course you want your children with you, but maybe God has seen that this solution would be better than letting the little ones suffer and probably starve to death, just as we are. They would be unable to survive in the harsh conditions we are enduring." Some of the mothers realised what she was saying was right, and those Catholics amongst them started to say prayers with the nuns. The Jewish mothers followed, saying Kadish, and gradually the crying and weeping stopped. They realised the nun was right, but would always remember their children.

During the winter more and more prisoners arrived, mostly men, and the guards were doubled in case they decided to try and escape. Each day these men were taken to the Quarry staircase, which the women heard was rumoured to be called "The Stairs of Death." Whilst the women worked on the stones, taking them further and further up the slope, they often saw some of the men being forced to carry much bigger blocks up the "staircase", often collapsing on top of the man behind him and then they would all come tumbling down, the huge blocks they were carrying crashing into them. If this did not kill them they were promptly shot on the spot by the guards. The women working closely with the men saw that even if they were bent double putting their stones in place on the "staircase" they were expected to stand and salute a German officer if he came near them. If he failed to do this he was then sent up to the edge of the cliff and forced to push the prisoner in front of him off to his death, then wait for his turn. Rosa could not believe such brutality could exist. She was horrified at the atrocities that were carried out each day, wondering why they were forced to work until they died if they needed the workers so badly. "Is it because there are now so many of us it doesn't matter if we die?" she asked herself. There had been more new arrivals in their hut each week, and it was now so overcrowded they all had to share a bunk so she had gone down to Elsa's. Fortunately, they had been given a second bucket of soup and more bread each night to feed the extra women, which Rosa and Elsa were still rationing out, but it was never enough. Now all the women were suffering from starvation, becoming walking skeletons. Rosa had sores on her legs and arms, her hair was falling out and she and Elsa had lice crawling in their armpits, on their heads and in their pubic hair. When she scratched her skin bled, and the sores were then getting infected. Not all the new women were Jewish, but Catholics and Christians whose only "crime" was the job they had done each day in Germany, Austria and Czechoslovakia. Some were teachers, others had worked in banks or shops and there were several nuns. Rosa felt very sorry for them, as they had been forced out of their black habits and made to wear the same rags as the rest of them. She admired them for their faith, as they never complained and were heard praying when they could during the day whilst they were working.

It was 1939 and spring was on the way. Each day was slightly warmer and the snow was rapidly melting. Rosa and several of the inmates from her hut had been taken away from the "staircase" and were working near the camp on a large farm, tending and milking the cattle, planting crops, herding sheep, and clearing out the pigsties. The work was much easier and all of them were thankful to be away from the Quarry with the daily beatings, deaths and atrocities carried out there. When the guards were covering another group and not watching them they would try and find a raw potato or swede to eat; squirt a mouthful of warm milk into their mouths and, if they were lucky, find an egg before the farmer came to collect them. In this way, the group's health gradually improved. Rosa's hands and nails had healed and were no longer bleeding and the blisters and open wounds on her feet were improving. She felt able to deal with the daily routine, always wondering how her family in England was, and how much she missed them. "Has anyone from the orchestra been able to get word to them that I was taken prisoner? Maybe no-one knows. Perhaps they think I was shot and died on that dreadful night." As she was thinking these thoughts a guard came up to her and Gretchen, who was working beside her as they planted seedlings in the furrows they had been making all morning. "You two, come with me," he said. They stood up and saw most of the other women who had been working were now standing in a large group. "Schnell. Don't lag behind. You have work to do. Follow me," he said. The women all walked behind him for about half an hour until they saw a large river ahead of them. There were already many men and women prisoners working there and, as they approached, saw they were piling earth up high onto the banks. Their guard stopped and turned to them. "The river is in danger of bursting its bank now that the snow is melting, and if it does this whole area will be flooded, including the farm you have just left, and others around here. Get to work shovelling earth up on to the banks which the others are making. Hurry, there is not much time as the water is rising rapidly. Shovels are over there, so take one and get to work."

Rosa picked up a spade and began shovelling with the others but the earth was still hard to dig and soon she was sweating with the exertion. The banks of earth were getting higher and higher on either side of the river, but the waters kept rising until, suddenly, she spotted a thin trickle of water breaking through the banking. "Quick, over here," she cried, frantically heaping more earth over the break. The soft earth was slipping down, the water was coming through faster and faster, the earth was giving way, the trickle became a stream and then, with a rush, the bank completely gave way, swirling around Rosa and three other women. The guards were yelling "Run. Run to higher ground." The prisoners dropped their spades and ran. Faster and faster it came; higher and higher, until they were waist deep. Rosa was trying to run through the water. It was up around her chest when suddenly she was hit from behind by a huge deluge. She fell forward, floundering, trying to get back on her feet, but the water was rising so rapidly she was swept forward, arms flailing, battling to try and keep from going under. She panicked and screamed "I can't swim. Help me, please. Save me," before swallowing huge mouthfuls of water, but the others were all fighting the rapidly rising torrent and saving themselves. Suddenly she was grabbed by the collar and pulled on her back through the water. It was one of the guards! "Come on, get on your feet, we are now out of danger and in the shallows," he said. Rosa was coughing and spluttering, coughing up the water she had swallowed. She looked at him, not believing that one of the guards had actually saved her. She was on her knees, water streaming from her clothes, her hair plastered to her face and neck. Great bouts of liquid was coming out of her mouth and she was choking. The guard banged her several times on her back to help her get rid of the water she had swallowed. At last she stopped coughing and was able to sit up. "I will be alright now, but how can we stop the river flooding the farm. It is so close." The guard looked at her and said "There's nothing we can do. We've tried to stop it, but couldn't. Hopefully the bank on the other side will hold now that some of the water has escaped over here." He waded away, and left Rosa standing alone, soaking wet, her clothes sticking to her, the water swirling around her ankles as she made her way to higher ground. She knew that she had been in danger of drowning, but at least she was now much cleaner!

As she dried her clothes that night in the hut Rosa told those around her bunk what had happened. Gretchen said "The guard who saved you is called Herman. I have seen the way he looks at you when we have been working on the farm. Maybe he likes you." Elsa said "No German likes a Jew, particularly not when we are so thin and covered in sores." Rosa said "I never got the chance to thank him, but I don't understand why he saved me when most of the time they are trying to kill us." Elsa said "Be careful. Even if you are a Jew you are still a woman. If he wants you he will take you, there will be nothing you can do to stop him. Try not to let him think you are grateful he saved you or he might want payment!" The buckets of the noxious liquid arrived, together with the hunks of bread, for Rosa and Elsa to dish out everyone's ration. One bucket was full, but the other was half empty – not nearly enough to feed almost one hundred women who were now in their hut. Gretchen and two others shouted out to the guards "Why have we only got half a bucket. There are dozens of us in

here. There will not be nearly enough to feed us all."
"Quiet," said the guard. "You are lucky to get this for
half of you did not work today because of the floods.
Those who didn't work should not have food." With that,
she dropped the basket of bread on the floor and the two
of them left. There was a mad scramble from the women
who had come up from the back of the hut, grabbing at
the bread and trying to dip their pots in the liquid. Elsa
yelled out "Stop. Stop. You know we have a system. We
must share the food out. If we do not keep to the ration
some of us will die." "You were not working on the
staircase. You did not have to break stones and carry
them up to the men. You were having an easy time on
the farm. How much food did you manage to steal?"
someone said loudly. Rosa shouted out "Alright. Keep
calm. Those who worked on the staircase today can have
more soup than the rest of us and a piece of bread. What
is left we will share with those of us who were on the
farm, although we did not get a chance to find any
potatoes or swede today as we were forced to try to stop
the bank breaking." There was a murmur of assent from
some of the women, but many others were grumbling,
whilst secretly knowing Rosa was right.

The smell of drying clothes filled the hut with a
cloying smell and Rosa felt the need for some air. She
put on her dry skirt and top, picked up her violin, and
went outside. Sitting on the steps in the dusk she took
out her fiddle and began to play. It soothed and calmed
her. She was so wrapped up in the melody that she was
unaware that Herman, the Guard, was standing nearby,
leaning up against the next hut, until he clapped when
she finished playing. "Does anyone here know you play
so well?" he asked. "I only play inside the hut usually,
but the smell of wet clothes forced me to come outside for

some air. As it is not dark yet and not been locked in for the night I thought it would be alright. I am going back in now." She put her violin in its case, closed it and stood up. With that Herman grabbed her, holding her tightly against him, forcing his mouth on hers. She could not scream or cry out as he was smothering her with kisses. Then he pushed her legs apart with his knees. "Come on, Juden, you know you want it." He grabbed her skirt and pulled it up around her hips. She was naked from the waist down and before she could do anything to try and stop him he had pushed her to the ground, falling heavily on top of her, entering her with such force that she screamed and screamed in agony. The searing pain was shooting through her body as Herman pummelled and pounded her, grunting and thrusting, until suddenly he gave out a huge groan, stopped heaving and lay on top of her. Finally, he stood, did his trousers up, spat on Rosa and walked away, grabbing his rifle as he went. Rosa was sobbing. She was in agony. She had been raped! The door of the hut opened and some of the women rushed out, saw Rosa lying on the ground, naked and bloody, and realised what had happened. They helped her to stand, pulled down her skirt, and half carried her inside, laying her on the bunk. One of the women brought her violin. Elsa was crying. "I knew this was going to happen when I saw him looking at you. You should never have gone outside. Pray to God this does not happen again now that he has had his fill of you." Rosa said through her tears "I could not understand why he saved me from the flood and now I know why. He was waiting his chance." She was bleeding and in a great deal of pain, but there was nothing she could do but lay in Elsa's arms that night and try to sleep.

Summer came, bringing its own terrors in the huts as

more and more of the inmates died from starvation and working in the unbearable heat on the "staircase". They died during the night and most of the women were too weak to carry the bodies outside to rid the hut of the stench of death, but Rosa and Gretchen, and a few other inmates working on the farms, were slightly stronger so were able to pull the dead from their bunks, carry them out and lay them on the ground in front of the hut. Many were dying in all the huts and the dead were piled in several heaps, waiting for the Kapos to come with carts to carry them off. Now the fear was cholera! Rosa knew she must try to keep herself clean to avoid catching the disease but with just two taps for use in the latrines amongst all of them, and only a few minutes allowed each day, this was very difficult, so she began washing under the tap on the farm when the guards were not looking. She would let the water run over her head and through her hair, scratching her scalp as hard as she could to get rid of the lice, not minding that her dirty clothes were getting wet – they would dry in the heat whilst she worked.

Autumn, bringing with it flurries of snow at night, and cold, windy days, a sign of worse to come. The ground at the farm was now too hard to till, but all the planting had been finished, and Rosa was still working there, milking the cows, tending the pigs and getting sheep in from the fields. She was always ready for milking, sitting in the comparative warmth of the barn, pressing her head up against the flank of a cow, able to swiftly direct a jet of milk into her mouth when the guard was not there. Even mucking out the dirty straw was better than working on the "staircase", which many of her friends were doing. More and more men were arriving daily, gathering in huge crowds on the other side of the camp for segregation, and the rumour was that they had been brought in to work on the "staircase", as hundreds of men had died whilst working on the site, their emaciated bodies unable to stand the heavy work and beatings which were inflicted when they fell or collapsed. The progress had also slowed down during the cholera epidemic, which had caused so many deaths, and the new arrivals were quickly put to work on the construction.

Rosa and the other prisoners arrived back at the hut after a long working day. It was almost dark, which meant they had no time to visit the latrines before being locked in for the night. The two guards came, carrying the buckets of soup and basket of bread, placing them on the floor as usual. She and Elsa still rationed out the portions, which were now so meagre amongst the many women begging for more. "Quiet, you Juden. We have something to tell you. Tomorrow you will be moved from Mauthausen and taken to another camp. These barracks are needed for the men who are coming here, as they will be fitter and stronger than you and able to work on the "staircase". Commandant Ziereis is not satisfied with the progress so far and has issued an order that the work has to be speeded up so the men will take over. You will be ready at dawn. Those not fit enough to travel will be taken to the Krankenrevier and if they recover will be sent to join you." The women knew they would never recover once sent to that fearful place. They were all asking questions, "Where are we going?" "Are we walking?" "Will we all be together?" The guard just looked at them, turned and walked out of the hut.

Dawn came, the door of the hut was thrown open, and the customary whistle blow. "Line up, schnell, schnell.

Quickly. Follow me." Rosa put on her boots, grabbed her violin and rushed to join the other women leaving the hut. It was a bitterly cold morning, and the snow was falling as they left the camp, the frozen ground making walking difficult. They were joined by the women prisoners from all the huts in their block, until there were hundreds of them in the line. They reached the railway tracks, where several cattle trucks stood silent, doors open, the engine at the front puffing steam from its funnel. "Schnell. Raus, Raus," came the cry. "Get in the wagons, be quick, or you will be shot. Move." The Alsatian dogs were barking and straining at the leads, ready to bite the ankles of anyone who got too near to them, the guards goading them to rush at the women to make them run. Pandemonium broke out as they realised they had to endure maybe days and nights of being confined in the trucks. Rosa climbed aboard, grabbing the hand of Gretchen to help her up. "Where is Elsa," she said, then to her horror saw she was lying on the ground, trying to get up, being beaten about the body by one of the guards with the butt of his rifle. Finally she laid still, and Rosa knew she was dead. As her friend for all this time she was distraught, wanting to leave the truck and go to Elsa, but Gretchen grabbed her, pulling her back. "Stay here, you can't get to her. She is now at rest. God knows what is in store for us, so maybe she is better off." Rosa turned and sobbed in Gretchen's arms, not just for herself but for the plight of all of them. The guards came down the line of trucks, slamming the doors shut, and they were in semi-darkness, with only the cracks in the panels letting in shafts of light. The women were crammed in, just as they had been on that dreadful journey a year ago, the stench from the filthy straw on the floor of the truck overpowering. The train moved off, swaying on the rails, jolting the women together. Rosa remembered how they had coped on the last journey so called out "If half of us squash up on one side of the truck it will leave a space so some of us can sit for a while, then we can let the others have their turn." "Good idea," someone said. Gretchen was first to move and she and Rosa squeezed up against the other women, who were all doing the same. "Who is going to sit on the floor first," called a voice. "Let the older women sit down to start, and anyone who is ill," called another, and the system worked. They travelled all day, the train hurtling along, stopping a few times presumably to fill up with water or coal, cries coming from nearby carriages to be let out, but the guards ignored them. It was freezing cold inside the truck, their breath coming out in huge clouds as they spoke to each other, so they stamped their feet and clapped their hands as much as they could in the confined space. By now it was dark and the train was slowing down, slower and slower, finally stopping. All was quiet for a few moments and then the familiar "Schnell. Schnell. Raus. Raus," and the barking of the dogs. The doors were flung open and the guards ordered them out. "Quickly, get out you filthy Juden. Move. We need to get this train moving again. I said move." He was prodding the women with his rifle, and grabbing their arms to pull them off. Some of the women were screaming in terror, but Rosa leapt down, took her violin which Gretchen passed to her, and joined the queue of women gathering on the platform.

There was pandemonium amongst the hundreds of women. They were frightened, scared of the dogs which were threatening to bite them, crying out in agony if they were bitten. They were asking each other "Where are we?" "What place is this?" Searchlights were being played on them, the whole area brilliantly lit. Sentries were standing in a long line, rifles at the ready, in case anyone tried to run. A huge metal fence stood alongside the track and the guards were yelling at them to start marching. They began walking, the guards pushing them along with their rifles. It was bitterly cold, and snow was falling. After walking past the fence for some distance they arrived at a pair of huge iron gates with large words on them "Arbeit Macht Frei". Rosa's heart sank and she gave an involuntary groan. She had been brought to the camp of horrors - Auschwitz - that dreaded name. They were still walking, being herded along by the soldiers, using their now-familiar rifle butts. The railway tracks ran along the path, with high fencing running down the side until they passed another gate. There was whistling and shouting from within the fenced compounds as they passed. Loud shouts of "Austehen, alles austehen zum Zahlappell." They all looked at each other, whispering in terror. What were they doing? "Stand and be counted." Why were they being counted, in the middle of the night?

There were so many women that Rosa was soon separated from Gretchen and the others she knew. The soldiers were roughly pushing everyone ahead, automatically segregating children and old women from the others. As the little ones were dragged away, the women screamed and desperately tried to cling on to their little hands. Cries of "Mama, mama, don't let them take me away." "Mama, don't leave me," were all around her, and suddenly a baby was snatched from the woman next to Rosa. Involuntarily she screamed "Give her back, she is mine," but was slapped heavily across her face and butted with a rifle. "Quiet, you Juden, keep walking." The other mothers, fearing they had lost their children forever, were now screaming hysterically and crying. The noise was deafening but try as they might they could not retrieve their children. In horror, Rosa watched the guard who had grabbed the baby toss it to another soldier nearby, shouting as he did so "This one is already dead, it will help keep the fires burning." He laughed, horribly, as the child was thrown on to a small heap, which she then realised were dead babies and small children. The guard dogs were howling and barking as they reared up, trying to lunge at the women nearest to them, adding to the noise, and the whips were lashing at their legs, making their feet move in the mud and they had no alternative but to march forward, trying to comfort those around them whose babies, children or old mothers' had been taken from them. There was no way of knowing what was to happen to them, and no one had the courage to say what was secretly in all their hearts. A large building was ahead, and Rosa's group of about fifty women was marshalled in, joining the others already inside. As they entered, a tall blonde woman, in German uniform with the now-familiar SS sign on her armband, stood on a platform. Shouting to everyone to be quiet she said "The children and elderly have been taken to be de-loused and then showered. You will be dealt with in here and will form a work party. If you co-operate and try to act sensibly your children will be returned to you, as will the older women. Remember, if you co-operate you will see your families again." They all wanted to believe her and so, with a renewed sense of relief, all grew quiet and waited for further commands. She disappeared, leaving them all wondering what would happen next. Suddenly, through another door, came several creatures. At first no-one could tell if they were men or women for all had cropped heads and wore some kind of loose-fitting garments with red crosses painted on their backs. They started to shout, in screaming voices, cracking the long whips they all carried. As they got nearer Rosa could see a triangle, in green, with a number on their fronts, which was obviously some kind of identification number and mark. She then realised they were, in fact, female! They commanded all the women to strip, and then go to the showers. Rosa carefully placed her violin on the ground where she could see it and put it with her clothes as she undressed, watching it like a hawk, fearful that one of the "guards" would perhaps take it. The women gasped and screamed out as the freezing cold water hit them from the showers, but at least it was good to be rid of the stench stuck to their bodies from the truck. When the water was turned off they tried to cover themselves with their hands, shivering in the cold, the water streaming from their hair. Rosa turned to the woman next to her and said "There is nothing to dry ourselves with so I think we should put our clothes back on, at least it will help us keep warm. My hair will just have to dry by itself." The other woman nodded, but when they went back for them discovered the clothes had been taken away whilst they washed, including shoes and underwear. Rosa wondered what they would be given to wear, but before she could find out, all the women were forced to walk through a deep bath, up to their necks, in a revolting icy cold fluid, which was obviously some kind of disinfectant. "How much better than the disgusting powder we were sprayed with at Mauthausen. Any lice we might have picked up will be in our hair," she thought to herself, then realised those dreaded insects would never have a chance, for being herded through into yet another huge concrete shed, still wet and naked, she saw the "fryzerki" at work. These women were obviously prisoners, too, for they wore the same kind of uniform and, as batches of prisoners walked up to them, they had to hold out their arms, then legs, which were roughly shaved, then bend down so that their heads could be sheared. Lastly, the final humiliation for Rosa, as to her horror they proceeded to shave between her legs. Within minutes they were totally devoid of any body hair and looked a queer sight. On another command they went to the far end of the room and each woman was given some clothing. It was certainly not new and all Rosa had was a vest, skirt and loose top. She made a mistake when she asked "Are there any pants or stockings," as she received yet another blow across the mouth and told to keep quiet. Passing on down the line she was then given two odd shoes, which were much too big for her, but she now knew that you did not complain or ask for anything else if you wanted to escape a beating. "Anstellen, anstellen schneller," came the cry, so they formed lines again and were marched back to the first room they had come through. She raced over and picked up her violin, grateful that it was still lying there, before being roughly pushed into the line again, where they stood waiting for some time as the queues slowly moved forward. Soon it became apparent that everyone was being questioned by women sitting at desks.

They were obviously all inmates, wearing a kind of uniform of blouse and skirt, but again with a green triangle and number on their breast. Obviously some kind of "trusties", whom everyone looked wary of. "What is your name. Date of birth. Parents' names. Where are you from?" At the word "England" Rosa's interrogator looked up, raising her eyebrows. "Stand over there against the wall when I have given you your number and someone will come and see you." With that, she told Rosa to hold out her left arm and, with a series of very sharp pricks, proceeded to draw a small triangle and then five numbers. Spots of blood were oozing from the prick marks, where she had gone too deep, but she quickly dismissed her and Rosa made her way over to the corner, rubbing her arm to try and help the pain and stop the flow of blood. She watched the scene before her in fatal fascination. Dozens of women - were they really women now they had no hair? - all parading in long queues through the entire room, answering a few short, sharp questions; holding out their arms, then moving on - all in total silence as if their tongues had been ripped out of their mouths. Eventually, she was joined by three other women. They dared not speak above a whisper in case they were heard but quickly asked each other their names and where they were from. One was French - Lily; another was Eva, a Pole and the third another British woman called Ruth. At this point, the tall blonde woman re-appeared and came towards them. She had long leather boots on her feet and was tapping a small cane on her thigh as she walked. The uniform she wore was khaki; a shirt, tie and skirt. "So, you four are not German. You are all Jews, aren't you? My name is Irma Grese. You will address me as Madam and I am in command here. You will answer my questions. You are my prisoners." She stood there, her hands on her hips, feet astride, in the pose that they were to see over and over again. She called one of the interrogators over to her. "These four women must be questioned very closely. Make sure you do your job properly and find out where they are from and how they came to be here. They are probably spies working against the Third Reich." Rosa was grabbed by the elbow and roughly marshalled across to a desk. Irma Grese came and stood by her side, swishing her stick. "Name, date of birth, where are you from?" Rosa did not say she had already answered the same questions – she did not dare. She proceeded to give the interrogator the information she wanted and explained she had been working in Berlin as a violinist with the Philharmonic Orchestra. Rosa proudly confirmed she was Jewish, for which she received an instant cutting "swish" from Irma Grese's stick on her buttocks. She flinched with the pain but did not cry out - she would not let her see how frightened she was. Irma Grese asked what sort of music Rosa played, and how much Wagner did she know. She answered her as best she could, stressing she could play almost anything. "Are you a spy? How did you get into the Philharmonic? We have only the finest musicians playing for us in our orchestras." Rosa said "I am not a spy, I came over to Berlin in 1936, well before the troubles started. My sole ambition was to play with the Berlin Philharmonic to get good experience, as one day I hope to become lead violinist in an orchestra when I return to England. I thought my position in your orchestra would protect me from being interned, which was why I have not tried to return to England, even though many of my friends and colleagues tried to make me leave." When she stated that her Father had been Russian, and violin tutor to the Tsar, Irma Grese spat on the ground and called him some unspeakable, vile names, calling Rosa a filthy Russian whore, and an enemy of Germany. She started to say she was a naturalised Briton now, but Irma Grese would not listen, only continuing to scream loud abuse at her. However, after a while, she seemed to calm down and walked over to one of the other desks. She spent some time talking to Lily, the French woman and then brought her to where Rosa was still standing. "Here is someone for you to make music with, little Russian whore. This one plays the piano. No doubt you will be able to make music together - we have many fine musicians here. You Jews seem to do nothing but play music and sew clothes." Her abuse towards the two of them was unspeakable but they stood still, looking at her, trying not to flinch at her verbal attack. Lily and Rosa watched the other two women being marched away and wondered if they would see them again. Irma Grese called out to her guards "I am leaving now. Take these two Juden to Lager A for quarantine and then on to Block 18. Keep the violin here and make sure I get it." Rosa said "Please let me keep my fiddle. It is very precious, and I want to keep it with me." Irma Grese smiled. "Don't worry, it is safe with me. I have good use for it." Rosa was really worried by this – what did she intend to do with her violin? She must try and get it back. As they left the huts some music could be heard in the distance. "Where is it coming from?" whispered Rosa to Lily. "I think it is coming from the loudspeakers above the lookout towers?" The music grew louder and louder, until they realised it was a proper band. There was the insistent beating of a drum and then, in the floodlights, they saw a column of women marching towards them, marching in time to the music, wearing thin grey striped tunics which gave no protection against the bitterly cold weather, accompanied by guards walking beside them, with the now familiar dogs barking and howling. They all carried a variety of tools – spades, shovels, pickaxes - they were obviously going to work and it was not yet dawn. What place had they come to - this must be hell on earth!

Dawn was breaking as they followed their guards and made their way to the quarantine hut. The mud was ankle deep and the flimsy odd shoes Rosa wore squelched and plopped with every step. Lily was having trouble walking as she was exhausted - as was Rosa - but they clung on to each other and together got across the open square. On reaching a hut a large, heavily-built woman appeared at the doorway and the guards left them with her. She was plump and well dressed, obviously in charge of the hut, and known as the Blokowa. The two girls learned that each hut had its own boss, and she, in turn, had several assistants. These were mostly Czech girls, who had been interned when the camp was opened, and because they had survived the horrors so far were in positions of trust. They joined a group of about seventy women, standing or sitting on the cold, muddy ground, hoping that now they would be given some food and drink. It had been four days by Rosa's reckoning since she had last eaten and she was ravenous. The Blokowa chief strutted amongst them, swishing her stick, poking a woman here, a woman there. "So, you are the new intake. You are all pretty fit-looking at the moment, all ready for hard work, so make the most if it, for it won't be long before you are Muselmanns like the others." Rosa turned to look at Lily. "What is she talking about? What is this new word "Muselmann?" She was soon to find out - these living skeletons who could not be described as human beings were everywhere in the camp, crawling along the ground or just lying in one spot - ready to die! The two sat there, freezing cold, huddled together for warmth. Rosa wondered what had happened to her violin. She had not told Irma Grese that it had belonged to her father when she snatched it from her hands - that would probably have made her smash it instantly, but she hoped it was safe - she had said she had good use for it! One of the

Czech girls beckoned Lily and Rosa to the rear of the hut, and they slithered and slipped their way over in the greasy mud. She pointed to a small pile of battered tin mugs and said "Take one each, and guard it with your life as I won't give you another. It must stay with you at all times, tied to your waist with this bit of string. It is for eating and for your water ration." Lily said "What do we use for washing in?" but the girl just looked at her and said "Hah, you won't do much of that in this weather, but it's for washing too, and as a pot at night in your hut. The lavatory is out of bounds after curfew until dawn so this is what you have to use then." Rosa shuddered and heaved on hearing this, trying to stop herself being sick, and wondered how she could ever bring herself to use the container in such a way. The girl took them over to the latrines, which were indeed a primitive affair, consisting of rows of holes in the ground in a wooden hut, with several buckets which one was supposed to use. It was difficult to find a bucket available though, for the "trusties" were meant to use these, so all that was left for the women to do was perch across the hole, where the stench was so dreadful they began to vomit as soon as they squatted.

After a couple of hours, there was movement from one of the other buildings, which Rosa learned was the kitchen. Large containers were being carried out by several of the Czech girls, and from the sudden rush of all the women from nearby huts, she guessed they were to receive food at last. She watched from behind the fence as the containers were carried nearer to them, horrified to see women scraping up drops of the spilled liquid from the muddy ground and cramming the filth into their mouths in the hope of getting some of the food. She watched what all the other women did, and when

Rosa saw them scrambling to get close to the containers she copied them, holding out her small tin mug into which was doled a small spoonful of greasy, grey looking liquid, which looked the same as she had been given in Mauthausen. She was so hungry she drank the tepid liquid straight down, but promptly vomited it back as the disgusting flavour penetrated her brain. She thought she had become used to the vile concoction, but this was worse! Again it was to be their daily food, very occasionally supplemented by a piece of hard, black bread, usually crawling with weevils. Lily and Rosa sat on the ground for several hours, talking to those around them, most of whom had been there for a few weeks. They told the girls about the system which existed here, and how the "trusties" and privileged prisoners got the best of everything. Water, food, clothing. It appeared that the starving women called the "musselmanns" were mostly Jews or Gypsies, for by and large the political prisoners were not starved in the same way, being used as extra guards when new intakes of Jews arrived. Suddenly, in the evening, there was a shrill whistle. "Alles Anstellen. Zahlappell" came the shout. Everyone congregated by their huts and Rosa, Lily and the other new inmates followed suit for roll call as a woman in the same uniform as Irma Grese came striding into the compound. She proceeded to count them, strutting up and down the lines of women and noting down on a pad the number outside each of the compounds. She eventually went over to where a man in SS uniform was standing on a platform. One of the inmates whispered to Rosa that this was the hated and feared man called Taube, who was responsible for checking that all the inmates were present, even though it was almost impossible to escape from this place. Once the roll call was over Rosa and Lily were told by the "trusties" attached to their hut that they would now be locked up for the night and to line up ready to go in. Rosa was very curious to see inside, although secretly suspecting what she would find, and as she reached the doorway was handed a piece of dry black bread. She later discovered they would sometimes be given a small piece of margarine or sausage to supplement their ration, but it had to last through to noon the following day. As they began to enter the hut a large group of women, led by a tall, thin blonde woman in a green uniform, came into the compound. These women, Rosa was told, were the workers who had been out in the fields as a working party for most of the day. They could hardly walk as they appeared to be totally exhausted, and all were flimsily dressed in the now familiar grey striped uniform. Their only protection against the bitter freezing cold. Finding they would have to wait before entering their hut they fell to the ground, lying there moaning with their tiredness. The whip cracked. "Schnell, Schnell," came the words, and they struggled to their feet in an effort to start moving again. It was pitiful to see. The empty containers of liquid had been returned to the kitchens so they were not given any of the vile soup which had been doled out to everyone earlier, but instead were handed a small piece of bread – their repayment for their day's work!

Once inside the hut, Rosa's eyes became accustomed to the gloom, and she could see two aisles, with three-tier bunks down the length of them. They had been told that each section held fifty people when fully occupied, and each block about eight hundred. On one side of this block was a smaller area where the Blokowa chief and several of her "trusties" slept. About fifty of them were new to the hut and stood waiting to watch where the other women went. All the top and middle bunks were occupied so eventually Lily, Rosa and another woman called Ruth, climbed into a bottom one. They were packed into these bunks, with no room to move, and only one straw mattress and blanket between the three of them. No-one removed their clothing or shoes, as they had been warned by the longer-serving prisoners they would not be there in the morning if they did.

"Raus, raus. Schnell, schnell." The morning roll call came as dawn was breaking and Rosa wondered why it had been during the evening on the previous day – was it because there had been so many new prisoners arriving? Maybe it was twice a day. After they had been counted they were allowed to leave the huts to make their way to the latrines and to obtain some water. Rosa was terribly thirsty, for it had been hot and foetid in the bunk, and she also needed to wash her face as it was burning. She and Lily had decided they would share one pot for washing, and one for drinking and food until they became used to the system and saw a way of obtaining another dish. It appeared from the little conversation they had overheard that, if you had anything of value to barter, you could buy extra food or water, but they had nothing except the clothes they wore – not even a scarf or belt. All through that day, Rosa grew hotter and hotter. Her skin was burning and she shook from head to foot and felt very ill. Lily could obviously see something was wrong with her, for perspiration was standing out in beads on Rosa's forehead. She tore a strip off the bottom of her skirt and used a little of her precious water ration to put the damp cloth on her forehead. By mid-day she could not bring herself to drink the filthy liquid Lily brought her and handed it back, telling her to drink it, but she bartered it for a piece of bread and gave it to Rosa saying "Eat this, you must eat something, or you will be ill. You have obviously caught a chill. It is nothing." Her words did not reassure Rosa, for she knew she was very ill indeed; her head was throbbing and swimming; her legs like jelly. She had not felt like this for many years, only once as a child on that long trek across Russia in the snow. She laid in her bunk for the rest of the day, hoping that the Blokowa would not come into the hut and find her, and somehow managed to get up and go outside for roll-call. With the help of Lily and Ruth, she half-crawled, half-walked back to her bunk, where she laid, alternately freezing cold and boiling hot, her clothes soaking wet and clinging to her. For the whole of the night, she lay in that state, with Lily and Ruth on either side trying to keep her warm when she shook uncontrollably. Eventually, the spasms started to leave and her head cleared. By the time roll call came at dawn she had begun to feel better and, although very weak, was able to stumble out of the hut. "Thank God, I am not really ill," she thought. She already knew that each morning those who could not stand or get out of their bunks were sent off to some other part of the camp, never to be seen again. Ruth had told them that these prisoners were going to the extermination huts, but they did not believe her!

As they stood in the cold early-morning air, with the stench of stinking mud all around them, Rosa realised that what had happened to her the previous day had been a reaction to the horrors of the past week. She stood there, waiting for the headcount by the Blokowa. Lily was trembling with the cold, and Rosa turned to her.

"Come now, it was me who was shaking yesterday. We must be strong and not let them see that we are either cold or frightened of them. I am determined that they will not get the better of me. I will do everything I can to stay alive in this place." Lily smiled and nodded dumbly. And Rosa knew the strength of her words of determination had given Lily a small amount of courage too. As soon as the roll call was over, the working party was selected from those not in quarantine and Lily, Ruth and Rosa went into the compound. The ground was a sea of wet, stinking mud – stinking with the filth and excrement of those women incapable of getting to the latrines. There were bundles lying or sitting on the ground, which on closer examination proved to be human beings when they got closer. They were obviously very ill or dying, and the three girls backed away – frightened as they were of the unknown. Suddenly, there was a shrill whistle and a shout from the Blokowa for them all to stand to attention. Music could be heard approaching, getting louder and louder, with the steady beat of a drum above the tune. Gradually, a sorry-looking band of women, in the usual shapeless uniforms, came into sight – all playing a variety of instruments. As the drum was beaten the leader, a blonde, fat woman in SS uniform, shouted out "One, two. One, two. Keep moving there. One, two. Halt." The line of players came to a halt and, at the command, stopped playing. The women in the compound who were capable of taking notice had crossed to the wire fence to watch this display and then, emerging from the rear of the column, came Irma Grese. An involuntary groan came up from those around Lily and Rosa, who sensed that her presence meant disaster. She came over to the Blokowa, talked quietly to her, who then gave the customary "Heil Hitler" salute, and turned to walk towards the blockade. She came nearer to them both and, as she did so, called out "Prisoner Levinsky. Prisoner Marcel. Make yourselves known. You are wanted." They looked at each other in mute terror. This was it. They were going to be executed and clung to each other, Lily crying "Don't let them take me. Please, help me, help me." Rosa was unable to either move or say anything; she was rooted to the spot in terror. The Blokowa then called out their names and numbers again and, this time, sensing they must reply, Rosa called out "Over here, Mein Frau," raising her arm to show herself. As the woman approached the fence she was smiling cynically. "Well, well. What have you been up to, you two, to be singled out for Fraulein Grese. I've heard she is partial to little girls, but you are a bit old and stringy for her liking. Maybe she has another sport in mind for you two pigs. Get out of the compound. Come through the gateway when I unlock it and go to her. I'm glad to be rid of you – two less filthy Juden to worry about." Lily and Rosa went through the fencing and crossed over to Irma Grese. She stood there, in her normal position, flicking her whip across her thighs in impatience. "You are Levinsky and Marcel, the musicians?" They both nodded. "Come with me, you are wanted in the Commandant's quarters." They exchanged curious glances with each other, then followed her through the muddy quagmire, stumbling across the compound, picking their way through the bodies of still-alive skeletons, the musselmanns, scattered as if at random, like a lions' den after the kill. They watched Grese as she strutted ahead, horrified as she kicked out at this body, hit out at another with her whip as she passed, calling out abuse at them as they lay huddled or crouched on the ground. Their eyes were staring at the two girls who followed her – sunken black orbs in enormous caverns, they were pleading, beseeching for help. Rosa and Lily hurried as much as they could to get through the mud, anxious to get away from these poor pitiful wretches who they were powerless to help. Grese occasionally glanced over her shoulder at them. "Schnell, Schnell," she shouted. Two musselmanns, obviously with a little more strength than the others, were fighting furiously with each other as the three approached. She brought her stick down heavily across the back of one and, as they parted, Rosa saw that the fight was over a few pieces of potato peelings. There was no way of knowing how they had acquired them, but on seeing the scraps, Grese ground them into the mud with her boot and whipped both women for several seconds until they both lay inert in the mud. Deprived of this scant mouthful of food, they had been brought to this final degradation before they died.

Rosa and Lily stood outside a large wooden building, puzzled. Irma Grese had gone inside, cautioning them to wait, and she had been gone for some time. Suddenly two Blockowa, the wardresses, appeared – one of them carrying a violin – none too carefully. Rosa recognised it as her own and started to move forward, to take it from her, but with a shout from the woman, she stood still. She sensed not to move until told to do so and held her breath as she obeyed. "This is yours, I think," said the Blockowa. "That is my case, so I presume my own fiddle is inside it. I can't say until I look." She nodded her head at Rosa, indicating that she could open the case and look. The catches were released and the lid opened, and she caught her breath. "Yes, it is my fiddle. Thank goodness it is safe. Thank you for giving it back to me." "Let us say it is a loan, Juden, shall we. It is the property of the

Reich now." She turned to Lily. "You play the piano, I'm told." Lily nodded, casting a curious glance at Rosa. What was this all about? Why did they want to know? "Follow me, and keep quiet," said the Blockowa as she led them through the camp and, as they came to a section of the wire fencing, met up with three other women, all wearing similar odd items of clothing as themselves, accompanied by two other wardresses. They became one group and were led through the main gates, making their way between rows of huts, surrounded on all sides by the wire fencing. Gradually they left the camp, still walking in the freezing air, shivering continually. All Rosa was wearing was the vest, top, skirt and the odd shoes, with no stockings or underclothes, and there was snow lying on the ground. Soon they were walking across open snow-packed frozen fields and, taking a note of the surroundings, saw mountains in the distance. The trees and hedgerows around them could be anywhere and for a few moments, Rosa was transported in her dreams back to England. Suddenly the railway tracks were ahead of them, and as they walked beside them could make out some large sheds and sidings with several trucks standing silently there. As they got nearer they saw the people – men, women, children, babies. What were they doing here? Suddenly Lily spotted an ambulance with a large red cross painted on it. "Is this where you would have been brought if you had really been ill," she whispered to Rosa. They carried on marching; through the railway sidings and past the hundreds of people collected there, all standing silently, staring in curiosity at the little group of women going by. The only noise to be heard was the barking, whining and snarling of the dogs, a baby crying and the guards calling out for silence. They passed through a small wood, full of leafless birch trees, and the countryside was beautiful – even in winter. It was so clean and pure after the filth and horror of the camp. Soon they were out of the woods and there, in the clearing ahead of them, was an extraordinary sight. Four very long, low, red stone buildings with tall square chimneys. They went through the gates, staring in amazement at the gardens, shrubs and neat lawns, the snow brushed away, looking tidy and well-kept even in the stark months of winter. Over to the left was a large white house, again surrounded by lawns and flower beds, and both wondered who lived there. They were walking along a road; just like a road in any town or city anywhere. Running alongside it, on either side of this stood two lines of huts, with eight on each side, all looking well-kept and clean. Other buildings could be seen at the back of the huts, which appeared to be sauna's or latrines. At the rear of these were the inevitable wire fences and, behind them, another long, one-storey stone building with two long chimneys protruding from it. "What a queer place that looks," Rosa said to the other girls, who were also looking around in astonishment. Behind that building could be seen another, an almost identical looking place, and on the other side of the track were two further structures, again very similar. "It must be a factory of some sort, with all those chimneys. Obviously, we have been brought here to work. What do you think they make – ammunitions?" Lily was looking to right and left as she spoke, trying to get some clue as to what went on inside those huge factories. As they approached the end of the road and the huts, they saw two large piles ahead. At first, no-one realised what they were but gradually could make out individual things. Clothing! Shoes, hats, suitcases, a teddy bear. Rosa drew in her breath. Where had all this come from? It was like huge piles of jumble. What was it to be used for? Lily turned to her. "I know what this must be. It's a paper mill. They are making paper from old rags and suchlike. It is all going to be turned into paper." Rosa looked at Lily. "Do you know, I think you might be right." Little did they know.

They had reached a hut at the very end of the line. The two wardresses stood aside and told them to enter and, slightly wary at what they would find, the small group of women went inside. It was very spartan accommodation, but absolute luxury compared to their hut over in the main camp. There were the usual rows of bunks, but each one had a mattress and what joy! a blanket too. Rosa guessed that the hut held about twenty women, all of whom had stopped talking as they entered – silently watching as one of the wardresses indicated bunks to the five newcomers. In the middle of the floor stood a huge iron furnace, which appeared to be out, for the room was freezing cold and ice had formed on the insides of the four small windows. Still, it was heaven compared to the other hut they had first been in, and all five girls started discussing why they might have been selected to be brought here. The wardresses shouted to them to be quiet, turned on and left. As soon as they had slammed the door and the lock had been thrust home there was a quick rush towards the five of them. "What are your names? Where are you from? Is the war still going on?" Countless questions came quickly from the twenty or so women. Urging them all not to make so much noise, a tall, dark woman stepped forward. "My name is Ilsa. I am the leader of this orchestra. Please, introduce yourselves." Lily and Rosa looked quickly at each other, turning to stare at her. "Orchestra. What

orchestra?" they both asked. "The camp orchestra. We
play for Hoss and the officers. We are very privileged
and lucky," she said, turning around and scornfully
laughing with the rest of her group. "The only reason we
are here and not with the others is that we are all
musicians." As she said the word "others" she flung her
arm backwards towards the window, through which
could be seen one of the tall chimneys. Now it all became
clear to Rosa why her violin had been given back to her.
Thank God she had been able to keep it with her during
that nightmare journey here – it was now her lifeline!
"Quick, come and see. Then you will know where you are
and what is really going on in this hell hole." One of the
women was standing beside a window, beckoning them
over. Out of curiosity and, hoping for answers to all the
questions they had asked, they rushed over to peer
through. What met their eyes was unbelievable. Rosa
looked. She stared. She watched. Across the large lawn
stood two of the bigger huts. Outside, queues of people
were forming at each entrance. Men, women, children –
some old, some young, some toddlers, some babies. All
queuing and moving forward into the buildings, the men
and boys being separated from the women, girls and
babies. As they reached the doorways they were forced to
strip and the possessions they carried were placed in a
heap, presumably at the insistence of the guards who
were standing, feet apart, rifles at the ready, along the
columns. A doll was tugged away from a child and
thrown on one of the heaps. She screamed and tried to
retrieve it, her little arms outstretched as her mother
tried to quieten her. The scream she then emitted was
even more horrifying as she was butted to the ground by
one of the guards and the mother received the same
treatment when she immediately tried to shield the child

with her body. After what seemed like an eternity the beating finished and two guards picked up the dead woman by her ankles and threw her to one side and her dead child followed. Some men in the other queue had been trying to go and help the woman but the soldiers pushed and shoved them back in line, butting them heavily with their rifles so that many fell to the ground, whilst the remainder of the women's queue were forced to file into their building. What these people had not seen, but what Rosa and the other women in the hut could all see, was a soldier climbing a ladder towards an opening in the roof, carrying a large metal canister. He was wearing a face mask and, as he reached the aperture, pulled on long protective gloves. Next, he opened the tin, lifted the lid of the opening, and quickly threw the contents inside, closing the cover with a swift slam and rushed back down the ladder. As he reached the ground there came the most agonising screams from the buildings. The air was split with the noise of howls and yells of people; a noise which could even be heard through the thin walls of their hut. Lily, Rosa and the other three all slapped their hands over their ears as if this would stop the agonies which the people inside that place of horror were suffering.

They looked at each other in mute terror, then at the rest of the women in their hut, their eyes filling with tears at the sight they had just witnessed, all knowing they were powerless to help any of them. After a few seconds Ilsa gently took Lily's hands in hers. "It is over. They are dead. They are at peace." The whole thing had taken just a few minutes. She pointed again. "Look, watch what happens next. This goes on day in and day out." A large group of men, in the now-usual striped camp uniform, had appeared with large barrows. They proceeded to remove all the clothing and cases which the innocent people had left at the entrance to the buildings and were taking it over to the huge piles the five women had passed earlier. "Those men are in charge of the Crematorium," said Elsa. "They do not live for long, for the terrible job they carry out drives them mad, or else they commit suicide by throwing themselves at the electric fences. It's their job to remove all the bodies from the buildings, in time for the next batch, which will be later on today. It usually goes on three times a day, depending on the arrival of the trains. Watch. Just watch the chimneys." As she spoke, smoke began to appear out of the chimneys and, soon, flames were shooting their tongues high into the pale sky. In the still air, the smoke drifted straight up – a funeral pyre. The smoke gradually grew thicker and darker in colour. The flames had disappeared but in their place came the most odious smell. That of singeing hair and burning flesh. Rosa knew that none of the group of five had ever smelt human flesh before, but knew instinctively what it was. The sky grew darker and darker as the pall of smoke grew in density. The stench was everywhere – in the hut, in their clothes, in their nostrils. The five were crying; Lily and Rosa clutching each other, burying their heads in each other's shoulder, comforting one another as best they could at the sight of this dreadful nightmare. "Those are the gas chambers," said Ilsa. "Haven't you heard of them. What did you think happened inside them – in those factories? They are factories of death. When you are not playing in the orchestra your job will be to sort their clothing. It is a terrible task, but if you want to stay alive you will have to do it. None of us thought we would ever be able to stand it when we first arrived, but eventually, you close your mind to it and accept that it is God's will and each day is a step nearer to freedom – or death." With those chilling words she turned away from the window, and it was the cue for all of them to do the same.

About an hour passed. The bolts were flung back on the door of the hut and a wardress appeared. "Schnell, schnell. Raus, raus. Time for work, Juden," she called. The other women had already outlined to the newcomers what would happen, so they knew that now they were being taken to one of the huts to sort out the belongings of those people they had witnessed being murdered. Rosa was taken to a hut with two women called Nika and Kitty, both German Jews. This was obviously full of men's belongings and they briefly told Rosa what she must do. The clothing had to be folded and tied up in bundles of twelve – jackets, trousers, pullovers and the like. A strict time limit was set and when they finished they took them into an adjoining hut ready to be taken away. Rosa later learned that lorries came every day to take the good clothing away and the unwearable items were placed on the inevitable heap outside. "Why can't the prisoners here who are still alive wear them to keep warm," she asked Kitty. "They don't want you to be warm – they want you to die," she said. "You are just a thing to them. I suppose these clothes go back to the Germans who have been bombed out or are homeless, with nothing left to wear." Rosa continued to fold up the bundles as they were passed to her; jackets on that pile, trousers on another. After about an hour a soldier came over. "Move over to the other side of the room. Take over on that other trestle and go through all the pockets for belongings. Feel inside the linings, and make sure there is nothing hidden in lapels and cuffs. Anything you find, make sure you place it on one side. You will be searched, so don't try and smuggle anything out. You won't like our searches, little Juden." He laughed, showing his black stumpy teeth, and his rotten breath hit her like a blow to the face. She proceeded to do as she was told, taking out photographs, papers, bank notes, loose coins. She could not bring herself to look at the photographs – she wanted to try and forget that the people she had just seen going to their deaths had been alive and had worn these clothes only hours before. She was just about to place a jacket on one side, having removed some papers from the inside pocket, when she felt something hard in the seam. She fingered it, unsure what it could be. Something sharp and pointed was just poking through the lining, so she picked away at it, trying to release whatever it was caught up in there. Eventually, the lining gave way at the stitching and there, shining up at her, was a beautiful diamond ring. Clean and pure, it lay in her hands. She looked up quickly at the Guard "What do I do with this. It has obviously got caught in the seam," she said. He came over, looked at the ring lying in the palm of her hand and snatched it away. "Good. You have learned quickly, Juden, that the Fatherland needs this. It will go towards the cost of keeping you alive." He walked over to where an officer was sitting at a desk, writing in a ledger. He saluted and handed over the ring as if he personally had been the finder of such a valuable article. Rosa found many items on that first day; money, coins, jewellery and more photographs. These were all handed over, for she soon realised it would be too risky to try and keep any of the articles, even if she had wanted to. Towards nightfall the women were marshalled together and marched to their hut, passing two more long queues of men and women which were forming. The new arrivals stared at the group of women as they passed, and called out "Do you work here? What is made in the factories? Is it a good camp?" They all looked worried and tired after what must have been a similar journey for them as the one Rosa had experienced. A small boy ran from the line towards them, calling out "Come and play with me." Ilsa called out to him "Go back, go to your mother," but it was too late. A soldier had turned and, with his rifle, had knocked the child to the ground, where he proceeded to kick him savagely. His mother ran towards him, in a frenzy, screaming "Don't hit him. Oh, please, don't hurt him," throwing herself at the guard who then turned his attention on her. Several men were attempting to restrain the father who was in the other queue as he desperately tried to rush to the aid of his wife and son. By this time the woman had picked the boy up in her arms, screaming that he was dead and cursing the German officer, who then proceeded to club her to the ground, just as he had done with her child. The rest of the people, seeing what they got if they tried to help, gradually became quiet and moved back into line, keeping their children close to them, now fearful of what was in store.

"Right, all come with me. Bring your instruments if you've got any. We are going to rehearse." Rosa was surprised, for she had thought that once they had returned to the hut they would be locked up for the night, but now it seemed this was not the case. Ilsa led the way, accompanied by a wardress, and they crossed the compound towards the white house. The queue of people had gone – but the black, filthy smoke belched out of the chimneys, flames shooting up into the sky, whilst all around hung the pervading stench of burning flesh, hair and bone. Rosa brought the hem of her skirt up to her mouth – anything to alleviate the burning, acrid smell of the smoke – the smoke which filled every pore of her skin, her nostrils, her eyes, her mouth. Would she ever be able to forget this, or cleanse herself of its stench? They entered the house, looking around with curiosity, as all were ushered into a large room. There were no curtains or carpets, but a large grand piano stood in the corner at one end. Grouped around it were three rows of chairs, and music stands stood at intervals. Facing them were several other rows of chairs, some soft, cushioned and luxurious; others hard, upright and wooden, but it was immediately obvious that they were there for a future audience. The other chairs, by the piano, were for the orchestra. Ilsa took her place at the front and ruffled through some music on a stand. "Right, everyone, let's see what our five newcomers can do. We have half-an-hour to rehearse before we start and I think we should all familiarise ourselves with tonight's music. The Commandant has asked for some Wagner and I think we will all need to rehearse that." They practised the difficult Wagner music, which was not Rosa's favourite; she much preferred to play Tchaikovsky and Beethoven, but Ilsa was pleased with the way the newcomers played and could interpret the music. Suddenly the doors of the room were thrown open, heels clicked, arms raised in the customary salute by the two sentries posted there and a burly, short man walked through in Nazi uniform, the now familiar SS on his sleeve and hat, who Rosa immediately recognised. "It's Hoss," whispered a girl on Rosa's right. "Rudolph Hoss. He is the camp Commandant, and everyone is terrified of him. Luckily for us, he loves music and lets us play for him most nights." Beside him walked Irma Grese, smiling and chatting to him as if they were a normal couple about to listen to a concert. Several officers also entered the room behind Hoss and Grese, sitting down on the chairs, and Rosa noticed immediately that the higher ranking officers had the comfortable ones, whilst the junior men had to endure the upright wooden ones. Hoss barked "Begin." Ilsa raised her baton and they started to play. Rosa did not particularly enjoy playing Wagner but, as her bow flew over the strings of her violin, she could hear the melody and knew she was playing well - realising that her life depended on giving the best performance she could. They played for well over an hour; loudly, softly, sweetly, stridently. A variety of music, but Hoss sat there, a smile playing around his mouth, his eyes closed, fingers tapping in time to the music. Eventually, he gave the command to stop and the orchestra had to sit there whilst all the others left; Irma Grese holding on to one of the officer's arms, laughing and joking with him. Elsa folded the music as it was gathered up and returned it to Sonia, who had been put in charge of it, together with the girl who had played the piano. Lily had just turned the music for her and had not had a chance to play. They were then escorted back to their hut, where each of them received a ladle full of watery, warm liquid with bits of rotten vegetable floating in it, a hunk of black bread and, wonder of wonders, a piece of sausage. Sonia said they were always given something extra at night to eat as a reward if they had played well. Rosa lay on her bunk, watching the bright moonlight through the window. "How could anything as pure as that moon shine down on something as evil as this camp?" she whispered to herself. She looked back over the events of the past few days, realising how lucky it was she had been brought to this camp and not stayed in Mauthausen, for it might mean she would survive. She shivered as she thought of those poor people she had seen entering the execution huts today and the deaths they had experienced.

The next morning, as dawn was breaking, they were woken by the wardress with the usual shouts of "Schnell, schnell; raus, raus." Snow was falling heavily as they stumbled out of their bunks, anxious to get outside for the roll call with the minimum of delay. This was the first the five of them had attended in the new hut, and wondered if it would be the same as before. Shouting "Zahlappell. Alles anstellen. Achtung," a senior SS officer appeared, and to Rosa's horror it turned out to be Rapportfuhrer Hoss again. She saw that all the women stood to attention as best they could, so she did the same. Hoss walked down the line, looking at them, flicking his whip idly across this shoulder, that arm, to make them all stand straighter. By his side walked a large vicious dog, who snarled every time the whip was raised, his yellow teeth showing through his curling snout. They stood stationary for over an hour in the freezing cold, until the command came to return to their hut. As they entered they were given a ladle full of liquid, which Sonia whispered was "tea". It was black, bitter and tasted so foul that Rosa felt she would vomit the whole lot back, but drank it down, knowing that even just this liquid would help in her determination to stay alive. Her work party left the hut when they had finished the meagre meal and she soon realised she was lucky – the work was not difficult and if this was all she had to do in order to save her life and play her beloved violin then she thanked God. The days passed, and each morning they would go to the huts, sort out the clothing

– sometimes men's and sometimes women's and, heartbreakingly, some belonging to babies and children. She worked out the rota system for herself and when she knew that the next day would mean being put to work with the little coats, dresses and shoes she would save her meagre ration of bread or sausage and swop her shift to another section, at least giving her a chance to miss this terrible ordeal, no matter how hungry she was. Late afternoons were given over to rehearsals, and then the customary evening concert. Always Wagner and Bach – never Chopin, Tchaikovsky or Mendelsohn. Sometimes Hoss would ask for a special piece to be played but usually Ilsa had already received her instructions for the day. Rosa realised quite quickly that she looked very ugly with her shaved head, so bartered some of her bread for an old scarf which she tied around it, as many of the other women in the orchestra had done. Her hair was very unsightly as it was starting to grow in little clumps, but she felt that the scarf made her look less like a sexless freak. The weather was beginning to improve daily, with less and less snow, so they were only allowed to light the stove in the hut every other day for two hours, but during this time took the opportunity of rubbing their now-filthy dresses in the snow to clean them a little and dry them off by the stove. Rosa knew she had lice – they all did, but had to live with them.

"Schnell. Schnell." Mid-day, and suddenly a roll call! They were all taken from the huts where they were sorting the usual piles of clothes and belongings and made to stand to attention outside. It was Rudolph Hoss, walking down the line of women, stopping every now and again to lift a chin with the handle of his whip, tilt a head, lift up the hem of a skirt or dress and peer at the legs. He came to Rosa. "You are new, aren't you?" She nodded dumbly, unable to speak. "Answer the Commandant, Juden," shouted the officer who was with them. "Yes sir," she replied. "She will do, send her over," said Hoss. He turned and walked away, leaving her bewildered. "Do for what. Send me where?" she thought. Very soon she was to find out. Her elbow was grasped from behind by a woman she had never seen before, who had walked beside Hoss. Her name was Oberfuhresin Drechsler and she proceeded to half-run Rosa towards the large white house. She was led inside and a Blockowa came running at Drechsler's shouts. "Take this woman; make sure she bathes and has her head and body hair shaved. Hoss will be here shortly." So began an ordeal for Rosa which was to take place on an almost daily basis for several weeks. She bathed, welcoming the chance to clean herself of the dirt and grime which caked her body. Oh! How wonderful the water felt, and soap. Real soap! Her head was thickly encrusted with the lice which crawled over it, forming an instant skull cap. They had burrowed into her skin, but she had tried to resist the temptation to scratch them – her body was infected enough with scabs and boils. As she scrubbed away at herself and the dirt began to come away Rosa saw that her skin had taken on a grey hue, with red mottled patches. Where boils had burst, craters had formed, and these had not healed but remained gaping, oozing holes. Where the constant attack by fleas had taken place she had red spots, like nettle rash, and knew that she was not just dirty – she was rotting away. The Blockowa had stood in the room all the time she was washing and had nodded when Rosa asked if she could change the filthy water. The lice had sensed the danger lurking once she was in the hot water and had started to dart all over her, from under her arms, between her legs and coming out of the burrows in her scalp. She silently looked at the wardress. Realising what was in Rosa's mind she said bluntly "The fryzerki is here. She will shave you." She washed herself once more in the clean water and thought she would never feel so good after a bath again. It was wonderful, and to be rid of those lice now that all the hair had gone – what a blessed relief. Her scalp was red raw where the fryzerki had shaved the disgusting cap off and then doused her in vile-smelling disinfectant, but anything, anything, to be rid of those evil insects. It ran through her mind that as soon as she returned to the hut and spent a night there the fleas and lice would all be back. She was given a clean white dressing gown to put on, and then taken up a flight of stairs. Rosa wondered what was going to happen, and why she had been selected to come to the house, but when the double doors were thrust open by a guard on duty and she entered the room, she knew! Hoss was sitting on a long settee, his jack-booted foot casually resting on a low stool. His jacket was off and his shirt was undone at the neck. On one side of the room was a large bed and she knew. She knew why she was there!

For several weeks the routine was the same. Work, roll call, bath and then Hoss, but to Rosa it meant "life". She was alive even though the sexual ordeal she was put through was sickening to her. She had never been made love to in the past, and had often dreamed of the kind of man she would meet and marry, and eventually have children with, but now knew she could never offer herself to another man as long as she lived. After Hoss had used her he would get up and go over to the table, which would always have fruit and cheese on it, also coffee and perhaps pastries. He never spoke, but would occasionally give her a small apple or pastry. This, coupled with the daily bath and the removal of the lice and fleas, meant she had begun to put on a little weight and her skin had begun to heal. The craters no longer existed and the skin covering the holes was shiny and red in its newness. Her scalp, whilst naked, was rid of the deep holes made by the burrowing lice and, altogether, she knew that she was better off in her present situation than she had been for months. One particular day, however, Hoss was drunk. Filthy, stinking drunk. He had rolled on top of her, slobbering all over her body, but in his stupor had been unable to satisfy himself. He had slapped Rosa savagely again and again, shouting obscenities at her. Eventually he had stopped, got up and staggered across to the couch. "Play. Play now or I will shoot you," he shouted. She was whimpering in terror and from the pain of his blows on her body. "I don't have my fiddle, it is in my hut," she said. "Play. Play now, or you will die," he shouted. He stood up, pulling his gun from its holster on the table, waving it back and forth as he aimed. He fired. She felt the heat from the bullet as it whistled past her head and embedded itself in the pillow with a dull "thwack". She screamed loudly, and the door burst open as the guard rushed in to see what had happened. "She is to die, unless she plays for me," Hoss screamed. Rosa was sobbing and hysterical. "Please, get my fiddle, I cannot play for him until I get it. Oh! Please, get it for me." The guard could see that the Commandant was very drunk as he reeled around the room, naked, waving his pistol. He looked at her. "Quickly, get out of here, go and get your instrument." She hastily leapt off the bed, grabbing her dressing gown as she did so and, pulling it on, ran from the room, down the stairs and across the compound. The guard ran behind her, knowing that if she did not return to Hoss he would be shot. The bolt was not on the door of the hut, and she uttered up a prayer of thanks, for this meant that she could get her violin and return immediately. The Blockalteste looked on in amazement as Rosa rushed into the hut dressed only in a dressing gown, grabbed her violin from the foot of her bunk and raced back out again. She dashed across the compound again, holding it tightly, by now gasping and breathless, still with the guard hot on her heels. She ran up the stairs as quickly as she could, slowing now as she ran out of breath with all the exertion, and entered the room. Hoss was sitting quietly in a chair, his head slumped on his chest, humming a little tune to himself – it was Tchaikovsky – the forbidden music! He seemed to have sobered up. He looked up at Rosa, throwing his gun on to the table. "Do you know the music I just sang," he mumbled. She nodded, putting her case down, undoing the catches with shaking fingers, and lifted the violin out. She was trembling as she brought it up to her chin, and wondered if she would have the strength to hold the bow in her hand, which was still shaking uncontrollably. She was deeply troubled, but not sure why. Looking across at the dishevelled bed, and at Hoss who was still naked except for a towel now wound around his waist, she soon realised what was happening to her. Even though she was now no more than a prostitute she was playing as if her life depended on it. She was playing to stay alive! She played the music she loved – Tchaikovsky - which she had not played for many months, and Hoss was obviously delighted, for he smiled, nodded and hummed, tapping his fingers in time to the music. Eventually the melody lulled him to sleep for finally his head slumped forward on his chest and his quiet snores filled the air in the stillness after she stopped playing.

She gently placed the violin back in its case after wiping it, covered it with a cloth, and closed the lid, knowing her instrument was the only reason she was alive. She had come through yet another day.

Rosa and the other women in her hut now had a new task. Each day they were marched to the railway sidings, carrying their instruments, and as the trains arrived the Blockalteste ordered to them to play rousing music to "welcome" the new arrivals. They were forced to play for hours until the last batch of people had been removed from the trucks. Then in the autumn of 1942, there were more and more trains than usual arriving. The orchestra had to play all day without a break, and the trains kept coming! Full of hundreds of men, women and children, all wearing the Star of David on their armbands. They were quickly sorted in the usual way – men and boys, women and children. They were marched off and when Rosa and the others returned to their hut when darkness came, and the trains had stopped, the chimneys were belching out their usual flames and smoke, the sickly acrid smell they had come to recognise filling the air. Word went round – all these arrivals were Polish, and had come from the Warsaw Ghetto where all human lives had been virtually wiped out in a matter of days.

Rosa kept a watchful eye on the comings and goings at the camp. All the members of the orchestra were now wearing the customary black and grey striped uniforms, so they looked the same as all the other prisoners, but their shoes had long worn out and never been replaced. It was now 1943 and the queues of people going to their deaths had increased to four a day, sometimes five. More men had been enlisted from the outside working parties to come and load the bodies on to trucks and carts, and the furnaces worked non-stop, the flames reaching out and licking the sky with their menacing red tongues; the acrid black smoke now incessantly hanging over the camp. Hoss had recently left her alone, presumably tiring of her, for there had been several new members of the orchestra for him to choose from, and to replace Lily, her friend, and two others who had died. Poor Lily, she thought, remembering her with affection. What a terrible death she had suffered. She sat on her bunk, her mind reliving the last few days of Lily's life. It had started on a sunny Sunday afternoon, when the order had been given for all the living inmates of the camp "hospital" to be carried outside and laid in the compound, where the orchestra had been ordered to take their chairs, music and stands. Three guards had pushed the piano out, grunting and groaning under its weight, and the orchestra had commenced playing. Some of those poor, helpless creatures on the ground were very near death but several were delirious and alternating between laughing and crying. Suddenly, one of the demented creatures sprang up, with a strength which was unbelievable in view of its skeletal size, and threw itself on Lily, sobbing uncontrollably and begging her to stop. They had been playing some Greek music, accompanying some singers, and the creature – they could not be sure whether it was a man or a woman - had obviously recognised it, causing it great agitation. Lily had stood up quickly from the piano, and putting her arms around the helpless soul had tried to carry it back to lay amongst the others. What no-one knew was that Typhus had deranged the poor soul's mind. Within a couple of days Lily had become ill. She had tossed and turned in her bunk all night, rousing those around her, who heard her groans with increasing anxiety. Rosa had quietly slipped out of her bunk and was appalled when she realised how hot Lily was and, putting her hand on Lily's forehead, found it was covered in perspiration. She had her eyes half-open, moaning quietly, but did not seem to hear Rosa's voice. Thinking it was maybe a severe chill, or just a nightmare, she returned to her bunk, but in the morning, when the Blockaltests roused them in the normal way, Lily lay inert in her bunk, her eyes closed. Alma and Rosa tried to lift her, but as they got her out and on to the floor, so her knees gave way and she collapsed. They called out to the wardress, who instructed a couple of the other women to get hold of Lily and carry her to the "hospital". This was almost full to capacity with the Typhus which was multiplying daily in the heat of the summer. Lily was lain in a filthy dirty bunk, with stinking putrid straw under her, remaining after the last patient had been removed. At first she had been delirious, yelling out for water, and plagued by some dreadful dreams, but gradually her condition worsened until she sank in and out of consciousness, her delirious state causing her to scream and kick out at unknown and unseen enemies. Rosa did not know where she got her strength from. All around her other patients were in the same condition; always the cries for water, and then the quiet. The one inmate allotted to each hut as "nurse" could do nothing. Rosa was allowed to stay and help nurse Lily and some of the other women, even though she risked catching the deadly disease, but preferred to take this chance instead of sorting out the ever-increasing piles of clothing. There was very little water to give the sick and no drugs to help their condition, so she felt helpless. It was obvious that Lily was in great pain when she was conscious, for she screamed in agony and pleaded for death. The stench of dysentery filled the air and, from every bunk in the "hospital", now filled to overflowing with naked, rotting, putrefying half-alive corpses, came the shrill cries of agony as death took its toll. Rats were everywhere, running up and down the tiers of bunks, unafraid of either the sounds or the smells. They stopped to take a bite out of a body here; a bite of a body there; ignoring the frantic yells from any of their victims who were still aware of their surroundings; ignoring the flapping of hands from those trying to beat them off the living souls; so bold, knowing that their victims were oblivious to their presence. The "nurses" could not keep up with the demand for more and more space as the days wore on and new patients arrived, and pleaded with the Blockaltests for permission to remove those who were so near death. On the day that Lily died over four hundred were taken outside - every corpse; every patient. The officers and guards kept well away from the huge pile of bodies in front of the "hospital" and forced other inmates to pile them on to the waiting lorries for removal to the Crematoria. Once the hut was totally empty several dozen of the "nurses" were sent in to clear out the filthy, stinking straw and wash the whole place down with the green disinfectant liquid which had been placed in containers along the row of "hospital" huts. When the straw and old rags had been removed and heaped up outside on the grass a can of kerosene was thrown from a distance by a guard, protected by a face mask, and then ignited. In this way the SS hoped to get rid of the disease, but it would be an impossible task – too many of the inmates already had it, or were carriers. Those inmates who were sick but still alive were left lying on the ground, with no food or water, and so they all slowly died as well, and the lorries returned day after day to take them to the Crematoria.

A month or so had passed since Hoss had no more use for Rosa's body so she was not receiving a daily bath or the extra food he had given her, so she had grown thin and emaciated again. The lice and fleas had returned and were nesting in her body hair which had grown back, and her skin was again covered in the customary boils which they all suffered from. She tried not to scratch them, but sometimes this was impossible as she would do it in her sleep and in the morning would wake to find her legs or arms covered in dried blood and pus. Her condition was slowly deteriorating again, but she thanked God she was still alive and each day prayed He would allow her to live to tell the world what horrors had existed here.

The children who arrived at Auschwitz were like migrating birds; they would arrive one day, only to disappear the next, but Rosa had noticed over the last couple of years that not all of these children were sent to the gas chambers. She had watched furtively and noticed that many of them would be taken away from the queues of people, their parents screaming and begging for them to be brought back, and then after a period of time, they would re-appear in the compounds, apparently well-fed. She soon discovered that these children, who all seemed to be about eight or nine years old, were used to relay messages between the officers and their "trusties" – those prisoners who were in charge of whole huts and compounds. These inmates were never Jews, but mostly political German prisoners from before the war. They were reasonably well-fed, wore respectable uniforms and were allowed many privileges. Rosa had made friends with one of the children, who would give her snippets of information as to who was in Hoss's house; what his children had been doing; where Irma Grese had been. She then discovered, however, that there was another very sinister reason for the children's apparent escape from death, for they were being used for experimentation and Rosa soon found out how. She was recovering from a less severe attack of Typhus than Lily and was in the disinfected "hospital" after apparently being unconscious for many days - she did not know how long. Gradually she began to improve, probably because, as a member of the orchestra, she had been given a small amount of medication and fresh water to drink. At first, she found it impossible to sit or stand, but with a great deal of will-power and her indomitable spirit and desire to live, had been able to put her feet to the ground and take a few steps. As each day passed she grew stronger but was astonished at the sight of her legs and body. Only bones were showing through her sagging skin, and the muscles on her thighs had completely disappeared. Her pelvis was the same width as her shoulders with no flesh whatever remaining. The skin on her entire body was covered in abscesses, where she had lain in the wet, putrid straw, lying in her own excrement, and all her hair had completely disappeared. She knew she must not scratch the abscesses or boils for then they would burst and cause septicaemia, which could cause her death as easily as the Typhus might have done. She had become totally deaf and could only listen to the pounding in her eardrums which threatened to engulf her in its density. She soon realised she was living on borrowed time and if she was to stay alive she must get out of this dreadful place, back to the hut and its comparative cleanliness. As the deafness in her ears lessened over the next few days, a cough which she had developed got worse. Soon it racked her body from morning till night, making it impossible for her to eat the meagre rations which were handed out, and causing her to vomit with its force.

Day by day Rosa forced herself to get up and walk, and her determination to live helped her recover, the cough slightly improving. However, she was not allowed to leave the "hospital" for the officers were not sure just how long inmates remained contagious, so she was put to work inside the compound before she could return to the orchestra. Her principal task was that of emptying the pails of excrement into the long open trenches at the back of the huts. This task went on all day, without let-up, but when one of the other patients who had recovered dropped to the floor, dead, the "nurse" re-assigned Rosa to take over her job which had been to remove the dead from the bunks. She was still very weak, and in no fit state to lift a child, let alone a grown person, and so had no alternative but to tug and pull the bodies on to the ground and then, grabbing a hand and a foot, drag them along the floor and outside to the pile which grew taller and taller by the hour. It was during this time that she had seen Dr Mengele for the first time. She had heard about him, and the rumours of the terrible acts he carried out were in every part of the camp. He entered the compound, staying well away from the hut and the piles of dead bodies, whilst several of the senior guards and officers accompanying him shouted out that all who could walk must come outside and form lines. When all the inmates were in front of Dr Mengele he gave the order for everyone to strip, and then proceeded to walk up and down the rows of men and women, indicating with a flick of his hand whether they went to the right or to the left – left was death! When he reached Rosa he took a good look at her body. She was now one of the musselmen, and in a deplorable condition. "Aren't you the woman who played the violin in the orchestra?" he asked. She looked at him and nodded. "Yes sir," she replied. He made her turn around by rotating her with his stick. "Run on the spot," he said. She summoned up all her strength and forced herself to do so. To her relief he indicated right! She could not believe that she was to live! All around her the poor creatures were being dragged off to the left – to their death. Only a handful of people remained standing, watching Dr. Mengele as he walked back and forth, back and forth, his immaculate white gloves clutching the stick which he used to prod people into action. He walked back to Rosa and, turning to Oberfuhresin Drechsler, who had accompanied him, he said "Make sure this woman is given medical treatment and food to fatten her up. She interests me. I am curious as to why these people make such fine musicians." Rosa could hardly believe her ears. She was to be fattened up – helped to recover! Why was God being so good to her, she asked herself? They stood in their lines after Dr. Mengele left until they were dismissed, when she was taken back to her hut, the guard whispering to the Blockalteste his quiet instructions. She received double rations of bread and extra sausage, and each day allowed to visit the "trusties" wash house to clean herself. After several days she was well enough to re-join the orchestra, now led by Alma after Ilsa's death, and rehearse with them. It was an effort to hold her violin under her chin for very long and run the bow over its strings, as she was still so weak, but daily grew stronger until eventually, she was well enough to be able to play at a concert for the whole evening.

The orchestra was being used much more now, having to assemble each morning at dawn at the main gates to play resounding German music as new trainloads of inmates arrived. The sound of the band was supposed to help calm any fears these poor people had, after being herded into cattle trucks and transported for days on end. They imagined that the propaganda they had been fed was true – bring your families and your belongings. You are going to be re-settled; you will be well-fed and cared for! Not only did they bring luggage with them but also brought money and jewellery, which was then taken from them after they had been slaughtered and went to swell the coffers of the Third Reich. Rosa had not taken part in any of the morning assemblies for some time as she had been so ill but knew that eventually, she would be there again, playing the music, watching Alma swinging her baton up and down in time to the rhythm. On the second night after her return, the orchestra was ordered to play at an evening concert and was informed they were to be honoured with the presence of many of the senior officials of the camp. When the doors had opened the new Commandant, Josef Kramer and Grese were there, as always, but so was Mengele, Bormann and Hessler. The whole top brass had assembled. Mengele stared hard at Rosa, his now familiar white gloves clutching his stick, and she saw him raise his eyebrows slightly at the sight of her improved condition. He turned to Irma Grese and whispered something to her. She nodded and gave a sly, sickly smile, which did not go unnoticed by Rosa. "What are those two demons planning?" she asked herself.

Rosa found out the next day, for as dawn was

breaking she was summoned from her bunk by the Blockalteste and marched out of the compound towards one of the other buildings on the other side of the camp. As they entered a lawned garden surrounding Mengele's private hospital Rosa saw the wire enclosures which housed the dogs. There must have been fifty or more of them in there, nearly all Alsations, snapping and snarling as they passed, the smell of an "inmate" rousing them and inciting them to attack. They jumped up viciously at the wire, beating it with their claws, trying to bite their way through. She cringed but knew she was safe whilst they were inside their cages. She wondered why there were so many dogs locked up, as she had only seen a few walking around the huts with a guard, or patrolling the trainloads of new arrivals. The Blockalteste marched Rosa inside the building which, to her amazement, smelt like a real hospital – clean, fresh and of disinfectant. "This is probably their own hospital if one of them becomes ill," she thought to herself. Before she left the Blockalteste told her to sit on the hard wooden bench, along with several other people already there, all wearing the familiar striped uniform with the Star of David on it. A guard came down the line, squirting them all over with disinfectant from a hand-spray, warning them not to speak. Rosa looked curiously at the others and her eyes widened in surprise. Twins! She was looking at twenty pairs of eyes, peering out from twenty pairs of identical faces. Even with their shaved heads and skeletal bodies, it was not difficult to see they were identical. Further down the room were two small twin girls playing on the floor, aged about five or six, looking plump and well, dressed in clean, bright dresses. They laughed and chuckled as they played, quite oblivious to the other strange looking beings near them.

A man in a white coat came out and, bending down, took their hands in his and led them through a set of doors which had the word "Theatre" written on them. Rosa wondered why they had gone through there. Very gradually the pairs of twins sitting with her were taken through the same doors, two by two. Not a sound could be heard from within and only the ticking from the wall clock penetrated the silence. Now and again the doors would swing open and a white-coated man or woman would pass through, carrying a metal dish, a length of tubing, or some other surgical equipment. "Why am I here?" Rosa asked herself. Even though she was very frightened and unsure she couldn't help but mutter to herself "All it needs is a small table with magazines on and I could be back in Dr Pfeffer's surgery in Leeds." What a long time ago that seemed – how were her parents and the family? Were they well? They must be wondering where she was. Was she alive or dead? She felt the tears spring to her eyes as she thought of them all but quickly wiped her hand across them before anyone noticed. Eventually, her name and number was called and she walked up to those doors and went through – through to horrors she would never have thought existed, and which even the most gruesome of individuals would recoil from.

Rosa was stripped and washed down by two white-coated women, silently rubbing away at her skin with strong-smelling soap and disinfectant. They shaved her head where her hair had begun to grow again, ensuring it was clean, and then under her arms and between her legs. When this was done they called out "Ready, Herr Doctor," to the screens placed across the end of the room and Dr Mengele walked out, smiling benignly at her. "Well, well, you have certainly improved. Now you look quite human – no more the musselmann. Come over here and be weighed and measured." Although extremely frightened, she was very curious as to what this was all about, and after the weighing and measuring had taken place was given a clean cotton shift to put on and, together with Dr Mengele, ushered through yet another set of doors. She stopped. Gazing in horror at the sight before her she screamed out, taking it all in, before passing out into oblivion at the sight of the butchery laying before her. Six pairs of operating tables lay side by side, with six pairs of twins strapped, naked, on to them. Some were obviously unconscious, but others were alive, turning their heads in mute silence at the sound of the approaching footsteps. One pair of males had obviously been castrated, their testicles removed. Others had tubes running from their noses or mouths. Hanging from a rail along the wall were several bodies, in various stages of disembowelling, and on the ground were the bodies of two dogs. A single trolley was on one side of the room opposite those of the twins, and on it lay an unconscious woman whose breasts had been removed. Rosa could not have known then that Adolf Hitler's newest craze was to have lampshades made out of the stretched skin of women's breasts. Nor could she know that the work being carried out here in this macabre "House of Death" was the transplanting of animal organs into human beings: the artificial insemination of women with the sperm of a dog; the removal of various parts of the body and the measurements of the internal and external organs of twins to see if they differed. Children were used for the purposes of experiments and also for the sexual pleasures of some of the more perverted officers – both male and female. Dr. Mengele was trying to achieve the ultimate goal – the perfection of the Aryan race in order to improve the quality of the children of the Fatherland. Adolf Hitler had given his approval to this idea and Mengele, in his madness, decided that the "Juden" were the ones to try out his ideas on first.

Rosa's head was muzzy. She felt sick. Her throat was dry. Water! She needed water. She tried to move but realised she was strapped to the bed. She wanted to raise her head but had not got the strength to do so. Her hands were firmly beside her thighs, also strapped in place, and she realised she was in a lot of pain between her legs but could move them. Why was she being held down? What had they done to her? Gradually she became more conscious and called out for water. A white-coated woman appeared and placed the spout of a drinking cup to her mouth, enabling her to have a drink. The woman did not look at Rosa, or speak, but placed the container by the side of the bed and walked out. She soon realised she also had bandages around her chest. What had they done? Why was she unable to move? She laid there all day in that room, the woman occasionally returning to give her water, the pain between her legs getting worse, and she knew she was lying in a pool of blood. Turning her head from left to right she could see two other people stretched out on tables. Were they dead or alive, she wondered. They did not move or make a sound. The room was quite small, very clean, and tiled throughout. It was not the same place where she had witnessed the atrocities which gradually she was remembering, and her body shook uncontrollably with fear as she did so. "God in Heaven, what is in this place?" she asked herself, now knowing the tales of horrific experiments being carried out by Dr Mengele were obviously true. She grew more and more terrified at the thought of what could have been done to her and wondered why she was encased in thick bandages. One of the "bodies" groaned. Rosa turned her head to look. At least "it" was alive! She could not see if it was a man or woman, but very quietly called out "Don't be afraid. I am a friend. Are you alright? Can you hear me? What is your name?" In answer, the body groaned and apparently fell back into unconsciousness. It was then that the other person answered. "My name is Ira Chilowicz, I am a Jew. Who are you, what is your name?" She answered him briefly, still feeling too hazy and unwell to say very much. He told her his twin brother was on the next table and was certain they had both been castrated. He was not sure because he could not see, but felt very numb in that part of his body. "What good will it do them? Are they scared I will rear some Jewish children? We are no longer a threat to them; they have murdered so many of us that we must surely be wiped off the face of the earth." "Hush," Rosa said. "You must not talk that way. Although many of us might have died here, and on the journey, we will never be beaten. You must be brave. Try not to think about what has happened, or what is going on. Keep thinking about the future and when we will all be released." He seemed to drift off into unconsciousness for a while, like his brother, but when he roused himself again he muttered "We will all be murdered. We are never going to get out of here." Then he was quiet. She did not know if he was alive or dead but kept on whispering to him and his brother, but neither answered.

From time to time a nurse would come in, briefly check the three of them, and leave. Eventually, when it was dark, and the moonlight was streaming through the window, the door opened and in walked Mengele, accompanied by two other men in white coats, presumably also doctors. They examined the two men who both woke as their dressings were removed; yelling and screaming in agony as Mengele prodded and poked them. He appeared to be satisfied with his work, for he ordered them to be returned to the hospital. Rosa wondered whether they would end up in the hell-hole she had so recently left or whether there was another "hospital" here. She watched the procession make its way over to where she lay, her eyes wide open in terror. "Why am I here? What have you done to me?" she asked. "Quiet, Juden," said one of the men. "Dr Mengele needs to examine you. Do not speak unless you are spoken to." She felt the straps on her wrists being undone so she could move her hands, then she was raised up and the bandages were slowly undone. She was bound around her chest and back, and up across both shoulders, and it seemed that the bandages would never end. Eventually, the dressings were reached and, using a fine pair of pliers, the pads were removed. Rosa looked down quickly, drawing in her breath sharply with the pain of whatever was there, pulling at those pads. As the whole area of her chest was exposed the full impact of the atrocity they had committed on her was revealed. Running from each shoulder, in a diagonal line to her waist, then straight across to her side and up to her armpits, were rows of stitches; the black knots pulling the half-gaping skin together in an ugly endeavour to close it. Her entire chest was black and mauve with the bruising and she saw that both her breasts had gone! She moaned loudly and uttered a cry of sheer terror. Pulling her lips tightly across her teeth she threw her head back as if to try and escape from the sight of her body. "What have you done? What have you done to me?" she cried, the tears streaming down her face. Dr Mengele touched the stitches, feeling the tautness of the hot, burning skin; nodding and smiling grimly as she cried out in pain. "Obviously there is some infection here which is probably due to her poor state of health. I am anxious to see how these scars heal, so do what you can to stop it spreading. Now, woman, you should feel honoured. You are serving the Fatherland, for I am trying to perfect the treatment of cancer of the breast. Without your help," smiling sickly as he said the word "help", "and that of the other Jewish whores who I have performed this operation on I would not see what problems might arise, or how the scars heal. I have also implanted you with sperm from one of my prize dogs and will wait to see if there is a result in a few weeks. We might even have a Jewish baby with a dog's head!" At these terrible words, he sneered and the other two men with him laughed loudly. "You will remain here for several days under observation until your wounds heal and the stitches removed, and should be grateful that you will be spared from your normal work. Stop that snivelling." With these last words, his voice rose to a loud yell, which caused Rosa to cower away from him on the bed and cringe in terror, fearing she would be struck by this man whom she now knew to be mad. The three men then left, giving an order for a nurse to clean up the blood she was lying in and put fresh dressings and bandages on her chest. She could no longer call them "breasts" – they had gone!

Rosa remained in the hospital for several days. The pain between her legs and the infected stitches around her chest gradually improved and she began to get her strength back. Each time a nurse removed the dressings Rosa would gaze in horror at her body, her eyes riveted to the terrible scars she now wore – her badge of office!

As she did so she swore an oath to herself that she would do two things; one, stay alive and get out of this place. The other to expose Mengele and everyone else in this place of unspeakable horrors. She had thought about this constantly, clear in her own mind what she must do, and convinced that the atrocities which were taking place around her, day and night, could not possibly be known by mankind. She must stay alive so that all the nations of the world would know what happened here in this "house of death."

It was late summer. Rosa's wounds had healed, but the scars reminded her every day of the tortures she had suffered. About a month after he had operated Mengele had examined her, before her release from the hospital, pulling her legs apart roughly and inserting some kind of metal object inside her. He let her know how disappointed he was that the sperm he had inserted in her body had not formed into a living thing by beating her around the back and legs, and slapping her face, shouting abuse that she was a "sterile whore". She was then returned to the orchestra but had been put into a different hut along with four other musicians. She realised that all five of them were classed as "privileged" as they had been there for five years and were spared the task of marching with the band at dawn. They continued to receive a little more food than the others in the orchestra and were still allowed to wash when they were giving a concert, but each day were sent to sort out the ever-present piles of clothing, shoes, glasses and toys, then either rehearse or give the usual concert in the evening. Each week one or two of the women would mysteriously disappear, to be replaced by a new violinist; a new pianist; a new clarinet player. Most of these girls had come from other camps, so there were constantly differing reports on how the war was going. Many said that they had been brought to Auschwitz as the Allies were approaching their camps, which had quickly been closed down, but no-one really knew the facts. Their hut was adjoined by a Common Room used by the S.S. officers and many of the German staff, but the walls were so thin that it was possible to hear a great deal of what was going on, and what was being said in there. One of the girls found a small knot hole in the planking and when the other room was deserted she scraped at it with her fingers to enlarge it, then by putting her eye to the hole could see inside the room. Very often they heard singing and laughing and, on looking through the opening, could see bottles of wine and plates of food on the table. There was a radio, which blared out music for most of the time the officers and staff were in there and, occasionally, they saw the men and women dancing together. Unfortunately, the radio was never left on when the room was empty as no-one seemed interested in listening to any reports on the situation of the war. Rosa and the rest of the women in her hut knew that things must be getting worse, for the Crematoria was working constantly day and night, and across the four compounds huge pits had been dug by the inmates. She had not witnessed anything for herself, but the rumours were flying around the camp that when the inmates had dug the pits they would then be lined up, marched into them, and machine-gunned where they stood. Once they were dead quicklime was poured on the bodies, and more inmates were brought in to fill in the pits. She knew there must be some truth in this, for it was on everyone's lips, and the sounds of rifle and machine-gun fire were heard many times during the day. One of the musicians in another hut told them of something else which was happening. It seemed that because hundreds of new prisoners were arriving daily the gas chambers could not cope with the volume, and so the number of people they forced inside these chambers had doubled. In consequence, when the doors were opened for the removal of the bodies, they were piled high on top of each other, their arms out-stretched in death, in an effort to reach the holes in the roof where the gas was poured in. Those on the ground must have died much more slowly and in a more agonising way, being trampled on by others clawing their way up to what they thought were the ventilation holes. Rosa made a mental note of everything she saw or heard, storing it away, still more determined than ever that she would seek revenge for these mass murders and tell the world.

One morning, quite early, the five of them were awakened by a lot of activity in the adjoining room. Loud voices could be heard, talking quickly, and the noise of people running back and forth. Something was going on, and they all looked at each other in puzzlement. When they were ordered out of the hut by the Blockaltests for roll call and to take up the never-ending work of sorting clothing and belongings, they saw dozens of men and women inmates, and even the mussellmanns who could stand, digging trenches. These were appearing everywhere around the camp, whilst lorries were driving back and forth with logs and bundles of kindling which they stacked at intervals by the trenches. What were they doing? Was it some kind of camouflage? Were they going to burn the wood? As the word "burn" came to mind Rosa looked at the others. "Have they run out of the deadly chemicals they use? Have they now got to set fire to all the bodies?" she asked. They could not imagine what was going to happen, and all day the activity continued – even when they were rehearsing for the evening's concert, and after dark in the light of the overhead searchlights. That night the women kept watching the activity in the adjoining room through the spy hole until eventually some of the senior ranking officers of the camp came in. Kramer, Hessler, Grese – they were all there, talking to the junior officers. As the five women all listened with their ears pressed to the wall the whole horrific plan was revealed. It seemed that the Camp had received a direct order from Berlin – from Eichmann himself – that twenty thousand prisoners were to be executed each day. They did not know how they would dispose of that many bodies, for neither the gas chambers nor the Crematoria could cope with such a vast amount. They discussed various ways and means of how this could be achieved but were all sure of one thing. With so many more prisoners arriving this would mean much more money and valuables to swell the pockets of the Third Reich. Apparently, the plan was that all those Jews remaining in Hungary would be rounded up and "persuaded" to leave their hometowns, with the promise of well-paid work. They would be "encouraged" to take any possessions or objects of value with them, as these would be needed to barter with on arrival at their destination. This way they knew that the "foolish Jews" would bring anything of value they still had with them. Three more sorting huts would be opened and those new inmates who were put to work in these huts would be executed the following day so that no one could report on what they had found. The officers were obviously in high spirits at the thought of so much more wealth coming to them that soon the usual drunken party was underway.

Each day, on their way to the sorting huts where the five women and the rest of their colleagues worked, they saw more wood being stacked and discovered that the railway line was being extended. Women were being employed to do this work, for the men seemed to have disappeared! "Were they cutting wood?" Rosa asked herself. One morning, after about five days of activity, they were woken at dawn as usual and ordered by the Blockalteste to get up and attend roll call in the Compound. "There will be no work this morning for we are to be honoured with a visit from a very senior member of the Third Reich who is coming to this camp, and every inmate has to be present," she said. They all stood outside for over an hour, waiting, until eventually a large black saloon car, bearing two flags with the now infamous SS sign attached to the bonnet, entered the camp. When an officer wearing the traditional black uniform of the Gestapo stepped out of the car the whisper went up – it was Eichmann himself! He had come to the camp! This meant certain death for many of them, and everyone stood silently, terrified by his presence. He walked along the lines of women, his white silk scarf held up against his nose to try and mask the stench in the air, only removing it to jot down notes on the pad he held, not saying a word to the other officers who accompanied him. Still as silently, he returned to his car which moved on slowly to another area of the camp. Whilst standing in line waiting to be told to return to their huts they could see that there were several stationery trains standing silently on the new length of railway track; trains which had not been there the previous day. Rosa knew then, knew with a certainty, that the first of the poor Hungarians the officers had talked about had obviously begun to arrive. She and the other women returned to their hut when they were dismissed, rushing quickly to the small window to watch what was happening. They saw the trains being unloaded and hundreds and hundreds of people swarming off them, mostly carrying cases and bundles, many with small children. They watched as the crowds were divided into two sections as usual; one directed to the Crematoria, which was already belching forth its usual flames and smoke, whilst the others went towards a large sign which bore the words "Disinfection Area". The smoke was coming from the chimneys; thick, black and dense. The stench of burning flesh filled the air and then as if to accompany this, smoke was pouring forth from the ground – the trenches had been set on fire! Rosa and the other women in her hut coughed and spluttered as the fumes and smoke crept inside – through the cracks; under the door; around the window frame. The smoke was everywhere. They could not breathe. They raced for the door. Pulling it open they rushed outside, and then the noise hit them. Screaming and howling from hundreds of people, dying slowly in the most agonising and horrific of deaths – being burnt alive. Rosa fell to the ground, sobbing wildly, calling to God for help. Maria and Sonia, two of the women with her, unable to stand the noise of the people being murdered in their hundreds, ran to the electrified fence, throwing themselves against it, crying out to God as they did so, and instantly dying their own horrific death. She could not comprehend what was going on around her. She only knew that she had to blot out the sound and escape from the noise and smell of death. Her two friends had died – for a brief moment she wanted to join them, but a voice was saying over and over in her head "Revenge. You must have your revenge. Stay alive."

For days the smoking chimneys belched forth, never stopping, and the trenches continued to burn. Bodies lay in every empty corner of the compounds, piled high on top of each other, waiting for their eventual cremation, and throughout the night the grinding gears of lorries could be heard as they brought load after load of wood in from other areas to burn in the trenches. Rosa wondered if it would ever end, but knew that the plotting they had overheard had worked - those poor people had really been hoodwinked into thinking they were coming to a new life – the gold, jewellery and prized possessions, which she helped to sort every day, bore the truth of it. Some of the whispered stories that passed around those who worked amongst the dead were hard to believe for it seemed that, desperate as it was for gold, the Fatherland had sent an order that all gold fillings must be removed from the corpse's teeth before cremation or burial, and hair was to be shaved off the heads for other uses. She had no way of knowing if this was true or not, for those unfortunate souls who carried out these gruesome tasks on the dead were living on borrowed time themselves – each day seeing a new intake of workers doing these tasks. She thought to herself it was incredible she had been spared but knew it was because of her precious violin – the one thing which had saved her. She was now leader of the orchestra, for many of the other members had died or been spirited away to the brothels, or Dr Mengele, and never returned. She felt sure she would also be put to death eventually, when someone else could play the violin for Herr Kramer. She knew too much and had seen too much!

Rosa wondered how long it would be before there was some sort of retaliation. She knew that it would never come from the musselmanns, they were far too weak, and were now depleted in numbers as they either died or were cremated. She did not have to wait long, for on one occasion when a train load of Jews arrived a "trustie", who was working among the dead, recognised his sister in the line. He ran forward, shouting and yelling at her to run, screaming what they would do to them all. The crowd became hysterical, fighting and clawing their way out of the trucks, and there were so many of them that, although they were being mown down by the machine guns, some of them escaped unhurt, lashing out at the soldiers, grabbing their weapons and turning the guns on them, firing at point blank range, so that several soldiers were injured or died. These Jews were shot, of course, by the sheer weight of numbers of the Germans, but it raised the hope of every remaining Jew in the camp who had witnessed the attack and gave them a little courage to carry on until it would be their turn to join their fellow men in a grave. During the end of the summer, the entire Gypsy camp was put to death. There were many thousands of them, for they had been sent to Auschwitz from all over Europe, but had not suffered the same atrocities as the Jews. There had been rumours for several days they were to be moved to another camp, as it was thought the Russians were approaching, but instead, they were put to death in the gas chambers, their bodies joining the huge piles of skeletons in every corner of the camp. The mass executions were being carried out on a daily basis, although the Germans were hampered in this work after a fire destroyed one of the Crematoria which meant they could not dispose of bodies as quickly as before. Lorries had stopped coming in, loaded with wood; instead, they were coming in empty and taking away corpses. The word went round that the dead Gypsies were being buried in the woods, in huge pits, but no one knew for sure if this was true. The piles of clothes had lessened, and soon there was no work to be done for the privileged orchestra girls. They had not been told to play at night for several days and it was thought that Kramer and Grese had left the camp. They were forced to do other work instead and Rosa, along with several other men and women, was sent to clear out the bodies from the gas chambers. The grotesque sight of naked bodies, arms and legs was beyond imagination and all the while she worked she tried to put her thoughts on other things – with always the same resolve that she would stay alive to seek revenge for her people – the millions of Jews who had been murdered here.

Gunfire! Where was it coming from? Rosa raised herself up in her bunk, whispering in the dark to the others to wake up. All around the camp could be heard the noise of guns, and then planes were overhead. Could it be the Allies? Were they going to be rescued at last? The guns and whine of bombs being dropped could be heard in the distance all through the night and before dawn they were woken by the Blockalteste who ordered them out of the hut for a roll call – taking place much earlier than usual. From the closeness of the gunfire it was obvious the allies were very near at hand as officers were scurrying back and forth, shouting commands to each other. None of the women dared to let the Blockaltest see that they were overjoyed at the noise, but they were very happy. Very soon, every living inmate of the camp who could walk was assembled in the compounds and in the dawn light, Rosa could see there were several hundred prisoners gathered together. She wondered what on earth was going to happen to them all. There was no time for everyone to be executed – the Allies were coming! A guard ran up to the Blockalteste and said "I have received orders that you are to bring your group of musicians immediately and make for the trains standing over in the sidings." She said "You heard the guard, go to the hut and get whatever you have and return here straight away." At least this meant they were not going to be killed yet, and every reprieve meant one step nearer to freedom for them all. The women rushed to pick up their few belongings and instruments and when they reached the hut Rosa grabbed her precious violin then hurried as much as she could to the train, slipping and sliding in the snow and mud, to the well-remembered shouts of "Schnell. Schnell." "Rauss. Rauss," the cracking of whips and the barking of dogs. As she boarded the truck with the women from the orchestra and several others they were prodded forward by a guard, using his rifle to hit them across their shoulders and backs to make them move quickly, the well-remembered stench of rotting straw hit her, but she tried to ignore it and pushed herself in as fast as she could. None of them wanted to feel the lash of a whip on their back, or a bite on the ankle from one of the vicious dogs. The gunfire was definitely nearer, and explosions could be heard every few minutes after the whine of a bomb being dropped. They had no idea where they were going as the doors of the truck were noisily slammed shut. Rosa and the other women all asked each other where they were going, how long the journey would take, how long they would be locked up, or whether they would in fact survive the bitterly cold conditions as they were without food or water. Rosa well remembered the horror of the journey she had experienced all those years ago when she had first been brought to Auschwitz in the freezing cold weather. This truck was much smaller and smelled of coal, as well as stale urine and excrement. There were no cracks in the sides for air to penetrate through, and she knew that it was almost airtight. They sat or lay in the truck for the first two days without being let out, whilst it grew colder and colder inside, with rivulets of condensation running down the sides. No-one talked, for fear of using up the precious air, just listened to the noise of the wheels running along the track; over points; through junctions. They had no way of knowing where their destination might take them but all longed for the journey to end.

The nightmare lasted for several days. The train stopping and starting, and at the beginning, they often heard the noise of aircraft above, strafing the train with bullets. They received no food or water until the fourth day when they were allowed out of the truck to relieve themselves and given some hunks of black bread and green slimy water, which none of them dared drink for fear of either dysentery or typhus. They still had no idea where they were going, for the guards kept silent when Rosa and another of the women dared to ask, and each day their numbers lessened as friends died in the dreadful conditions or from the cold. After travelling forwards and backwards, dodging the air raids, and presumably damaged railway lines, they finally came to a stop and the familiar "Schnell. Schnell." "Raus. Raus," orders came. "Alles raus, anstellen." Rosa and eleven of her companions were virtually dead when the doors were finally thrust open. The other twenty-seven women in with them had died during the last twenty-four hours, due to a combination of starvation and suffocation. Those of them who had stayed alive had clambered on top of the bodies to try and get some air at the top of the truck, for that was the only way they could try to survive.

Rosa crawled along the ground after she had lowered herself from the truck. She could not stand and her head was spinning, but she was clutching her violin to her. As desperate as she was she had held it tightly throughout the journey. Although it was bitterly cold, and the snow was thick on the ground, the air was so clean and fresh after being locked in the truck she just lay there, taking in huge gulps, trying not to vomit at the memory of those last hours in that hell hole, risking the lash of a whip or a bite from one of the dogs. The whole train load of prisoners still alive had been forced out of the trucks and Rosa could not believe her eyes, for out of the hundreds who had been packed into the train at the beginning of the journey, and who she had seen emerge at some of the stopping places, only a hundred or so were actually alive, and she was one of them! A woman bent over her and whispered "You must get up, or you will be beaten, and they will kill you. That is all they want to do with us. Come, let me help you." As frail as the woman was she helped Rosa, who finally managed to stand, but she was dizzy and faint from the lack of food and water. They were all marshalled together and forced to march but many were incapable of walking, for the journey had finally taken its toll, and as they fell to the ground the others with them who still remained standing knew they were dead or dying. The guards would not let them stop to help them get up, shouting the familiar "Schnell. Schnell." "Raus. Raus," prodding and poking them with their rifles, forcing them to walk on. As they reached the camp the whisper spread through the line of prisoners. "Belsen. We've come to Belsen." Rosa heard the words with dread in her heart, for she knew from everything she had heard that they had come to a place far worse than anywhere she or the others had been before. They entered the compound, looking up at the towers positioned all around the electrified fences. There were hundreds of bodies lying on the snowy ground, as far as the eye could see. Worse than Auschwitz! Some were naked. Some partly clothed. All musselmanns. Those who were still alive looked at the new arrivals with beseeching eyes; pleading for death and release from the starvation, disease and the freezing cold conditions from which they were all suffering. As Rosa and the other women with her stumbled through the compound they had to pick their way between the bodies and those of the half-dead. Those of them still alive tried to raise themselves up and hold out a hand to beg for food or water. It was obvious that these poor creatures had not received any for a very long time. The weather was much colder here and the majority of them had no clothing whatever, only a few rags covering their bodies. It went through Rosa's mind that their clothes had probably ended up in the same kind of sorting sheds as she had been working in at Auschwitz. She turned to the woman by her side, who had suddenly grabbed her. "My God. My God. I cannot believe it. Why has this been allowed to happen? What have they done to deserve this?" she said. Rosa could not reply, nor did she want to, as she was covering her mouth and nose with her free hand to try and stifle the stench that rose all around them. She realised that here was something far more terrible than she had ever experienced during all her time in Auschwitz.

Rosa and the eleven other women from the orchestra who were still alive were taken to a hut at the far end of the compound, joining a group of others from the train. They recognised the woman SS guard, Oberfurhesin Bormann, who shouted at them, and pushed and prodded them towards it with the end of her whip. They entered the hut, which was windowless, and as daylight filtered through the doorway they recoiled in horror. The place was full of dozens of dead bodies, their limbs sticking out of the bunks into which they were tightly packed. In the half-light the rats could be seen scurrying across the floor, darting hither and thither amongst them. Bormann shouted out "Get in there, you stinking Juden, clear out the dead and dump their bodies outside, for this is where you will be housed." They knew there was no way they could refuse. Rosa placed her violin carefully against the wall of the hut and promptly ripped off the bottom of her tunic. When she had done this she wound the strip of material around her face and nose, the others following her example, as they all knew there was no way they could manage this grisly task without some small protection from the stench. They removed the bodies, stiff and rigid in death, many with mouths wide open in their last dying hours, and as they pulled an arm or a leg to free it from the bunk there would be a loud 'crack' as limbs broke. The filthy straw in the wooden bunks was covered in excrement, and the rats were running around the floor, squeaking and squealing as Rosa and the others kept kicking out at them so they would not get bitten. She was desperately fighting the urge to flee and run from the horror of the work as she helped carry the bodies, taking them across the compound and placing them on a huge pile of skeletons already there, but knew if she did so her own body would soon join them. These skeletons were so emaciated there was hardly any flesh left remaining, most having been gnawed by the rats, leaving gaping holes in what skin did remain. Similar piles were everywhere, waiting for burial, but there were just too many for this task to be carried out. When the last body had been removed the women stayed outside the hut, all afraid to go back in, for the rats had not left when the bodies had gone. They sat in the snow on the cold, hard ground, shivering in the night air, for all they had on were their thin tunics and, since they had torn the bottoms off to protect their faces, their legs were bare. Suddenly Bormann was striding towards them. "Where is Rosa Levinsky?" she shouted. Rosa stood up. "Here," she replied. "The Commandant has ordered that you will now re-form the orchestra here. You will receive some food each day, which is more than the other filthy Juden will get, and each morning at dawn you will work on the burial party until sunset. You will play at night for the Commandant. You and your musicians," sneering at the word 'musicians', "will all go with the guard now, who will take you to the quarters where you will stay. Take whatever instruments you have with you and leave them there. You are forbidden to take them out." She turned to walk away and, fearing nothing now as Rosa was sure none of them would remain alive for very long, she called out to her "Madam, who is the Commandant here?" She slowly turned and, looking at Rosa with scorn and contempt, said "The Commandant is Josef Kramer and the senior woman officer here is Irma Grese. You will already know them, I am sure, for they have both come from Auschwitz to carry out our beloved Fuhrer's work. They will exterminate you all." As the last three words were uttered her voice rose to a high crescendo note, and she raised her fist as if to strike her. Rosa stood her ground, unafraid. "With permission, Madam, I would like to have some time for rehearsal. Because of our long journey, none of us has played for many days and those who do not have instruments will need to become familiar with any you are providing. We have all played for the Commandant many times and know he loves his music and will not be pleased if we do not play well." She stood, waiting, fearing some violent punishment at her audacity. Bormann looked at her, and at the others, then said "Very well. Come with me and I will allow you a short time to organise yourselves. There is no music here in the camp. You will have to play from memory and if you are so familiar with the likes and dislikes of our beloved Commandant you will have no problem. There is a piano and some other instruments in the room where you will play, left behind by those who did not please him, which you can use." As she uttered the word 'familiar' her mouth twisted into a grotesque smile and her voice took on an oily tone. Rosa then realised that Bormann was well aware how they had all been used on numerous occasions to satisfy the lust of not only the Commandant, but that of many other senior officers as well. They still had not received any food or water since arriving at the camp and no-one had the courage to ask for any, but as Bormann had said they would receive some each day, they knew they would have to wait until tomorrow, even though they were all thirsty and weak from hunger.

Rosa collected her violin from outside the hut, telling the others who had their own instruments to bring them along. They followed Bormann as she led them through a high wire fence towards a long, low building, with smoke coming from a chimney. This was obviously the officers' quarters, for it was very clean; painted white, the snow cleared from the neat gardens in the front and well away from the stinking, rotting piles of putrefying bodies in the compounds. They were led into a large room, with an old upright piano at one end, and several chairs and tables scattered around. There were empty wine bottles and cigarette packets littering the place and it was evident that this was the general 'mess' area. Bormann barked some orders to the guard who had accompanied her, turned and left. Rosa compared it with the neat and tidy music room at Auschwitz and wondered how long it would be before Kramer insisted that this room be cleaned up. The guard stood laconically in the doorway, leaning up against the door jamb, watching the women as they placed some chairs in a semi-circle around the piano. Esther was the pianist and she started tinkling away on the keys, whilst Gittle and Kitty, both clarinet players, started to tune their instruments. There were three other violinists, a cellist, a saxophone player and three oboists. The cellist and two of the oboists had no instruments with them and Rosa wondered if there were any in the camp. Kitty had obviously read her thoughts and said "With all the people who have died here they must have some instruments hidden away somewhere." She turned to the guard and politely asked him if he could arrange for them to see whether there were any instruments available. He spat on the floor, shifted his position and ignored her, so she asked him again, but still he stood there, not even glancing at her. Rosa went over to him and said "Sir, we have been chosen to play for Herr Kramer himself tonight. He will expect the same standard of music as we played when we were at Auschwitz, and I think he will be very angry if we do not have at least one more oboe and, I hope, a cello to help the orchestra sound more professional. All we are asking is that you let us inquire if there are any instruments anywhere here." He looked at Rosa as he opened a door into a small side room and said "There are some instruments in there from other stinking Juden who are no longer with us," leering at her when he said those words, and nodded to her to go in. To her delight, there was a Cello laying on the floor, with several other instruments, including an oboe, so Rosa called out to the girls to come and choose what they wanted. There was no music but Rosa did have a small selection with her, tucked inside her violin case, which she had been carrying around for the last few months, always fearful she would be moved to another camp, so they were able to make use of it. They rehearsed the music she knew Kramer enjoyed as best they could and gradually, as each of them became engrossed in the melodies, for a few brief moments they all forgot the horrors outside those four walls. They were all there that first night; Kramer, Grese, Bormann, Hoss, Drechsler, sitting facing the small group of women as they played for them. Playing with as much skill and talent as they could muster in their determination to use their tools as a means of staying alive.

Spring had arrived, the snow had gone, but conditions were just as terrible and the camp was still packed full to capacity, the piles of skeletons scattered around the whole area. For four days now there had been no food or water for the orchestra, nor had they been taken to the mess room to play their music. Large German staff cars had been seen coming and going out of the camp and rumours were running rife that all the senior officers had left, including Kramer and Grese. It was April, and Spring! Gunfire was all around them, bullets were whistling overhead. The noise of bombs dropping could be heard in the distance. Grenades! Bullets. More gunfire. Those who could walk or run darted for cover, thinking the end had come for all of them, and it was the Germans firing on them at random. Others too ill to move just laid on the ground, whimpering and crying out. Rosa and her companions all stayed in the safety of their hut and she hid under her bunk, clutching her violin close to her, like a child; a precious thing. She was trembling, but had the courage to call out to the others to keep quiet. "They will not hurt any of us, we are all Kramer's property." She did not know if they were safe or not, but was trying to calm Kitty and Gittle, who were screaming with terror, urging the noise to stop. The others were too scared to make a sound in case their hiding place was discovered. Suddenly they realised it had grown very quiet and the gunfire had ceased, and all that could be heard was a low rumble. Rosa could not make it out. It was not a familiar noise. She called out to the others in a whisper "What is that noise? It sounds very odd, that rumbling, squeaking noise." "I know what it is. It's a tank," said Kitty. "Tanks here? Why would tanks be here?" Rosa asked." As she said these words, half to herself, the door was thrust open and two soldiers in strange uniforms, wearing steel helmets, stood on the threshold. They were free. Free. And she was alive.

The women threw themselves at the door of the hut, darting past the soldiers, anxious to be out of that house of horrors, and an incredible sight met their eyes. There were dozens of tanks situated around the fences of the compound, and inside all the jeeps and army vehicles were stationary. There was silence - the drivers all too numb with shock at the sight of the horror of what lay around them to move. Many soldiers were kneeling on the ground, weeping unashamedly, whilst others were being violently sick. Officers were so appalled at the mounds of skeletons on view everywhere, and those poor souls still clinging to life crawling on the ground towards them, that they were unable to give the order for the troops to go to their assistance until they, too, had ceased crying at man's inhumanity to man!

There was no yelling and shouting from the men and women of the camp with the joys of liberation. Those of them who were still alive had finally given in and had no strength to move, just lying on the ground or in their bunks waiting for help, whilst those who came to their aid were so moved by the horrific sights around them they had to muster up more courage for this task than at any time throughout the war. This, then, was the horror of it all. This, then, was Belsen.

Rosa lay in a hospital in Hanover for many weeks, tended by British and American doctors. They asked her many questions and when she was examined and the terrible scars on her chest were revealed they treated her with tenderness and compassion, visibly moved when she told them what Mengele had done and how he had experimented on her with dogs' sperm. The nurses were gentle and caring, giving her so much love and attention she could not believe she was receiving such kindness after so long. She knew when they saw her scars the tears had sprung to their eyes and they had turned away, unable to control their emotions, hoping she had not noticed. She had forgotten that people could be so kind and have feelings for their fellow man. Many of the patients in the hospital were dying as a result of the starvation and disease, their bodies too wasted to recover, but Rosa was able to eat a small amount each day and gradually improved. After four months she was finally brought back to England and put in an isolation hospital in Surrey. Her Mother, Helena and little sister Gittle were allowed to visit and she knew they were horrified at her appearance, but bravely tried not to show it. They had brought her fruit and some chocolates

– what a treat - joking with her that all the family had pooled their coupons to get the small box. They were allowed to stay for about an hour, holding her hand, telling her how proud they were of her, how much they missed her, until Matron came and asked them to leave as she was not to get tired. They promised to return, Mama saying she knew Israel would be visiting her soon.

She began to gain a little weight, the many ulcers on her legs and arms had healed, leaving awful scars, and her hair had started to grow back, but to her dismay, it was iron grey. She had lost her beautiful blonde hair! But it gave her the will to survive, knowing that many were still dying, too ill to ever recover. At last, she felt she had the strength to play her violin again, and the Matron brought it to her. She took it from its case, wiping it gently with its cloth, and drew the bow across the strings. It needed tuning badly after not being played for such a long time so she plucked at the strings, tightening them until she was satisfied. The melody poured forth from the violin as she began to play. Other patients in the ward turned towards her to listen. The Matron and Nurses stood in their office doorway, entranced at the music, their duties temporarily forgotten. She was lost in the Chopin she was playing until finally, she was unable to hold the violin for any longer. She stopped playing. There was silence. Then the clapping started and went on for several minutes. Rosa was embarrassed but secretly pleased that she was still able to play well enough to give the patients and nurses some pleasure.

The following day three army officers came to see her. She had been shown to a pleasant sitting room with a sofa and armchairs and they were waiting for her. "Miss

Levinsky, we have come to tell you that proceedings are about to begin in Nuremberg against those German officers, both men and women, who have been captured. The case is likely to last for many weeks, even months. Present will be many of Hitler's senior officers, and the commandants from the concentration camps will also be on trial. Are you willing to give evidence as a witness and relate what you saw? What you experienced and how you were treated in both Auschwitz and Belsen? Having been a prisoner in both your testimony will be invaluable, as very few people who have survived are well enough to attend." Rosa said "All that kept me alive during those terrible times was my determination to tell the world what had been carried out in both the camps where I was sent. To tell the world how those maniacs tortured us. How they caused thousands to suffer an agonising death, not only the Jews but many others. How we were beaten, starved, experimented on. I am alive, but only because I was able to play my violin and was useful to them, otherwise I would not be here. Gentlemen, I will be prepared to go back to Germany and testify, whenever you are ready, but hope it is soon as I have TB and my health is not good. I am not sure if I will fully recover."

Rosa's mother and Helena were allowed a further visit before she left for Germany, and brought a parcel with a smart dress and jacket which her sister Esther had sent from America, together with shoes and underwear. She was flown back to Germany the day after the Trial began and she was given into the care of the nearby hospital. The day arrived for her testimony and she wore her new clothes and one of the nurses did her hair and lent her a lipstick. She felt ready to face the ordeal. Her name was called and she was ushered into the courtroom. There were eight Judges sitting on the Bench, with the English, American and other flags displayed behind them. Most appeared to be wearing headphones so Rosa realised they needed an interpreter, as she had been told the proceedings would be mainly carried out in English. Then she felt faint and almost swooned, putting her hand out to steady herself, for there in the dock sat many German officers, a row of Military Police behind them. She immediately recognised Hess, Goering and Speer from photographs she had seen, but no sign of Kramer, Eichman or Mengele or some of the other officers who had attended the concerts in the camps – where were they, she wondered? She was sworn in and allowed to sit, the Judge fully aware how sick she still was. Hour after hour that morning Rosa was questioned, giving evidence, telling the Court what she had suffered and endured, and at whose hands. Then they recessed for lunch. She was already completely exhausted, and one of the doctors saw she was very distraught and came to talk to her. "You can now be excused, you know, if you are not feeling up to any more questions. You have already given the Court a great deal of information," Rosa said "No. I am alright. I still have much to tell the court – I want to tell them everything. Leave nothing out. Every horrific detail. The world must know what these monsters did. What despicable acts they committed and what for? What has been gained except the mass extermination of many of my race, and others as well? We all suffered a harrowing ordeal, and this must be told."

It was over. Her terrible revelations, which had taken several days to be heard, and the questions constantly put to her by the Prosecution, had come to an end and now Rosa was free to start a new life. She had vowed to seek her revenge and tell the world what she and others had experienced and seen in those terrible camps, and she had done it. The trials in Nuremberg at the Palace of Justice had started in the November and would go on for a very long time, but she had given her testimony against them all – Kramer, Grese, Hoss, Mengele, Ziereis and the many others who had persecuted not only her but the millions of her fellow men, women and children. She was free – and alive – but knew she was very ill, and the cough which racked her body day and night was gradually weakening her. The doctors who had told her she had TB said they would help her to recover, but she knew she never would. She was too weak after nine years in the camps. Her revenge was over – she had testified – her belief in God and her determination to survive had given her the strength to bear witness against the atrocities carried out by the Germans. Now she could go home to die in peace, knowing the world would soon learn the full story of the horrors which had befallen all of those in the camps of death.

Sydney Israel Levinsky

PART THREE – ISRAEL'S STORY

It was the summer of 1947. The rain was falling heavily as Israel led Anna and Helena away from the Cemetery. Nathan walked behind with Esther and Gittle, and the rest of the family followed. The Rabbi smiled sadly at them as they got into the cars and soon they were heading out of the Cemetery and on their way home. Anna was still crying, the tears coursing down her work-worn face. Israel knew his mother was not just crying for her little Rosa, whom they had just buried, she was crying for her husband Abraham, who had died so long ago, and for her other two sons, Isaac and David, who had died in concentration camps during the war. They had all been taken from her. Israel wanted to console her that even in the aftermath of the holocaust, she had five of her children alive, and safe.

The cars pulled up at the house and Israel turned to her, saying gently: "Mama, stop crying, please. The children will not understand, for they thought the tears were over. Come, dry your eyes, and let us try and start a new life. Rosa and the boys would not want you to keep mourning them – we have all mourned long enough. We must be brave and try to forget our sorrow for the sake of the children. Papa would not have wanted to see you crying like this and Rosa made you promise not to grieve for her after she died." She smiled up at him, and, dabbing her face with the handkerchief he had given her, said "You are right, Sonny, I must give my love to all of you who are still left, and not those who have been taken from me." Since Israel had gone to school he had been nicknamed "Sonny," and he knew it suited him. He always tried to be cheerful, always smiling, so was now known by that name to everyone. His mother, Anna, still spoke in her Russian tongue, for although she had now been in England for nearly thirty years she had only learned a smattering of English. The people she met and served every day in her shop were mostly from Europe too, and no-one spoke fluent English in their community – Yiddish prevailed, above all else. The children, however, had learned to speak English at school and they were all fluent in both languages. Israel had been fortunate, for he had an ear for accents and his closest friend before the war had been a Polish boy from Lublin called Leo Franck. Leo only spoke Polish, whilst Israel spoke Russian and the Polish he had learned when living with Mala and Moshe, so the two boys had mutually learned each others' language like natives, filling in with English as they were taught it.

As they got out of the car the front door opened and Anna's three grandchildren came running down the path, followed by Julie, Israel's wife. Anna knelt down and gathered them to her – Natalia, the eldest and her favourite. Jacqueline, Esther's daughter, and Rodney, Helena's son. They were all holding on to her hands and tugging at her to come in, for they adored their grandmother and had been told that they must show her a lot of love now that Aunt Rosa had died. The house was full of people; the family and friends who had all come to say goodbye to Rosa. Anna had said she did not know how they would all fit into her little house, but the rain had stopped so maybe some could go out into the small back garden. She turned to him and said: "Sonny, I know what I have to do, and it is time. Time to fulfil the last wish of my beloved daughter, when she was so sick from the TB which she contracted whilst in Auschwitz and Belsen for all those years." Anna excused herself from the Rabbi and her friends and, beckoning to him, she turned and went up the stairs. "Sonny, bring Julie with you," she called out. They entered her bedroom and she opened the cupboard, taking Rosa's violin from the shelf, placing it in his hands. He opened the case and gently lifted out the instrument, lovingly caressing the strings and gently plucking them. "Sonny. Rosa made me promise that on her death the fiddle was to come to you. It should be played every day, and Rosa wanted you to use it in your work and look upon it as a friend, as it was to her, for you know it saved her life. It belonged to your Father first, then to Rosa, and now it is yours. Promise me you will never part with it, and give it to Natalia one day. I know she does not play yet, but perhaps you will teach her." He looked at his Mother. "Mama, I know what the fiddle means to you, and that it kept Rosa alive during the war. I promise to keep it and cherish it as long as I live. Thank you. I will always remember." He looked at his wife, and taking up the bow, played a few notes on the strings. "It needs tuning and some attention, but seems fine," he smiled with pride at the honour she had given him.

"Oh, how good it is to play this beautiful fiddle again," thought Israel, remembering the many times all those years ago in Russia when his father had let him play it after his own violin had been left behind when they fled from their home. He shuddered as he remembered the long trek for almost a year, which seemed would never end. Every day he took the violin out of its case, tuned it, practised scales, arpeggios, Tzigany music, until he was exhausted. It had not been played for many months before Rosa died. She had lain in her hospital bed, unable to play, until the fight she had put up in her determination to stay alive and seek revenge for all the Jews who had been persecuted in the camps took its toll, and she had finally died after her harrowing ordeal at Nuremberg. Israel was a fine classical violinist, but his first preference was Tzigany music. He loved the strident, rapid beat of the music when he could imagine the gypsy couples whirling and dancing around a campfire, and he would take the bow furiously across the strings of the violin as he accompanied the other musicians grouped around him, all with the same love. He was now in uniform based in an army camp, and each evening got the opportunity to play with other members of the orchestra to entertain the troops. The boys and girls in uniform would whistle and clap, shouting "Encore, encore," so the band would play more and more of the good old tunes and the crowd would join in and sing along with them.

Israel sat at the wooden table, a sheaf of papers in front of him, bearing eleven names. He signed first one, then another. "This will take all day, possibly longer," he thought. Sometimes he could be sure in less than an hour if the person sitting opposite him was genuine, but on other occasions, he had been well and truly hoodwinked, and it could be a whole day before a little slip, often nearly missed, would expose them as being an imposter. The windows had the familiar brown sticky tape crisscrossed over the glass and he smiled ruefully to himself. It would probably be another year before they got round to removing it – the war had been over for two years and still, the air-raid shelters had not been dismantled! The guards stood on either side of the door, at ease, and he reached forward and pressed a bell on the corner of the table. The door opened and a small,

Natalie Cumming

thin man entered. He saluted Israel and sat on the chair.
The papers indicated that his name was Mita Vychodil,
from Stradom Street, Cracow, and he had served with
the Polish army until captured by the Germans in 1944,
spending the remainder of the war in Lublin
concentration camp. Vychodil sat nervously in front of
Israel, his hands wringing each other. Israel noticed this,
but it did not always follow that he might be a German
on the run or an imposter. He spoke to him in Polish.
"Tell me a little about yourself. Your family, wife, any
children. Where did you go to school? Where did your
Father work?" Vychodil then began telling his story of
where he was educated and his family background. He
talked about a wife and children, and their town, but did
not know if they were alive or dead. Israel sat there,
listening intently. Listening for anything which did not
quite tally; did not quite ring true. He stopped talking
and Israel read the scribbled notes in front of him. "Do
you know a store called Buchheister in Stradom Street?"
Vychodil nodded. "Oh yes, it is a fine store," he replied.
"But of course, I have not seen it for several years."
"What did it sell?" asked Israel. "It was a wholesalers, I
think, supplying cloth to the trade. I don't think it sold to
the public at all." Israel asked him one or two more
questions, but was happy that at least this man was
genuine. There was no doubt that he was not a German,
trying to escape capture, but a genuine D.P. "We will do
all we can to arrange for you to be returned to your
home. If you take this form to the officer at the desk
outside he will help you make the necessary
arrangements." He smiled at Israel, thanked him
profusely, saluted and left. Israel leaned back in his
chair, smoking, deep in thought. "Thank God that had
been an easy one." So many of them became desperate

and stuttered their answers, knowing they were being interrogated. Yesterday he had seen seven men, all of whom were supposedly Russian or Polish soldiers. He knew with a certainty that four had been German, but how? How could be prove it? He just knew they were lying, but could not put his finger on it. Something nagged at his brain. There was a clue there somewhere, but where? He must try and go back over the whole thing in his mind, then perhaps it would become clearer when he questioned them again. He sat back in his chair, thinking of all that had gone on during the past few years. Was it really eight years ago when it all started?

When Israel had received his call-up papers he was with the Halle Orchestra, playing second fiddle and enjoying his work immensely. He loved to play and knew that he was a good musician. His gratitude to his Father for allowing him to study music was immense but knew it was his own ability which had won him the scholarship to the Royal Academy in London when he was thirteen, just after his barmitzvah. Oh! What celebrations there had been at the little house in Leeds when the letter had arrived. His mother, Anna, once she had got over the initial excitement, had only one practical thought in her mind – "What will you do for boots? You don't have any boots. Uncle Nathan must make you some new trousers, as you cannot go to London in your old ones," she said. Ever practical, Abraham had laughed at his wife and said "Don't worry, Mama, we will find a way of getting what Sonny needs. Our son is going to London. We must send him off like a hero, for he is like one to us. Sonny, my boy, we are so proud of you. All the years I have taught you the violin, and you have rewarded me ten times over." Israel beamed at his parents. He was so pleased, and his first thought was that he must tell Rosa, for she would be so glad he had passed the scholarship. Secretly, he knew that it should be her who was going to London and not him, for she was a far better player, but he knew his parents would never allow her to go away from them whilst she was so young. Finally, everything was ready. His few possessions were packed into an old battered suitcase which a neighbour had brought in. Uncle Nathan had made him trousers and a jacket, and the Rabbi had miraculously appeared with a pair of boots – not new, but good enough to get him to London. He had also arranged for him to lodge with a good Jewish family and the scholarship would provide him with just enough money to pay for this. He studied music for five years at the Academy, sometimes hitching a lift on a lorry to get home for a weekend to see his family. When the dreadful news had come through in 1930 that his father had died the Cohen's, where he lodged, had immediately given him the money for his train fare home so he could attend the funeral. He begged and pleaded with his mother and Uncle Nathan to let him stay so he could go out to work and help support the family as the eldest son, but they had been adamant that he must return to London, to continue his studies at the Academy, as this would be what his father would want. When the scholarship finally came to an end when he was eighteen and his tuition was over he was ready to leave the Academy, and thanks to his Professor, had secured a position with the Halle Orchestra immediately. They travelled all over England, playing in concert halls and theatres, and he knew that this experience was of the greatest value to his career. His ambition was to become first violinist but knew this was many years ahead. He was able to send a little money home each month, as he was aware how difficult life was for his mother, Nathan, Rula, and all the family now his father was dead, and his only bitter disappointment was that Abraham had not lived to see him perform with the orchestra – he would have been so proud of him. He thought of his sister, Rosa. She was already a truly accomplished and well-known violinist, now playing with the London Philharmonic Orchestra. She seemed very happy living in London and had made friends with some girls in the orchestra and together they were sharing a flat there. When she and Israel last met she had told him she would like to travel to get more experience and had applied to the Conservatoire in Paris and the Berlin Philharmonic to see if they would be prepared to engage her.

In the early spring of 1935, when Sonny was twenty-three, the orchestra was playing in Paris. One evening, after the performance was over, Israel and several of his friends decided to go and see the Folies Bergere cabaret, which was the talk of the city. "Come on, Sonny, let's go and find out what all the fuss is about. I bet they are not a patch on our own dancers in London," said Joe, a particular pal. "Alright," said Israel, "But I think we should have a couple more chaps with us. Someone who speaks good French – mine is very poor." Joe went over to a few of the others and quickly rounded up three more, and the five found themselves in the darkened theatre, at a good table near the front, waiting for the lights to go up. The music began, the curtain rose, and what a sight! Twenty or so naked ladies, standing on plinths, sitting on seats, posing for the audience, clad only in thin veiling or feathers, their beautiful bodies clearly on view through the flimsy material. They were not moving, but those with feathers waved them tantalisingly around themselves, giving the briefest glimpse of what lay behind. Dancers then came on the stage, wearing the scantiest of costumes, performing a beautiful routine with male partners. Israel and his friends could not believe their eyes – nothing like this was on the stage in London! Joe and Frank were clapping, but Israel had spotted one girl, standing on a plinth who was smiling down on him – at least he was telling himself she was looking directly at him. He grinned at her, clapped with the others, the curtain came down and the lights went up for the interval. Joe said "Sonny, I think the brunette on the plinth was looking at you. Wasn't she lovely?" Israel nodded, said "Yes, she was," sipped his drink, and kept quiet – thinking secret thoughts. The second act came. The curtain rose, and this time the brunette was sitting on a bench, near the front, cleverly waving her feathers around herself, but Israel could see her lovely long legs, the toss of her head and, yes, she was smiling directly at him – he knew this for sure. The third act came, and there she was again, but this time dressed as a nymph, in a beautiful filmy peach coloured dress which came to her knees, tied around the hips with a satin ribbon, and the smallest of silk slippers on her feet. She danced like a cloud, light as a feather as her partner lifted her high, slipping back to the ground with ease. The music ceased, the female statues remained in their positions, the dancers bowed, and the mainly male audience went wild, clapping and cheering, calling for more, watching the curtain come down several times. Israel had stood up when he clapped, and knew the brunette had winked at him. He must get to meet her! After this he went to see the show several times on his own, watching her perform, until he could pluck up courage to leave a note at the stage door, asking her to meet him. Finally, he went to the Porter and said in his faltering French "What is the name of the girl who stands on a plinth on the right of the stage in the first act, sits on a seat in the second, and dances in the third?" "Ah, monsieur, you mean our Julie," said the Porter. "All the men come and ask the same question." "Is she French?" said Israel. "No, monsieur, she comes from England, but is our darling. Everyone loves her." Israel was very relieved to learn she was English and wrote his note to her there and then, balancing on the Porter's desk. "Dear Julie, I am the man who has been here several times watching your performance, usually sitting at the second table on the right. You have seen me there and smiled each time. Please, will you have dinner with me after tomorrow night's show? If you agree, please let the Porter know and I will be waiting at the Stage Door when you have finished." He signed it 'Ever yours, Sonny.' then handed the note to the Porter, asking him to give it to her that night, who said "Au Revoir, monsieur. If it is a meeting you want I do not think Mademoiselle Julie will be interested, she turns all the fine gentlemen down." Israel smiled and said "I think she might meet me – let's wait and see. I will be here tomorrow, then we will know."

Israel and Julie had a whirlwind romance, which lasted for five weeks before he returned to London in May 1935, with a promise from Julie to write every day until she finished her contract the following August. Israel had written to his mother, telling her that he had met a wonderful English girl, called Julie Wood and that they were going to be married after she returned to England in the summer. He decided not to mention she was a dancer; it would be easier to tell her face to face when she met Julie. She was so beautiful and had such a lovely nature, he knew his mother and the rest of the family would love her as much as he did. The letters came regularly as promised, full of her love for him, and Israel was happier than he had ever been before. He answered every one, telling Julie it was only his contract with the Orchestra which was keeping him from returning to France to see her, but as they were always on the road, playing at this Concert Hall, or that Theatre, the time sped quickly by and August had arrived. Her train was due into Victoria at 11.00a.m that day, but Israel was there at 10.30a.m.wearing a new suit and trilby hat, clutching a bouquet of flowers, as he stood on the platform. He could hardly contain his excitement as the train drew into the station, and there she was, leaning out of the window waving eagerly to him, blowing kisses, until the train stopped. He ran down the platform towards her carriage as she stepped off. They were together again – finally! They clung to each other, saying "I love you, I love you," the poor flowers getting crushed between their two bodies until Julie remembered her luggage was still in her compartment. They both got on and she pointed out her two large cases and hat box on the luggage rack. Luckily a porter was going by empty-handed so Israel whistled to him and called out "Porter!" who helped them load the cases on his trolley, wheeling them to the taxi rank, as Israel and Julie clung to each other, laughing and kissing as they walked behind.

Israel had taken a week's holiday from the orchestra, so he took Julie to Leeds to meet his mother and the family and to obtain a special licence for their wedding. As he guessed, his mother was enchanted by her, and his brothers and the rest of the family could understand how he had fallen in love with this beautiful girl. When his mother had asked "What job were you doing in France when you and Sonny met?" she replied "I was a dancer at the Follies Bergere in Paris." His mother merely smiled and said "I knew you were a dancer, you move so gracefully." Israel and Julie looked at each other, secretly pleased there had been no further questioning, as he knew it could be embarrassing for her if it was revealed she had posed each night almost naked on the stage. He had met Julie's parents, who lived in Putney, the day she arrived back from France and they had immediately taken to the young man who obviously adored their daughter. The Wood family had also come from the north of England, settling in London, and were very happy and content that Julie was marrying Israel. Secretly they hoped this would mean she would not be returning to France – as their youngest child they wanted to know she was nearer to them. After their marriage, Israel rented a flat in Streatham and Julie joined the Bluebell Girls in London. The orchestra was often on the road, but they usually managed to have their weekends together, and Sunday was their day alone. On fine days they would walk in Hyde Park, feed the ducks, have lunch at a small restaurant and return home in the late afternoon. Wet days found them reading the papers, a cooked brunch, and an evening listening to the radio until that one weekend in late April when Israel returned home from a week in Manchester. When he walked through the door Julie rushed to him, threw her arms around him and said "Don't squash me with your hugs, Sonny. You had better be easier with me from now on." He pushed her gently away from him, saw her grin, and knew. Knew he was going to be a father at last! Their little daughter was born on October 16, 1937 and they named her Natalia. Israel was so proud when he and Julie took the baby to Leeds when she was just over a year old to meet all the family, Anna holding her first grandchild close to her, murmuring soft words in Russian. "She is the image of my little Rosa, except she has dark hair," she said. Rosa had been in Germany since 1936, playing with the Berlin Philharmonic, but no word had been heard from her for some months. The whole family wondered where she was. The stories and rumours of what was happening in Germany ran amongst them all, first saying one thing, then another, but out of it came one grim fact – no one knew what had happened to Rosa, nor others who had been in the orchestra with her from England. They had all disappeared.

Israel received his call-up papers just after war was declared in 1939. He was 27 years old. Most of the younger members of the orchestra had also been called up so they all said their goodbyes, with promises of keeping in touch "after the war – only be a few months!" Everyone was saying the war would not last long, but Israel and some of his friends were fearing it could be longer, particularly as Hitler had conquered Czechoslovakia and Poland already. He said a tearful goodbye to Julie and the baby, with promises to write every day, and keep safe. This was happening in many houses throughout the country at that exact moment. Men and women, saying goodbye to their loved ones – some never to return. He reported to the camp near Hounslow as instructed and joined the long queues of young men, many there willingly, ready for some excitement in their lives, whilst others wished they could just run and hide. He was a little afraid of the unknown. Would he be expected to shoot another man? Would he be able to survive long enough to see Julie and little

Natalia again? The new recruits all stood in line outside a long, white building as ordered for an interminable period until finally a bellowing sergeant major strutted along their uneven lines, eyeing them up and down, shouting orders at them – "stand up, stop slouching, pull your stomachs in." They stood there for another hour, their names being called in alphabetical order, until finally it was Israel's turn to go into the hut. He was asked to fill in forms; answer questions; then go through for a medical. The doctor had been there all day looking at white-skinned shivering men, some thin, some fat, but not many good physical specimens. He said to one of the nurses "I wish I could get off duty but this is the last batch today, thank goodness, so the quicker I get on with it, the sooner it will be over." The new intake kept coming in. "You're OK. You're OK," and so it went on. Then he came to Israel. "Breathe deeply. Turn round. Bend down. Cough. OK. Sit on that bench. Put out your feet. H'mm." He examined his feet carefully for some time and looked at Israel, standing in front of him. He looked a healthy young man, just what the army needed. Pity he would not be any use to them. "Sorry, son, can't use you. You have flat feet and fallen arches. You must have been allowed to walk badly, or your shoes were too tight when you were a child." Israel laughed out loud. "I walked well over a thousand miles as a small boy, sir, from St. Petersburg to Odessa, much of the time without shoes, and never thought I would have to rely on my feet again." The doctor looked at him in amazement. "Walked. Walked a thousand miles. I don't believe it." Israel looked at him. "I swear to you, sir, on my Father's grave, that I did. My whole family walked to escape the Bolsheviks and took many months to do it. We arrived in Odessa and then came by boat to England, where we were settled in Leeds with hundreds of other immigrants from Russia and Poland." The doctor knew this young man in front of him was telling the truth, and smiled. "I am proud of you. No wonder you have bad feet!" At that, they both started laughing and heads turned in all directions to see what the joke was. "It's a pity that you are turning me down, for I really wanted to be a soldier and fight for the country which has been so good to my family and me. Two of my brothers enlisted as soon as war was declared and both have already gone overseas." The doctor, his curiosity aroused by this young man who had walked so far, asked him what he did for a living. "I'm a musician. I was playing second fiddle with the Halle Orchestra until my call-up papers arrived." "Well, well. You might be of use to us after all," said the doctor. "Look, son, if you go through that door there, with the sign 'Rejected' you will see an office straight in front of you marked 'Entertainment Officer'. Go in, and tell him I sent you. Dr. Wilson's my name. Tell him you play the violin and see if there is anything you can do. If you really want to be involved, that is one way you can be. Better than going into munitions work, eh?" Israel thanked him, turned and went through the Rejection door. He felt very disappointed not to be joining the army, but secretly relieved that he was not going to have to fight. He knocked on the door and a voice called to him to enter. A jolly-looking middle-aged man sat at the desk and, seeing Israel, beckoned him forward. "Dr. Wilson sent me," said Israel. "He told me to tell you that I am not able to join up for active duty, but thought you might be able to use me." He spent several hours with the Entertainment Officer, whose name was Ron Bishop, who had formed an organisation called ENSA. His job was to get together musicians, comedians, vaudeville acts, singers and the like to go round the camps in England and overseas to entertain the troops. So far, they had a couple of girl singers, Ann Shelton and Vera Lynn, some comedians, but nowhere near enough musicians as most of them had been called up for active duty. He said he was keen to have young Sonny, as he had asked to be called, particularly as he played tenor sax and clarinet as well as the violin, and signed him up straight away. He said "Get yourself up to Kimmel Bay Camp in Wales within the next two or three days, where a band is being formed. Here is a travel warrant. You will be kitted out with a uniform when you get there."

Two days later Israel walked through the gates of Kimmel after a long train journey across London, changing on to a train bound for Wales. He had sat on his case for the whole journey, stuck in the corridor with dozens of other men and women – some in uniform, others reporting for active service, finally reaching Kimmel, jumping on a bus and reporting to the Camp Officer as instructed. A fierce looking sergeant had shouted at him to join the ranks of civilians who were standing around in groups, looking lost, and who had obviously just arrived in the backs of lorries. They were a motley looking bunch of men – young, all of them, some thin, some fat, some well-dressed, some scruffy. Israel thought to himself they would all look the same when they got their uniforms on in an hour or so. Most of the men carried small cases or hold-alls, and so he picked up his instruments, hoisted his haversack on his back and went to join them. After a short time an officer strutted towards them, together with a huge, tall sergeant major who bellowed at them "Get in line, you miserable lot," and the two men proceeded to walk up and down the three rows of men, making a remark here, a remark there. "You, stand up straight. You, pull your stomach in." Giving orders to many of them, until he came to Israel. "You, get your hair cut or get a violin." Israel grinned at him and, holding his violin case up at waist level, said "Sorry sir, but I've got a violin." A huge roar of laughter came from the ranks of men, including the officer, who saw the funny side of it – it had broken the ice; given them a break from the thoughts of the dangers facing them, and put him firmly down as the camp comic. The Sergeant Major had the grace to smile too but glared at him. "You think you're a comedian, do you, sonny Jim?" "No sir, just a musician. I've come to join the band," he said. "What's your name?" asked the sergeant major. "Sonny Levinsky" he replied. Again more guffaws of laughter and the Sergeant Major grew red in the face and said "You may think you are funny, young man, but let me tell you, I've got your number. I'm going to make it hell for you in here – then we will see whether you are still 'Sunny'." He carried on down the line, shouting directions at most of them, then stood in the middle of the square and said "You are here to learn to be soldiers. You will drill every minute of every day until I turn you into those men. Believe me, you will wish you hadn't been born. Stay in line until your name is called, then go through into those barracks over there. You, Levinsky, you miserable little toad. You shouldn't be here at all. You should be over in the large mess, where they are collecting you lot together. Clear off." He pointed over the campus towards a brick building so Israel picked up his violin, adjusted his haversack, got his other instrument case and walked off in the direction the Sergeant major had indicated.

The hall was full of people; men and women, some in uniform, some not. There were a couple of pianos, with groups of singers around them obviously practising, and a crowd of musicians were sitting ready to start playing, their music spread out before them and their instruments being wiped or tuned up. There was a lot of activity going on and, as Israel entered, he turned and looked to the back of the hall, where a group of young women were practising a dance routine, their tap shoes making a staccato beat on the wooden floorboards. He walked up to one of the pianos. "Excuse me, I've been told to report here to join ENSA." The band leader slapped him on the back. "Welcome aboard, we're very pleased to have you. My name is Nat Gonella. What instrument do you play?" Israel said "The fiddle, but I play a fair clarinet and tenor sax, although I don't have my own sax. If you've got a spare I don't mind playing any music which doesn't call for strings." "Do you read music?" asked Nat. "Oh, yes, I've been a musician all my life. Got a scholarship to the Royal Academy when I was a boy, and played with the Halle for a number of years, before becoming second fiddle." "Oh, ho. A real musician, boys, not just another busker," said Nat. "He'll make you sit up and take notice. What's your name?" He told him, calling himself Sonny Levy as he thought this would be easier than "Levinsky," although he was very proud of his name. He was then introduced to all the boys in the band, shown where to leave his bag, and within fifteen minutes they were well into their first rehearsal. It seemed to Israel that the bandleader, a man called Sid, was keen to find out what all of them were capable of, and just how much they knew. The sound they made together wasn't bad for a first attempt, but he knew they needed a lot of practice, not just to learn the pieces they would play, but to find out how much they needed to know about each other's ability. He soon realised that the majority of them were definitely not "buskers', but good, competent musicians, whose main love in life was to play music.

In the winter of 1941, when Natalia was four years old, Julie had finally persuaded Israel that she wanted to get back to dancing and join ENSA too, instead of having to work in the munitions factory near Streatham where she was living in the house they had rented when Natalia was born. This meant that most of the time she was being left with neighbours, and now there was the risk of bombing it would be better if she could be evacuated to the country as many children had been. Israel was very concerned about Natalia, but Julie had done her homework and discovered that, in some cases, the Army would put children in boarding schools if their parents were doing essential war work. He pointed out that 'dancing' could not exactly be called 'essential war work', but finally agreed that if their daughter could be placed in a good school then he would see if he could use his influence to get Julie a job dancing with the chorus girls who travelled with them from show to show. He knew that when she was single, before meeting him, she had worked in Paris at the Lido before the Folies Bergere and, with this experience behind her, she had got through the audition to join the Bluebell Girls in London, so was a very talented dancer – far more than a chorus girl - but that was what she wanted to do – not stuck in a factory, or even volunteering to work on a farm as a land girl. He sensed her heart lay in the theatre, and she was very keen to get back on the stage. It might even mean that they would be together some of the time.

In March 1942 news came through to Julie that

Natalia had finally been given a place at Queenswood Girls School, in Potters Bar, Middlesex, with an army scholarship. This meant she would be safe from the air raids and bombing which were taking place almost nightly over London. Julie had been in tears when she and Israel said goodbye to their little daughter, looking so grown up in her navy blue blazer with red trim, and her cream Panama hat. "Mummy, why are you leaving me here. When will you be back? Will it be soon?" All the questions that the little girl could think of. "I will be back very soon, Dushka, but I have to go and be with Daddy for a little while. Aunty Mem and Uncle Bill will visit you often, and when you have any holidays you can stay with them at their house, and I can come there and be with you too. Won't that be fun?" Israel knew that Emily, Julie's sister, and Bill her brother-in-law, were Natalia's favourites, and now that their two sons, Sid and Len, had both been called up they could devote all their attention to their little niece. She would be safe with them. The Headmistress had told them they were a very mixed bunch of girls at the school, and as most of the teachers had been called up or were doing essential war work many had been replaced by nuns from a local teaching order. She said the children came from all over the country – the daughters of army personnel, some Catholic, some Church of England, some Jewish, but there had been a large intake of Polish girls, whose fathers' had managed to get to England and bring their families with them. Israel knew Natalia seemed very happy there, from the news he received from Emily, but wished he could get to visit her more often.

During the early years of the war Israel travelled all over Europe and the Far and Near East, playing in camps in the pouring rain; the icy wind and snow; and the boiling sun. He and Julie managed to spend some time together at first, but in 1943 Julie joined another dance troupe, which was immediately sent to the Middle East, and so they lost touch with each other, only rarely receiving letters as mail was not getting through – most of it being lost in bombing raids or going down with the many ships which were being sunk in the Atlantic and Pacific Oceans. He knew they both missed their little daughter very much, but was encouraged by the letters from Emily and Bill which did reach him, saying she appeared happy at school, was making friends and coming to them for every one of the holidays. England was at war! A war which secretly everyone feared was being lost. It meant being parted from wives, husbands, children and families, and Israel never failed to admire the courage of all the soldiers, sailors and air force crews he met, who all talked longingly of "home", and whilst he wished he could have been in the thick of the fighting he felt pleased that he was at least contributing something to the war effort, even if it was only to boost the morale of all the brave men and women he met on a daily basis. Many famous names in show business were always joining them to entertain the troops, either to sing or tell jokes, and one of the highlights had been when Glenn Miller arrived with his band, the Squadronaires. What a great musical sound they made, really unique, and how the troops loved to dance when they played. The Americans had shown them how to 'jitterbug' and at every musical show, when he and his band played, the floor would be full of boys and girls doing the crazy dance routine. Israel had been allowed to form his own small group, called Sonnelli and his Tzigany music, when he found four other violinists all specialising in Tzigany and Gypsy music. They had found time to rehearse between shows for several weeks before they knew they were ready to appear, and he was very pleased with his 'boys'. There was Phil Benjamin, a young Jewish lad from Golders Green; Larry Barnes from Liverpool; Roy Williams from Coulsdon and Frankie Goldberg, another Jewish boy, from Sheffield. Frankie's father was a tailor and after he had begged some faulty parachute silk from one of the factories they visited, he made them some wonderful costumes in the traditional Hungarian style – tops with the Magyar full sleeves, dyeing the sashes and throat scarves with red dye, and colouring the strips for the sleeve trims with green ink. The ingenuity that went into their costumes amazed Israel and, teamed up with normal black dinner suit trousers, they made a dashing group and really looked the part. They played all the popular music – Black Eyes, Czardas, and when they met a group of Polish officers who had managed to escape to England they were delighted to learn some of their music too. His group were all accomplished musicians and once they had heard a melody being hummed a few times could easily play it by ear. Their reputation spread, and soon they were as much in demand as the bands of Billy Cotton, Harry Roy and Sid Millward, all formed through ENSA to entertain the troops and to play in munition factories all over England. The big break came one day when Israel was up in Scotland, playing his Tzigany music at an army camp in Ochtamuchty. A man approached him and said "I understand you have formed this group yourself." He nodded and then introduced all of them. "My name is George Elrick and I was a music agent in peacetime. I like the sound you make and I think you have something which would go down well on radio. I have got together a new radio programme called 'Workers Playtime' which goes out live from factories all over England at lunchtime. If you are interested I will give you a spot." Israel beamed at the others. "Interested? I should say we are. When do we start, and where do we go?" George outlined his plans, saying he would make all the necessary arrangements, asking them to report to a factory in Manchester in a week's time, stressing that they were never to talk about where they would be playing, not even amongst themselves, as the locations must never be revealed to the enemy in case they then bombed the factories.

The broadcast was over in the factory, and Israel knew that it had gone well. The audience, always rapturous in their applause, had whistled and clapped for some time and the others doing the show with him – Jimmy Edwards, Terry Thomas and Ann Shelton, had congratulated them all, saying how good the music had sounded. He had rung his brother, Nat, to tell him to listen to the radio on the day they were due to broadcast and about a week later, when they met, Nat kept telling him how great it had been and how much all the family had enjoyed listening to it. That was the beginning, and after this Sonnelli and his Tzigany Music, as they were now called, could not keep up with the demand for them to appear. Shows were being broadcast from theatres, music halls, munition factories and ENSA – they were never in one place for more than a couple of days. The boys' wives had learned to live with this – at least they were safe and not away fighting in the war, but London was being attacked night after night in heavy air raids, as were most of the large cities throughout the country, and so they were in just as much danger during their travels as if they were fighting. Israel heard from Julie at long last, after a silence of several months, and was relieved to learn that she had returned to England, dancing at the Windmill Theatre, 'The theatre which never closes', in London with her friend Peggy Hunterman. Her husband, Abe, was a trumpet player with Billy Cotton, and Israel and Abe had been at school together in Leeds as boys, so he took the opportunity of meeting up with him again when they were playing at the same camp. Both men were glad their wives were no longer overseas – although there was heavy bombing in London they somehow felt they were safer in their own country than abroad. Julie was living in the basement at the Windmill Theatre with all the other girls, which was as safe as the Underground stations where most Londoners were sheltering during the raids, and getting to and from Streatham to their house was difficult with the shortage of buses, particularly at night. She wrote to Israel to let him know she had not been able to get to Potters Bar to see Natalia since her return to England but had promised she would go to Emily's at Christmas so that they could all be together. Israel knew there was no chance of him getting down south then – he was stuck in the North most of the time as that was where many of the factories and military camps were based. His sister, Gittle, was working as a Land Girl on a farm near Bradford, and he had managed to see her a couple of times when he was able to visit his Mother in Leeds. She had found herself a really nice boy, Ronny, who was in the Air Force and he had asked Israel's permission, as head of the family to get married "as soon as the war was over." Both his brothers, David and Isaac, were reported "Missing, presumed dead," which his Mother took very badly, crying out that God was punishing her for some unknown sin she had committed, blaming herself for allowing them to join up, despite Israel telling her over and over again they would have been called up anyway. He tried to stress to her that until they received word that the boys were actually dead there was still hope. He reminded her that all through that terrible journey across Russia neither she nor his father had ever given up hope.

Israel had now been given the rank of Captain, and his men were all sergeants, wearing their army uniforms with pride. In early 1944 he was finally able to visit his little daughter at her school. It was three years since he had seen her and she was now nearly seven years old. He didn't recognise her as she came flying down the main steps to greet him when he arrived. "Daddy, Daddy, you've come. You're here. I couldn't believe it when the Headmistress said you were coming. Is that your car. How posh – just like my friend Barbara Oyler's." He was as thrilled as she was to be reunited. She had certainly changed! She was very thin, with long black plaits, horn-rimmed glasses and her teeth stuck out. He hoped that something could be done about her teeth – he must speak to Matron before leaving that day. He opened up the boot of the car and got out a bike he had been able to find. Although second-hand he had cleaned it up and it didn't look too bad. Natalia was overjoyed – the best present she had ever had. She jumped up and down with glee "Can I take it home with me to Aunty Mems next holidays?" she asked. "Of course you can. But can you ride it?" he said. She beamed up at him. "Oh yes. When I go to Barbara's she lets me ride hers. I'm really good, and I have wished for ages that I could have my own bike. Now I have one. Oh, Daddy, thank you so much." Sonny felt the tears welling up in his eyes as she threw her arms around his waist. He had been worried that she would resent the fact that he had not visited her for such a long time but she did not seem to mind at all. At least she seemed happy. He took hold of her hand and they went into the school, with Natalia pulling him along to the Head's office, impatient to be off for the promised treat in the village tea shop. The Head welcomed him and asked Natalia to wait outside whilst she talked to her father. He felt a bit anxious at this – was there a problem? Was she misbehaving? Somehow he didn't think so. She looked at him and smiled. "Capt. Levinsky, your daughter is such a joy. A really lovely girl. She is willing to help any of the new girls, particularly the foreign ones who don't speak English, and she gets her school work done without any complaints. She is good at history and arithmetic, and excels at English, but does find Latin and Geography difficult. As you know, she doesn't play any sports because of her slight heart condition, which is a pity, but she always sits on the sidelines and cheers on her particular favourites. However, from my point of view, she tries hard – which is all we can ask. She has some special friends, mostly day girls, and spends Exeats with them when she is not going to Putney to your sister-in-law. All in all, she is doing well." Israel looked at her and smiled. "It's a great relief to my wife and I to know that she is in such good hands. If she was unhappy her behaviour and work would have been affected, but when she is with Emily she chatters away about what she has done, where she has been, and whose house she has visited. I agree it would be better if she could play tennis and netball, but doesn't seem to mind at all. Does the school doctor think her condition is serious?" The head looked across her desk at him. "Oh no. She simply drops one in eight heartbeats, which means her heart has a minor fault, which prevents her from any real activity, but she enjoys riding her friends' bikes, and is often seen running across the playing fields to join her class. The doctor has stressed that she is very fit, but should not take any heavy exercise. I understand she sleeps and eats well, which is more than can be said for some of my other pupils." Israel said to her "I hope it is alright with you, but I managed to get hold of a small bike in really good condition so I have brought it with me today. Can she keep it here at the school?" "Of course," said the Head. "Many of our boarders have their bikes here, and they are stored in one of the outbuildings, so are safe. It is a pity that you and your wife are not able to visit more often, but I fully understand why you can't, and have to say that I really enjoy hearing you play on the radio. Maybe when this ghastly war is over you would bring your band here on Founders Day." He said "I would be delighted. Nothing would give my boys and I greater pleasure. I know that you have lots of Polish children here and they would know some of my Tzigany music. Maybe we can get some of their parents here too, if they are still in Britain. The situation does seem to be easing and Mr. Churchill seems to think we have reached the 'beginning of the end' – what a great way with words he has, don't you think? Thank you so much for the news of my daughter. It is a great relief to know that she seems to be doing so well. I plan to take her out for tea now, and will make sure she is back in time for supper. It would have been nice if we could have ridden into the village together so she could try out her new bike, but that will have to wait for another time." The Head looked at him. "If you want to cycle, then there is a perfectly good man's bike in the shed, which the Gardener uses when he is riding around the grounds. You can use that, if you want." Israel was delighted, and said "That will be a real treat for Natalia, so I will take you up on your kind offer. We will not be too long as I have a show to do this evening. Entertaining some Canadians – can't tell you where, of course, but as I am based just outside London at the moment it will not take me too long to get back." He grinned at her with a twinkle in his eye and she smiled back. "Have a good time with Natalia, and we look forward to seeing you here again as soon as you can. She talks about you and your wife all the time, but she really does understand that it is very difficult for you to visit. Your in-laws have really helped with this. When the staff know you are going to be on the radio we let her listen if possible. You should see her beaming smile when you play." He said goodbye, with a promise to keep in touch and left her office. Natalia was skipping up and down the corridor and rushed to his side when she saw him. "Can we go now, Daddy? I am really very hungry." He took her small hand in his and they went outside.

The village was not very far away and soon they were cycling through the countryside, Natalia's little legs peddling furiously to keep up with him. It was a beautiful day, warm and sunny, perfect for a bike ride. "Shall we stop for tea soon, midget?" Israel said, after they had ridden a few miles. 'Midget' was his pet name for her – why, he didn't know. "Yes please, Daddy, I'm awfully hungry and tired. I would love a drink." "Right, as soon as we see somewhere we will stop." They had got off their bikes now, puffing and panting, to walk up the steep hill. They reached the top and, looking down the road, he could see a small teashop at the bottom with tables and chairs outside. "We'll go there. Race you to the bottom." They set off, Israel free-wheeling, letting his bike pick up momentum, with his little daughter peddling away beside him. "Slow down, darling, you are going too fast. Put your brakes on," he cried out to her, for she had now gone ahead of him and he could see that she was trying to brake. "Daddy, daddy, the brakes won't work. I can't stop." She was yelling now, obviously frightened, for the hill was quite steep and she was going very fast. He started to peddle so that he could catch up with her, for he had seen to his horror that the teashop stood on a crossroad, and there was traffic going across, obviously a main road. He was sweating. Not just with the heat but with the panic that was building up inside him. "God, I must somehow stop her. I must do something before we reach the crossroad," he thought. "Hang on, Natalia, keep upright. I'm coming." The road was getting nearer and nearer to them as they sped faster and faster down the hill. He knew what he had to do. He cycled up level with her and, reaching out, grabbed the handlebars of the little bike. He braked furiously on his own bike, tugging at the other one in an effort to slow it down. The next thing he knew they were both lying in a muddled heap in the road, with Natalia crying, and both cycles tangled up together, their wheels still spinning wildly from the speed they had built up. Luckily she was not badly hurt, only a grazed knee and hand, and a bit bruised and shaken, but he could see blood running down his leg through a large tear in his trousers. "Oh Daddy, you're hurt," she cried. "It is nothing, Dushka, just a cut." He knew it was more than a cut, though, from the amount of blood he was losing. He took his handkerchief out and, lifting up his leg he saw a large hole, which he quickly bound up. He knew what had caused it – the pedal had stuck in his calf as he had fallen. A woman rushed out of the teashop. She had obviously seen what had happened for she quickly came over to them, tut tutting over Natalia and helping to brush her down. "There, there, dear, don't cry. You're alright. A nasty turn you had. What happened?" Israel explained to her what had occurred and she took them both into the teashop, through to the back and into her own sitting room. Getting a bowl of warm water she undid the handkerchief on his leg and got some clean bandage to do it up. "There," she said "you'll live. Nasty old cut, though. You'll have to keep it clean." He thanked her, grateful for her help, and watched as she bathed Natalia's knees and hands, removing some of the grit and dirt from the grazes. "Lucky it wasn't worse, dear," she said. Natalia, sniffing, now smiling through her tears, said she was alright, but could she have a drink. "Course you can. Nice cup of tea and some toasted teacakes will make you feel much better, won't it?" Natalia nodded and smiled at her father. Soon they were tucking into a really good tea, with real butter and jam on the bread, scones, and some little cakes. What a treat. Natalie looked up at him and said "We never have butter on our bread, you know. We get jam or marge, but never both. I hate the cabbage. It is pink when it is served up, it's been boiled too long. So Mrs. Oyler and Aunty Mem say. As for the custard! It is really, really horrid. So thick they cut it up in chunks and we have to eat it. I promise you when I leave school I will never eat custard, semolina or tapioca ever again." "Darling, you might be here for a long time yet. The war is still going on, and Mummy and I are never home for more than a couple of days together. The good thing is you have your friends to go to at Exeat and you love going to Emily and Bill. You are safe here, so I want you to be brave and stick it out." She looked at him and said, tearfully, "At least I still have you and Mummy. Some of the girls here don't have any parents at all and are really sad. Some of the Jewish girls in my dorm with me cry every night as they have been told their parents have died, particularly the Polish and French ones. Do you know, some of them were smuggled out of their countries before the Germans could take them prisoner and had the most awful time getting to England." Israel looked at her. "I know exactly what they have been through. When I was a small boy I had to walk across Russia with my parents, your aunts Helena and Rosa, and your Great Uncle Nathan and his family. We were fleeing from the Bolsheviks. You won't remember them, I suppose, as you were only a baby when we were all last together in Leeds. Maybe they will teach you about them in your history lessons. Your Headmistress told me you did not really like Geography but if you can remember the names you should ask your teacher to show you St. Petersburg, Minsk and Odessa on the map, and you will see where we all walked to escape. It took us many months. When you are older I will tell you all about it, and you must get your aunts and Grandmother to tell you too. It was a really terrible journey, and even though I was too young to understand then, I know now what a difficult time it was for us all, and often wonder how we managed to survive. Thank God for some very kind people we met on our journey." He took a piece of paper out of his breast pocket and wrote down the names of the three places he had mentioned so that she could look them up on the Atlas. Natalia was looking at him in amazement at what he had just told her and said "I am really going to try much harder to understand geography and I will ask the teacher to show me a map of Russia and the places you have told me about. Maybe I can try to make sense out of all those coloured squares on the map of Africa. Some of the place names are so difficult to pronounce, but I will try my best."

When they had eaten their tea and got over the shock of their accident Israel said it was time to leave. He thanked the owner of the teashop once again for all her help, and then picked up the bikes from the garden at the side where he had placed them. Miraculously they were not badly damaged and could still be ridden, so they made their way slowly back to school, only riding on the flat road and walking up and down the hill. Sonny felt very guilty at not having checked the brakes on Natalia's bike, but it had never occurred to him to do so. It had looked in such good condition. When they arrived back he took her to Matron's office, telling her what had happened, and apologised for the dirty marks and slight tear in her skirt. He asked if she could arrange for his daughter to be seen by a dentist to try and straighten her teeth, and he would contact her as soon as he could get to London again to pay for any treatment which was necessary. He also gave her some money, asking her to ensure that the brakes on the bike were repaired before it was ridden again. Israel wrapped his arms around Natalia as he said goodbye. He would not let her see his face for she would see the tears welling up, but the damage was done. She was crying and clinging on to him, and soon they were crying together. He knelt down, looked at her, and took out his handkerchief. "Come now. No more tears. We have had a lovely afternoon, even if we did have a crash and I tore my trousers, but I must get back to London as I am on the radio tonight. No doubt your teacher will let you listen. Dry your eyes and give me a smile. I don't want to remember you with a long face, now do I?" She dried her eyes and gave him a final hug, then turned and ran up the steps, calling out "Thank you for my lovely bicycle. I love you." And she was gone. He sighed, climbed into the car and set off for his barracks. He promised himself he would not leave it so long before his next visit, and maybe could even manage to bring Julie with him. He thought he must try and get the Oyler's address from the Head and drop them a note to thank them for their kindness to Natalia. She was obviously very fond of her school friend, Barbara, and her family. She had chatted about two other girls, Marilyn Kane and Sally Schaffler, and it seemed as if all three families were farmers in the area. Children exaggerate, he knew, but from what she had told him about their houses and their cars, and the fun they had on the farms, they all seemed pretty well off. Maybe after the war, he would be able to provide Julie and her with a nice house and fancy car and she could have her friends to stay, and he could repay their kindness. Certainly, the car he had borrowed for the day from the barracks left a lot to be desired, but at least it was transport and the chief mechanic had made sure there was sufficient petrol in it to get him back there.

The war was finally over! 'Peace in our time' were the words Churchill had used. Israel and his group had been in Cairo for several months where they had been touring the camps, playing their music and joining other artists who were with ENSA. Now finally they were back in England. What celebrations there were! All over England, the crowds had been out in their hundreds, singing and dancing in the streets throughout the night; streets decorated with strings of bunting; wives, mothers and girlfriends joyously greeting their men as they arrived at the railway stations and docks. Hordes of people had streamed into the Mall, singing Rule

Brittania and cheering the King and Queen when they appeared on the balcony of Buckingham Palace, not letting them go until the two Princesses joined them, both in uniform, laughing and waving at the crowd. But the war wasn't over for all of them. The Japanese had not yet surrendered, so the battles were still raging in the Far East. Julie was dancing at the Windmill every night, and told Israel she had managed to see Natalia a few times, whose letters had been full of how well she was doing, how grown up she looked with her short curly hair now that her plaits had been cut off, and she was wearing braces on her teeth, complaining how uncomfortable they were, but Israel knew that she would be grateful they had been fitted when she was a bit older. Julia told him she was going to get hold of a camera if possible and take some photos when they were next together.

One morning after the band had returned to England he was asked to report to the Colonel's office. He entered the room and sat down on the chair indicated, puzzled as to why he should be asked there, together with two five-star generals, a colonel and another captain. "Captain Levinsky, we understand that you speak fluent Russian and excellent Polish. Is that right?" asked the Colonel. He said yes, wondering what this was all leading up to. "We have a proposition to put to you. What we are about to discuss is highly confidential, you understand, and if you decide that you cannot accept, then we will need your absolute assurance that you will not disclose our idea to anyone. Is that understood?" Israel nodded and again said yes, so the Colonel continued. "We want you to become a DADPR - Deputy Assistant Director, Public Relations. This will just be a nominal title for you, as a cover-up for the work you would really be doing. You will be attached to a special unit which has been formed here in England to try and ferret out some of the spies who are inevitably coming over with the Polish officers, and the SS men who are managing to escape here from Europe. There are also some Russians amongst them, although most of them are still over there, but we are very short of interpreters. The work is top secret, of course, and you won't be able to continue in ENSA whilst you are doing it. What your job would be mainly concerns the interrogation of these men, and some women too, in an attempt to check their stories. You may be sent over to Germany if the situation arises. These people will have good, solid backgrounds if they are spies and will need intense questioning, but with some training from our specialists in this field it would not be too difficult for you to tackle - it is the language which is our main problem." He looked at Israel. "What do you say, Levinsky?" He was flattered – flattered that they should pick him and, secondly, that they thought his Polish good enough to be of use to them. "My Polish is not that brilliant. I only learned it from my aunt and two cousins when I was a small boy, and from a school friend in Leeds who couldn't speak Russian or English. It was a case of both of us learning each other's language in order to be able to talk to each other. Of course, Russian is my mother tongue, but I am a bit rusty on that, too." "Don't worry," said the Colonel. "First of all, you will go on a special course for a month, where you will speak nothing but the two languages – no English at all. You will be briefed in everything you need to know and trained in the special kind of interrogation required for this work. What's your answer?" Israel looked at all of them, not really believing for one minute that he was to be given a choice anyway. "I am very flattered that you have asked me, and of course I am prepared to do it. When do you want me to leave ENSA?" "You will get your orders in a couple of days, and told where to report, but you must understand that this is top secret. When the training is over you will be based somewhere in middle England – I cannot be more precise at this moment in time. We will concoct some story for ENSA, and just tell your band you are moving to a different area. You will not be able to leave your new base for any reason because of security, and in case you are recognized," said the Colonel. Israel nodded, then rising with the other men, who had remained silent throughout the conversation, he gave a salute and turned to leave. "One more thing, Levinsky. Whatever you see, or hear, say nothing - it will be the best advice."

Israel was able to spend a brief spell of leave with Julia and Natalia before reporting for his new assignment. He knew his wife was very disappointed that they could not be together now the war was finally over, particularly as he could not tell her what work he was doing, nor where he was based. The address was just the usual "BFPO" and its number, and he was not allowed any phone calls, which he knew she found strange. Natalia remained at school and Julia continued with ENSA, travelling to the camps still situated throughout England.

Then came the dreadful news – his sister Rosa had been found, barely alive, in Belsen Concentration Camp. She was suffering from starvation as well as TB, but was being looked after by the Army doctors in Germany, who hoped she would recover. She was too ill to travel at the moment, and the information the Red Cross had given Mama was that it would be many months before she would be returned to the UK. But for the moment she was alive. They also had confirmation that his two brothers, David and Isaac, had both died in concentration camps; David in Treblinka in 1943 and Isaac in 1944 in Auschwitz Birkenau, Lager BII, next to the camp where Rosa had been, so now the family knew they were not "missing" but would never see them again. Israel asked for some compassionate leave, and although his Commanding Officer had stressed that he would not be allowed to leave the base once he took up his new post, agreed that these were extenuating circumstances and he should be allowed to be with his family. He also agreed that Israel could phone the Windmill and leave a message for Julia. He travelled home with a heavy heart, knowing how distressed his Mother and the rest of the family would be at the news. "Two brothers gone – what use has it all been," he asked himself.

Israel arrived home to find the house in darkness, all the mirrors covered, and his Mother and sisters dressed in black, sitting on hard wooden seats, surrounded by the rest of the family. He gathered his mother's frail body up in his arms, tears streaming down his face, trying to console her weeping, but without success. "Come, Mama. Try and stop crying. David and Isaac would not want you to mourn them in this way. You will make yourself ill. You must be strong, as you always have been, for the rest of us." Finally, her sobs stopped, and she looked up at her son and said "You are such a comfort to me. You are right, we must mourn the dead, but go on with life for the living." There was no food in the house and it was obvious that no-one had eaten since the terrible news had been received but once he was home he took over from Ronnie, Gittle's fiancé, and the Rabbi arranged Kaddish for the following day. Israel spoke to his brother, Nathan, after the prayers had been said. "You are now the man of the house here. I cannot stay any longer as I was only given a forty-eight-hour pass, and have to get back. Look after Mama, and I will try and get home again in a couple of weeks, but I am not supposed to leave the base so let me know how she is. Ronnie, you have been such a comfort to Gittle, Helena and Esther. I look on you as a brother already, and part of our family, even though you are not yet married, and hope that you will be able to help them through this terrible time. Thank God one of them is still alive, even though the news about Rosa is not good. Let's hope and pray she will be well enough to come home soon." He left the house with a heavy heart, fearing that this might be the last time he saw his mother alive; she had appeared so frail and had aged a thousand years.

Israel received regular letters from Nathan which were encouraging, as his mother appeared to be coping well, and had returned to her normal way of life. He never mentioned the boys, but wrote constantly of Rosa, whose condition remained critical, but at least she was still alive. Esther had married her American boyfriend and returned to the States with him when his unit was sent home. Although his mother and the rest of the family were sad to see her go they knew she was going to have a much better life over there. Israel had been in his new job for some months, after being put through a gruelling few weeks at the language school and an intense training course. He had felt both flattered and honoured that he should have been chosen for this job, but it was a tremendous drain on him mentally and emotionally, for so many of the men broke under the strain of the interrogation and confessed that they were runaway S.S. officers, or ordinary German soldiers fearing execution for desertion at the front as the war in Europe had drawn to a close and finally ended. So many of them had been found hiding in barns and haylofts as the Allies made their way across Germany, but they had been rounded up and put into POW camps, nothing like the terrible places which had been discovered in Germany and Poland, full of Jews, who had died in their millions. He knew with a certainty that the atrocities of those camps would never occur again, and with the help of his sister Rosa, who had miraculously survived, the culprits would be found and put to death. She was still very ill when she was brought back to England, and was in an isolation hospital in Surrey, still suffering from malnutrition, but with the added complication of consumption. Israel knew he was not supposed to leave the large country house and grounds where he worked in case he was recognised but approached his Commanding Officer once again asking for compassionate leave, explaining the reason and giving a brief outline of what Rosa had been through during the war. His C.O. had agreed, but only on the condition that a staff car would take him to the hospital and the escort stay with him at all times for security. When the day arrived for his visit he entered the ward, wondering how he would be able to hold back the tears when he saw his sister. His escort stayed discreetly at the entrance as Israel walked down to the bed pointed out by the Ward Sister but he was not prepared for the shock of seeing how ill and emaciated Rosa still was. She had hung on to his hand and vowed she would live long enough to tell the world what had happened in those places of death. She told him it was not until she was finally brought back to England from the hospital in Germany, where she had been taken after the liberation of Belsen, that she had discovered her brother David had died in Treblinka and Isaac in Auschwitz Birkenau and could not believe the two of them had been so near to each other. She said she tried to keep it out of her mind how they would have been killed – Beaten? Starved? Tortured? Or even worse, experimented on as she had been. Israel hoped and prayed she would not die before she got her chance to give evidence – there were so many like her, with incredible tales of how they had survived, and how they all wanted the same thing – revenge!

Those four Germans he had interrogated yesterday. They were adamant they were Russians and had been wearing German uniforms because they were spies. They spoke fluent Russian and had known where they came from and names of places in and around their homes. Two of the men apparently came from the same village in the Urals, of which Israel had little or no knowledge, so he had asked that a colleague, Captain Ivan Sobovsky, deal with them – but these other two! The more he thought about their story, the more he thought they were lying. How to trap them - or prove their innocence. He drummed his fingers gently on the desk, oblivious to the fact that it was one of Bach's violin concertos he was tapping out. Suddenly it came to him. He sat up. Of course, that was it. That was why he was sure they were lying. He knew it. He was recalling those very early days, when he was six and the night they were leaving St. Petersburg. What was it his father had said, that night he had witnessed the massacre by the Bolsheviks. "The vast golden dome of St. Isaacs Cathedral, near the Arch of the Permskaya Zastava, with the Synagogue nearby." The two men had talked about St. Isaacs, with its silver dome and they said it had a spire. A spire! A silver dome. That was it! That was the clue. He reached forward and rang the bell. A soldier entered, saluted, and said "Yes, sir." "Please ask Sergei Bolstevsky and Igor Politovski to come and see me right away, and on your way, drop in on Captain Zukov and ask him if he could come immediately – tell him it's urgent." The soldier saluted, turned smartly on his heel, and went out of the door, shutting it quietly behind him. Within a few minutes, Captain Zukov knocked and entered. "You wanted me, Sonny." "Yes, Leo. You know yesterday I told you I had my doubts about those two supposed Russian soldiers, well, now I know why I was suspicious." He then related the story he remembered from his father, finishing off with a slap to his knee. "We've got them, Leo. We've got them. Let's see what the two devils have to say again. Play dumb, and see if we can't trap them. I'm now sure that they are either SS officers on the run, or genuine German spies, don't you agree?" Leo nodded, smiling. Sonny knew his friend admired his expertise in this game of cat and mouse. Every day he was wheedling out these criminals who were so cleverly trying to hide their true identities.

It was over! "What an ordeal that had been," said Israel to himself. Both men had been adamant right to the end that they were Russian officers unlawfully arrested. It was only when he had played his winning hand regarding St. Isaac's Cathedral that first one of the men and then the other had confessed. Both had been interrogated separately, and both caught out on the same details. Israel had one thing to say for them; they had both got their stories word-perfect and were obviously very senior German officers. Whether they were SS or not he would never know, for now, they would pass on to another section for trial. The Bach music was again going through his mind, and he found himself unconsciously humming the beautiful melody from the Concerto in A minor. He would be playing it for the officers at the house tonight and hoped the concert would be a huge success. Several of his old ENSA chums were also taking part and it was only now he realised just how much he had missed his music during the many months he had been there. He had made up his mind that he was going to speak to his Commanding Officer tomorrow. He wanted to go home. He wanted to be with Julia and Natalia, and the new baby when it arrived, and he wanted to be back in the world of music. He missed it so much.

Peace. Peace at last, and Israel was going home, after two years interrogating soldiers. After six long, hard years, peace had come in both Europe and Asia, as Japan had finally surrendered after bombs had been dropped on Hiroshima and Nagasaki. There had been singing in the streets, singing in the pubs, singing everywhere. Linking arms with total strangers and doing the Palais Glide, the Conga and the Hokey Kokey. People had been smiling, and nothing could make them sad at this time, only those who had lost loved ones during those terrible years. He walked down the street, his beloved violin in one hand, his clarinet in the other and a kit bag over his shoulder. There wasn't a taxi to be seen at the station, and the streets were so full of people, just milling about, that he knew it would be quicker to walk. As he neared his house his pace quickened. He was anxious to open it up in readiness for tomorrow when Julie was arriving from Wales, and then they would go and collect Natalia from his sister-in-law. He expected it would be pretty cold and damp inside, but hoped to be able to scrounge some coal and light the two fires downstairs, which would soon air the house through. After all, it was late summer and with some fresh air in the place, it would soon be back to normal. Normal, he thought to himself. Would the world ever be normal again? He wondered if he and Julie could pick up the threads of their lives again after so many years apart. He had only seen her three times in the last four years when they were both abroad, and then once for a weekend at the camp where he was stationed in England when she had managed to get a pass. She had seen Natalia on about five occasions, but even between them, they had not been able to see their little daughter as often as they would have wanted. Of course, they had written, but letters were not the same. Now she was expecting the baby very soon, and he wanted the house ready for when they came home from the hospital. He wondered if Natalia ever rode her bike now after that awful episode on the hill – she had written in her last little letter to him that she would like a scooter, they were so much safer! He chuckled to himself. There were only five more houses and he would be there. He looked ahead and stopped dead in his tracks. What the devil? The front door and windows were open. Some of the glass was smashed. "Oh, no. God. No. What has happened?" he asked himself. He started to run as fast as his awkward load would let him. He ran up the path and stood in horror in the open doorway. Where was the hall stand, the rugs, the stair carpet? He walked slowly in, sliding his kitbag off his shoulder and placing his violin gently on the floor as if it might also disappear like everything else if he was not careful. He opened the door into the dining room – it was totally empty – even the curtain rails had gone. He turned and went into the living room. Again, the place was bare, except for his beautiful walnut bureau, filled to capacity with all his musical scores, arrangements and pieces.

The glass fronts had been smashed by whoever had robbed them in an endeavour to open the doors, but Sonny knew the locks were foolproof, the bureau had been made by his cousin, Schicky. Obviously, it had been so heavy the thieves could not move it. The kitchen was devoid of everything, except for the old copper in the corner, attached to the wall with brackets. Every pot and plate had gone. He frantically opened and closed the cupboards, almost as if the missing china would be spirited back into place. What would Julie say – her home, her precious home, had all gone. Thank God most of the valuable stuff had been given to his brother Nathan to look after when Julie left, but that was silver and cutlery, and not the everyday things which he knew they could not possibly replace overnight. He walked up the stairs very slowly, as if he had lead weights in his shoes. It was the same story upstairs, except that the thieves had left the curtains fluttering at the bathroom window – big deal, that will get us a long way, he thought. He sat down on the top stair – desolate and in a quandary as to what he should do. He heard footsteps and sat very still, waiting to see who appeared. A woman stood in the doorway, but the light was behind her and he could not tell who it was. "Anybody there," she called out. "Who is it?" asked Israel. "Mrs. Murgatroyd, from next door. Who are you?" "Oh, Mrs. Murgatroyd, it's me, Sonny, you know, I own this house." "Oh, Mr. Levinsky, am I pleased to see you. Well, I never did, I thought you had moved up north. But what are you doing here, they said you was going. They took all your things." "Tell me, Mrs. Murgatroyd, come on, tell me, who took everything?" he asked. She sensed something was very wrong and said "Look, you come on in with me, and I'll make you a nice cup of tea, then we can talk." She gently took his hand. "Something's up, isn't it? I can tell. You can't fool an old girl like me." She was a kind soul, he remembered, so gratefully he gathered up his stuff, fearful of losing it if he left it at the house whilst he went next door.

After a cup of tea Ada, as she insisted on being called, told him what had happened. It seemed that a bomb had fallen about a mile away, one of the latest kind, and the blast shattered all the windows and blew the doors open in all the houses down the street, including his. Mr Murgatroyd had tied up the door handle with some rope and closed the windows which had not been smashed, but the ARP wardens would not give permission for the broken windows to be replaced as no-one was living there, and so the house had been open to anyone. Then one morning a large furniture truck turned up, and four men had gone into the house, all in the usual overalls and aprons which removal men wore, and Ada had gone round to see what was going on. "I hope you don't think I was being nosy," she said "but it seemed strange, like, with you not being there that you should be having all your stuff moved out." Israel shook his head but said nothing. She then went on to say how she had asked them where they were taking the stuff to and they had told her that the owner had contacted their firm, asking for all the furniture and household goods to be taken away and put in store, as the house had been blasted. Ada had thought this reasonable, and quite likely, and had even made them all a cup of tea. After about four hours the men had finished loading the van and driven off. There was no name on the van, so she was unable to give him any clue as to the destination of his furniture. She said she had later asked herself how Mr L, as she called him, would have known the house had been blasted, but thought the authorities had probably informed him. It was immediately obvious to both Ada and Israel that everything had been stolen - in broad daylight. What was he to do, with Julie and Natalia arriving tomorrow. He put his head in his hands and moaned. "What am I going to do, Ada? Julie is home tomorrow. What a way to repay us for being in the war and doing our bit. We don't deserve to have everything stolen like this." Ada felt very sorry for him, as she had liked both he and Mrs. L before they had gone their separate ways during the war. "Look, luv, my three boys have all left home and don't need their two rooms. There's only Stan and me now, so if it would help for a bit you and your wife and the little ones can move in here for a while, until you get yourselves sorted out, like. If you're on the spot, you might be able to do a bit of ferreting out what likely happened. You know, how did it get out that you were away and who knew your wife wasn't here. Someone will likely know, especially in the pub. If you go down there with Stan for a few evenings you'll maybe pick something up. You never know. In the meantime, he can take you along to the Town Hall where they're issuing extra clothing and furniture coupons to them who has been bombed out. You ought to tell the police, though, first, in case they can help you. Never know, they might have caught the blighters." Israel was relieved. Ada was very kind, although down to earth, and he knew that Julie would rather be here and on the spot. They could at least start doing some decorating, getting windows repaired, and getting the home back together during the day, for he had a job lined up for his band starting next Saturday at the Bagatelle restaurant in the West End, so he would be working every night. Ada's house was clean and comfortable, and no doubt she would keep her eye on the baby and Natalia until she went back to boarding school whilst he and Julie went shopping to try and replace some of their things. Maybe his cousin could help with some furniture from his factory in Leeds, even if it was a few of the rejects. It seemed that all his luck was not bad – at least he had got the opportunity to get a band together and get back into show business as soon as he was demobbed, and he had some money saved in the bank from the work he had been doing with the Secret Service. He knew that Julie had not touched much of her wages during the war, except for essentials, so she would have a bit of a nest egg too, but some of this would be spent on the baby. Natalia's education was secure – the Army had promised to continue to pay for her education as a boarder at Queenswood until she was fifteen, which would give her a great start for her future. He took a second to think of his new job "Sonnelli and his Tzigany Music". He thought the name sounded just right. He had also been offered a spot on Henry Hall's radio show the following week, which he hoped would make him well-known. He dreamt of stardom and hoped it was just around the corner. With the good salary he would be earning they could begin again – there were others far worse off than they were – he and Julie had each other, their lovely daughter and the new baby, and at least the house was still standing, and not just a heap of rubble and bricks.

His life had come full circle – as a boy he and his family had fled their home in Russia, leaving everything behind. Now he had the chance to rebuild one.

AFTERWORD

The author was approached by Ricochet, who made a documentary called *The Repair Shop* for BBC2, showing the violin in its original state, being restored by John Dilworth, a well-known violin maker and restorer, then finally brought back to its original condition and played by Christian Garrick on the programme on March 12, 2018.

The violin has now been donated to the Yehudi Menuhin School by Natalie Cumming and Debbie Rees for perpetuity in the name of Sydney Israel Levy.

JOHN DILWORTH
VIOLIN, VIOLA & CELLO
MAKER & RESTORER

Violin by F.F.Bottcher, Dresden 1883

The violin, bearing a facsimile label of Joseph Guarneri of Cremona, dated 1726, is signed internally by the maker 'F.F. Bottcher Geigenmacher (violin maker) Dresden 1883'. This maker is so far unrecorded in any published dictionary and probably worked mainly as an anonymous craftsman in a large commercial violin shop in Dresden. Its first known owner was Abraham Levinsky, the grandfather of the present owner, who was a violin teacher, born in St Petersburg in 1879. He fled Russia at the outset of the Revolution in 1917 and arrived in England in the following year, settling in Leeds. The violin subsequently passed to his daughter, Rosa, also a professional violinist, who went to Berlin in 1936 to join the Berlin Philharmonic Orchestra. On 'Kristallnacht' in November 1938, she was arrested and sent to Munchausen, and then in 1939 moved to Auschwitz, where she continued to play the violin. In 1945 she was taken to the camp at Bergen Belsen and finally returned home to Leeds, where she died in 1947. Her violin passed to her brother Sidney, who was also a professional player, often using the stage name 'Sonelli'. On his death in 1984 it was inherited by his daughter Natalie, the present owner.

It was restored by me in 2017, when it had major damage to the two upper ribs. The upper bass rib had a substantial puncture, crudely patched externally, and the upper treble rib had been partially replaced, and the joints had sprung open. It became obvious after cleaning and inspection that the treble rib had been repaired using a rib taken from another violin. It seemed reasonable to assume that these crude repairs may have been carried out under the oppressive conditions of the Auschwitz camp, and it was decided to leave this repair piece in place as a token of the remarkable history of the instrument, rather than renew the entire rib. The puncture in the bass rib was repaired, and the treble rib cleaned, realigned and refitted, and supported internally with patches over the joints.

The violin is now in good playing order.

49 CRESSWELL ROAD • EAST TWICKENHAM • MIDDLESEX • TW1 2EA
TELEPHONE 0208 892 7609
EMAIL jjdilworth@virginmedia.com

4th August 2017

No.0122

JOHN DILWORTH
VIOLIN, VIOLA & CELLO
MAKER & RESTORER

CERTIFICATE OF AUTHENTICITY

The violin shown in the photographs attached overleaf was made by F.F. Bottcher in Dresden in 1883. His signature appears on the interior surface of the front in the lower bouts. For details of its history please see the attached letter.

The back is made from two matched pieces of quarter-sawn maple with a regular narrow flame rining from the centre joint. The ribs are of mixed stock, generally showing a light flame, and the scroll is of similar wood to that of the back.

The front is of two matched pieces of spruce with very straight and even grain of fine to medium width.

The varnish is overall a dark reddish-brown.

E. Dilworth

Principal dimensions:	357mm
Length of back	357mm
Width of upper bouts	178mm
Width of middle bouts	113mm
Width of lower bouts	216mm

49 CRESSWELL ROAD • EAST TWICKENHAM • MIDDLESEX • TW1 2EA
TELEPHONE 0208 892 7609 • EMAIL jjdilworth@virginmedia.com

FAMILY HISTORY

Abraham David Levinsky

Born St. Petersburg, 1879

Died Aged 52, Leeds, 1930

Married Anna Davidov, 1908

Anna Davidov

Born St. Petersburg, 1887

Died Aged 66, Leeds, 1953

> Children:
>
> ### *Rosa Anna Levinsky*
> Born 1910, St. Petersburg (died 1947)
>
> ### *Sydney Israel Levinsky*
> Born 1912, St. Petersburg (died 1985)
> (Married Julie Wood, September 1935)
> (Natalia born October 1937)
> (Debra born August 1947)
>
> ### *Helena Ruth Levinsky*
> Born 1913, St. Petersburg (died 1990)
>
> ### *David Abraham Levinsky*
> Born 1919, Leeds (died 1943, Treblinka)
>
> ### *Isaac Reuben Levinsky*
> Born 1920, Leeds (died 1944, Birkenau)
>
> ### *Esther Naomi Levinsky*
> Born 1921, Leeds (died USA, 1995)
>
> ### *Nathan Isaac Levinsky*
> Born 1924, Leeds (died 1993)
>
> ### *Gittle Levinsky*
> Born 1925, Leeds (died 1969)

Nathan Jacob Levinsky

Born St. Petersburg, 1888

Died Aged 72, Leeds, 1960

Married Rula Walenska, 1910

Rula Wanda Walenska

Born Warsaw, 1892

Died Aged 76, Leeds, 1968

Children:

Moshe Aaron Levinsky

Born St. Petersburg, 1911 (died 1982)

Mala Katya Levinsky

Born St. Petersburg, 1913 (died 1987)

Katerina Ruth Levinsky

Born 1919, Leeds (died USA, 2000)

Nathalia Wanda Levinsky

Born 1922, Leeds (died Leeds, 1999)

ABOUT THE AUTHOR

Natalie Cumming started work aged 17 as a secretary at Gillette Industries. In 1970 she moved into merchant banking, as a personal assistant in the City of London with Lord Kissin of the Guinness Peat Group, finally working with Jacob Rothschild, Chairman of the Five Arrows Group, before retiring.

She became a Freeman of the City of London in 1983 and Member of the Guild of Freemen in 2003. After becoming a supporter of the Missing People Charity in 1986, she served as a Trustee from 1990 to 2007 and continues to be involved with them.

Natalie lives in Shropshire with her husband David. They have two sons, Richard and James.

Available worldwide from

Amazon

---

www.mtp.agency

www.facebook.com/mtp.agency

@mtp_agency

Printed in Great Britain
by Amazon

76294995R00163